RED-EYED FLIGHT

RED-EYED FLIGHT

THE LIAM AND BOO SERIES
BOOK THREE

WILLIAM MIERZEJEWSKI

DISCLAIMER

Quantity Purchases:
Companies, professional groups, clubs, and other organizations may qualify for special terms when ordering quantities of this title. For information, email info@ebooks2go.net, or call (847) 598-1150 ext. 4141.
www.ebooks2go.net

Published in the United States by eBooks2go, Inc.
1827 Walden Office Square, Suite 260, Schaumburg, IL 60173

ISBN: 978-1-5457-6317-9

Library of Congress Cataloging in Publication

TABLE OF CONTENTS

A MEETING OF THE NOBLEMEN

The year is 1894. It's Halloween night in the highlands of Poland. The old wooden wheels of a single-horse carriage crack and squeak as they bounce along the stone pathway. The coachman looks up at the rising crescent moon. He sees his warm exhaled breath drifting away from his mouth on this crisp clear evening. He whips the reins and exclaims, "Come on! Faster!" He looks back at the gentleman who's sitting inside the carriage. The older gentleman is wearing all black except for a small white collar symbolizing his membership into the Benedictine Monks. His short, curly red-and-gray hair lies along the sides of his bald head, his matching beard is long but groomed. The coachman exclaims, "Just a few more minutes until we reach the castle, Father!"

The priest replies, "Excellent, my son, and please make haste! We have no time to waste."

The carriage approaches the front gates guarded by two young men on horseback. The horsemen are wearing the red-and-white colors of their noble house. They stand ready at their post while trying to stay warm along the radiating torches on either side of the castle's arched entrance. They have their rifles over their shoulders and their secondary weapons—long swords—secured on their sheaths, alongside their horses. A lookout from the over-watch shouts down to the guards, "Watch! Watch! A carriage approaches!" The guards direct their horses in the direction of the carriage. One guard directs the other saying, "Quickly! Let's intercept them before they reach the castle gate." Both guards cock their long rifles, whip and kick their horses as they dash off toward the arriving carriage.

They position their horses a few yards in front of the carriage as they exclaim, "Halt! Who approaches?"

The coachman pulls back on the reins and says, "Woah! Watchmen, please raise the gate! I bring the priest and his cargo!"

The priest sticks his head out of the small carriage window and says, "Go, my sons! It is I!"

One of the watchmen nods his head and says, "Thank you, Father. The noblemen are gathered in the war room!"

The guards quickly turn their horses about-face and head back toward the gate. One of them shouts up to the guard on the lookout and exclaims, "Open the gate! It's the priest! He arrives with the cargo!"

The guard on the lookout runs over to the wheel crank and starts turning its long metal handles. He looks at another guard and says, "For God's sake! Help me with this damn thing!" The gate slowly glides upward with every crank of the wheel. The coachman slows down only for a minute as he waits for the gate to open enough to pass.

The priest yells up to the coachman and says, "Stop, my good man! Please, only for a moment."

The coachman pulls the reins and replies, "Father, you said we have no time to—"

The priest interjects saying, "I have a moment to help these brave men protecting their post." The priest signals one of the guards to come closer.

The guard approaches asking, "What do you need, Father?"

The priest answers, "I don't need anything, my son. But please wear one of these and give this other one to your fellow brother-in-arms." The priest reaches into his brown leather satchel and hands the guard two silver crosses on a long, thin necklaces, and says, "Let this help shield you from any evil that stands in front of you this night."

The guard looks at the priest with a tear in his eye and replies, "Thank you, Father. No evil shall cross this gate. Rest assured."

The priest gives the guard a sign of the holy cross and signals the coachman to proceed.

The carriage enters the courtyard. A young man, Jacek, sees the carriage arrive and quickly walks down the stone steps from the lookout. Jacek opens the carriage door and says, "Please let me help you, Father."

The priest hands him the wooden box and says, "Thank you, Jacek. Is your father in the war room with the others?"

Jacek answers, "Yes."

The priest replies, "Then I'll lead the way and get the doors for you." The priest and the young man briskly walk through one of the entrances to the main hall. They walk past the large walk-in fireplace as the fire rages and dances along the charred wood. Above the fireplace mantel is a large tapestry symbolizing the noble house's coat of arms.

Jacek tries to keep up with the priest as he says, "Father, I was wondering if you can give me a special blessing tonight."

The priest looks back as he cleans his glasses with a cloth from his jacket pocket. With his eyebrows raised, he answers, "If it makes you feel better while you stay here inside the walls of your father's house, then by all means."

Jacek replies, "Not at all, sir. Father is letting me join the hunt tonight."

The priest stops and turns toward Jacek asking, "Has he lost his mind? You're too young to be a part of something like this."

"I'm already in my teenage years."

The priest interjects, "Barely!"

Jacek continues, "Plus, Father mentioned it's time for me to become a true member of this family and its legacy."

The priest shakes his head in disapproval and continues walking toward the war room. He says, "Your father has been protecting you from the dark forces your entire life. Why would he want his son to—"

Jacek interjects, "Father lost men when that girl was seized by those women and her beasts."

The priest nods his head as says, "Very well. You have my blessing, my son. I baptized you and watched you grow within these walls. Before we go into that room, a few things. One, keep your mouth shut. And two, most importantly, listen to what is said. Your father and I will go over our strategy and tactics.

And whatever happens after we leave these walls, you stay close to the group. Understood?"

Jacek and the priest enter the war room. There they meet Jacek's father, Mikolaj, and other noblemen who are gathered around a large rectangular wooden table. Several other warriors stand alongside the noble leaders as they discuss their plan of action. Mikolaj turns toward the priest and says, "Oh, thank God! Good of you to join us, Father Pawal."

The priest approaches the table. Jacek is close behind. The priest replies, "Thank you, Mikolaj. And it sounds like I'm not the only addition to the hunting party this evening." The priest turns and looks at Jacek, still carrying the wooden box.

Mikolaj says, "It's time for him to be involved, Father. Have you bought everything we need?"

Father Pawal motions for Jacek to bring the wooden box forward. He instructs Jacek to place the box on the table. The priest opens the box and places several pieces of rolled parchment and a black book with weathered pages onto the table. The yellow pieces of aged parchment are unrolled, showing strange symbols and a map of the neighboring mountains with a vast forest woven along their flanks and valleys.

Mikolaj asks, "Where did you get this, Father?"

"This was taken off one of the slain witches who belong to Angelica's coven."

"And what do you make of it, Father?"

"I took these pieces of parchment with me during my long and fast journey to the church of the bishop. As some of you know, it's usually a two-day ride from there and back. My coachman and I managed to make it in less than a day. The bishop has dealt with covens in the past. One of the monks was able to translate some of the symbols."

Mikolaj asks, "What does it mean, Father?"

The priest answers, "Apparently, it's instructions on how to transfer the youthful life energy from one woman into that of an older witch host. And some of the other symbols, unfortunately, we weren't fully able to understand. But it has something do to with the rising of something evil. Resurrecting it below the rise of the midnight crescent moon."

One of the other noblemen interjects, "Well, we don't have time to waste, do we? It will be midnight within the next hour. We must leave now and try to save my daughter!"

Mikolaj replies, "We understand your concern for your daughter, Brother Filip! The night before last was a horrible night for many houses. Most of us lost men. Brother Piotr lost his son during the siege."

Piotr, a fellow nobleman, adds, "That's right! So, let's not waste time and hunt that witch and burn her coven to the ground!"

Mikolaj looks at the priests and asks, "Do you have anything else that can help us, Father? The cargo?"

Father Pawal picks up the black book and says, "This will be no help to us. The monks and the bishop believe that this is one of Angelica's coven books. Unfortunately, we couldn't open it. It seems to be protected by some type of spell." The priest pulls out a weapon from the box. It's an old handheld weapon in the shape of a war pick. The light brown wooden handle is tipped with a silver pick no bigger than a common dagger. The silver working end of the war pick is crested with sparkling sacred symbols and anchored to the wooden handle next to the symbol of the holy cross. Father Pawal hands it to Mikolaj and says, "This is a gift from the bishop. Something that he had in his armory. Designed generations ago. It's made of pure silver and is crested with symbols of the holy order and has been bathed in the oil of catechumens. The bishop said that this weapon has been used to end the mother of a few covens in the past. This is the weapon we must use if we are to stand a chance against Angelica. The bishop wishes he could provide more assistance and join us tonight. Unfortunately, he has his own mission to complete." The priest walks back over to the map and says, "The map shows the location of the coven. Hidden deep in the woods just east of the mountains along our territory's edge. That's where we need to go."

Mikolaj looks at the priest and then turns toward the rest of the congregation. He boldly says, "Then let's not waste any more time! Midnight approaches. All of you men to your horses! Spread out along a long line. I will lead the charge, and my son will be right next to me with his bow and the map." Everyone looks at Jacek who now appears to be worried and frazzled. The priest shakes his head, still not happy with Jacek joining the hunt.

The men make their way to their horses. The priest walks up to Jacek with the map and says, "Now remember what I told you. Stay close."

Jacek asks, "What weapons do you have, Father?"

The priest smiles as he re-positions his leather satchel around his shoulder and says, "Don't worry, my son. I have all the protection I need."

Jacek and the cavalry of brave warriors quickly ride their horses east toward the heights of the mountain range. Mikolaj utilizes the map and the clear night sky filled with endless stars and constellations to guide their way. They reach the top and form up their attack line. Mikolaj rides next to his son and takes a torch from one of the men in the line. He looks up and down his flanks. The men are in position. He rides his horse slightly down the valley. He points the torch in the direction of travel. Suddenly, there are several loud shrieks coming from the dark-filled sky. Some of the men look up. They hear movement along the tree line. The horses start to shuffle and neigh as they begin to sense danger. In a flash, there's quick movement along the tree line and the sound of large wings flapping through the chilly wind. The priest rides up alongside Jacek.

Piotr looks up only to see two massive hairy claws grab him by the shoulders and fly off into the night sky. He screams as the creature ascends high into the dark night and drops Piotr onto the mountainside. Piotr is silenced. Mikolaj looks at his son, the priest, and then the rest of the line as they start to break in a panic and exclaims, "Quickly! Down the mountain! The coven is down there in the valley!"

The line is broken as men quickly slide down the hill with their horses. The men blindly fire shots from their rifles into the darkness, wasting their ammunition. Most of the horses are unable to make the journey. Most lose their footing and flip their riders over the sides. Other horses are too frightened by the flying beasts and knock off their riders as they flee into the distance. The remaining men run down toward the valley. Some are picked off by what seems like several flying beasts working together to slay the human intruders. Mikolaj is still in front of the remaining pact. Father Pawal and Jacek are luckily still on their horses charging toward the valley where they see a small fire and a gathering of a few women in a circle. Abruptly, there's a horrible scream coming from a young woman near the fire. They see a turbulent purple mist reflect off the flames as it encircles the screaming woman. It's too late. Angelica has already taken the life of the captured young woman. She glares her blazing red eyes at her wicked coven followers. She sees the warriors approach she says, "Remember your lessons, ladies. Have fun with these fools."

Angelica backs up along her makeshift hut and grabs a long stick and her book. Mikolaj is greeted by three women belonging to Angelica's coven. One of the women grabs a stick off the ground. She quickly runs her hand along the stick and points it toward Mikolaj. A brilliant flash of violet light shoots out the working end of the stick. Instantly, Mikolaj's horse is turned into solid stone. Mikolaj flies through the air as he loses the grip of the war pick. The war pick bounces off a nearby tree and lands in a bush. Mikolaj is unarmed!

Jacek and Father Pawal are almost at bottom of the valley. The priest looks back as he hears a horrible scream. It's one of the members of the party being slain by one of the winged creatures. The creature flaps its huge wings and glares its red eyes at Jacek. The creature takes flight and heads straight toward Jacek like an arrow cutting through the air. Father Pawal grabs a small vile of holy water out of his satchel. The horrifying monster closes in on Jacek as it propels its long back hinge claws in front of itself. The priest turns his horse and throws the vile straight at the creature. The vile hits its mark and splashes the beast along its face. The creature screams out in pain as the holy water sizzles and burns. The priest's horse panics and knocks him off. Jacek gets off his horse and pulls his bow from over his shoulder. He looks back at the priest who grabs one of the party's unaccompanied horses and draws a sword from its side sheath. Father Pawal shouts, "Go! Help your father! I can handle myself!" The priest points the sword at the winged beast. The monstrous creature focuses on its prey.

Jacek grabs his sword out of his side sheath before his horse gallops and runs away. Mikolaj is in front of Jacek backing away from the women. Mikolaj backs up along the remains of the dead young woman. She looks withered as though her life energy was sucked from her now blue-and-gray decaying body. Jacek runs toward his father. His father looks back as he hears his son shout,

"Father, take my sword!" Mikolaj regains his footing and stands as his son throws the sword toward him. His father grabs it in midair. The witch in front tries to get her stick ready for her next attack. Mikolaj turns and jabs his sword right into the side of the witch, dropping her instantly. The two other women step back and cry out as they witness one of their sisters receive her death blow.

Jacek hears a ghastly inhuman scream coming from the direction of the priest. He turns, points his bow, and draws an arrow. He witnesses the unholy winged creature hit the ground. The priest stands victoriously over the monster. Only one other nobleman from the party remains as he makes his way toward the priest. It's Filip. Filip and the priest run toward Jacek. The priest shouts, "Jacek! For God's sake, help your father!" Jacek turns back toward his father.

Angelica turns the pages of her book by running her fingers through the air. She looks up at the midnight moon and says, "I still have time!" Angelica screams at her coven sisters and says, "Stop crying over spilled milk! Destroy Mikolaj and his priest while I complete the ceremony!" Mikolaj charges toward the remaining two women. One of the witches points her stick at Mikolaj. Flashes of purple electricity fly out of the end of the stick. Mikolaj screams out in pain. Jacek points his bow at the witch. He releases. The arrow hits its mark and strikes the witch's hand, ending the attack and throwing her into a spin while she screams in pain.

Filip and Father Pawal continue to run toward Mikolaj and Jacek. They are immediately stopped in their pursuit as another winged creature drops right in front of them. The unharmed witch sees Jacek drawing another arrow onto his bow. She takes her stick and points it at Jacek. Mikolaj notices the witch take aim at her intended target. He charges at the witch and throws the deadly edge of his sword directly into woman's chest like a javelin. She screams out in pain and drops to the ground. The wounded witch cries out as she continues to grab her hand. Angelica points her stick at the wounded witch and a bright green flash of light bursts out toward her. The witch is stunned as she freezes in place and shrinks down beneath her clothes. A small frog emerges from out of the clothes and hops away. Angelica says, "That's better. These apprentice witches are useless. Can't concentrate with all this racket! Now, where was I?

Oh yes." Angelica thrusts her stick into the ground over what appears to be a shallow grave. The purple mist continues to encircle as she starts to stay the words,

> "Crescent moon on the star-filled sky
> Hear the words of your dark servant cry
> Solutions, chemicals, and earthen oils
> Help resurrect my love as the cauldron boils."

Angelica looks up and sees Mikolaj remove the blood-stained sword from her fallen sister. He immediately charges at Angelica. She breaks away from her spell casting as she pulls her anchored stick out of the ground. She points the stick at Mikolaj and several sharp splinters rise off the ground. They shoot through the air quicker than an arrow from a bow toward Mikolaj. They rapidly pierce Mikolaj's skin, stopping him instantly. Jacek sees his father fall to his death. Angelica whips her beautiful long dark hair around her shoulders and says, "Finally. This menacing family's legacy is almost at an end." As she laughs over the body of her defeated enemy, the fire rises behind her. She bends down and smells the blood oozing from Mikolaj's body. She says, "That's the smell of a dying bloodline." As the fire rages, Jacek sees the war pick's silver tip shimmer from the bottom of a bush to the right flank of Angelica. He moves in a flash to try to retrieve the weapon before Angelica locks on to his position.

Meanwhile, Filip and Father Pawal work together attempting to slay the horrid, winged creature. The creature takes flight as he grabs Filip by the shoulder and digs under his skin. Filip screams out in agony as the priest throws another vile of holy water at the beast. The vile hits the creature's clawed back legs. The creature lets out a horrible sound as it's overcome by excruciating pain. The beast and Filip descend rapidly toward the ground. This misguided action by the creature gives Father Pawal the perfect opportunity to drive a fatal blow into its chest. The creature is finally silenced. The priest drops to Filip's side and attempts to help, but it's too late. The creature pierced several vital vessels during the battle. Father Pawal gives Filip his last rights before he takes his last few exhausting breaths.

Angelica breaks away from the spell as she hears the fatal death cry of her fallen creature and turns toward its direction. She sees Jacek before he vanishes behind the row of bushes. She looks up at the crescent moon and says, "Damn it! It's too late! Not to worry. Other pressing matters are at hand." The turbulent purple mist begins to slowly turn upward and fade into the night sky. She glides over the ground toward Jacek. She reaches for his foot as he tries to reach for the war pick with his outstretched hand. She pulls him from under the bush as he grabs hold of the weapon and drives the pick end directly into the posterior side of her hand. She screams in agony as she feels the pain derived by the holy weapon. She knows the power of this weapon and immediately backs away from Jacek. She covers her hand as she signals for her long tree branch and her book to meet her in retreat. Her long branch and spell book glide away from her hut. She grabs hold of the book and mounts the branch as she vanishes out into the night sky screaming, "I'll end your bloodline, Mikolaj! Rest assured!"

....

CHAPTER 1

THE MEETING ON THE MOUND

It's the present day in Chicago. The sun continues to set over the early evening sky in Chicago. The brilliant colors from the sunset fade and paint the setting of a fine summer evening. The colors transition from orange to pink and gracefully into a dark indigo as the moon begins to rise over the eastern sky. From Liam and Boo's house, it's a short walk over to the park where they play sports. This warm and dry evening is the setting host to Liam's baseball game. The overhead field lights perfectly illuminate the fields as several teams play the game Liam has grown to love. It has the perfect sounds and smells of summer. The sound of an aluminum bat echoes slightly behind a baseball as it glides into the outfield. The parents on the bleachers and friends from the dugout cheer as each player awaits their next pitch. Smoke rises from the far corner of the field and carries the smell of freshly grilled burgers and hot dogs.

Tommy, Liam and Boo's friend, is on the mound trying to deliver another strike with his curve ball. His curve ball has been Ryan's nemesis during practice and regular play. But late into this tied game, Tommy's curve ball is starting to fade. The bases are loaded with two outs. The player up to bat has two balls and two strikes. The batter takes his stance as he taps home plate with his bat. Ryan is behind the batter as catcher. He gives Tommy the sign for another curve ball. Tommy reads the sign and nods his head. He checks on his friend and teammate, Liam, who's playing shortstop. Liam, who's 12 years old, gives Tommy a nod and says, "Come on,

Tommy! You got this, dude!" Tommy nods back, checks the placement of his fingers around the baseball, and winds up for his pitch.

He throws the ball. It dips down low and out of the strike zone, resulting in another ball. The batter smiles and doesn't swing. He knows he's one pitch away from walking and his team taking the lead. Ryan receives the ball into his catcher's mitt. He shakes his head and says, "Shit." Ryan stands up, looks back to the umpire, and asks for a timeout. The umpire waves his hands into the air as he steps outside the batter's box and shouts, "Time!"

Ryan runs up to Tommy. Liam follows suit along with Timmy, Tommy's younger brother, who's playing first base. Tommy shakes his head and kicks the dirt as Ryan and the rest of the lads walk up and have a meeting on the mound. Ryan says, "Okay! Yeah, that's it, Tommy. Show that fine dry dirt who's boss!"

Tommy says, "Shut up, Ryan! You're not helping."

Ryan responds, "Yeah, well you're not helping us get out of this inning either, Tommy."

Tommy replies, "You don't think I know that dude—"

Liam interjects, "Ryan, just tap the brakes for a minute. Let's not be all Viking right now. And Tommy, just take a deep breath for a minute."

Timmy says, "I agree. Just take a minute and calm down."

"Okay. Okay. Deep breath. Got it." Tommy takes a couple deep breaths.

Liam says, "Now, this batter will be expecting another curve ball. And I know this guy. A couple of weeks back, one of our other pitchers struck him out with a high fast ball. He likes those."

Ryan says, "I agree. Even if he gets a piece of it, it will be a line drive or a ground ball over to Liam. He'll throw it straight over to second or third base and the inning is over."

The umpire, growing impatient, says, "Hey, guys! Time to wrap this up. Come on!"

Liam says, "Okay, guys. We got this." Liam looks straight at Tommy and continues, "Just give him what he wants, and I'll handle the rest."

Tommy takes one more deep breath and nods his head. Timmy runs back to first base. Ryan gives Tommy the ball and says,

"End this crap. I stress eat, and that delicious meat cooking at the concession stand is making me hungry."

Liam taps Tommy on the shoulder and says, "Come on, Tommy. You got this!"

The batter gets back into his stance and the umpire says, "Play ball!"

Ryan gets down into his stance and gives Tommy the sign for a fast ball. Tommy looks at the call, nods, and gets his hands ready in his windup. He throws the baseball right on target, and the batter quickly adjusts to the high fast ball. He swings and slightly taps the baseball on the lower portion of his bat. It's a ground ball close to second base. Liam runs up to quickly intercept the ball and throws it like an arrow from a bow straight over to second base. The second baseman catches the ball as he steps on the base, ending the inning. The crowd from Liam's side of the bleachers jump and cheer as the nail-biting inning finally comes to an end.

Boo, who's 10 years old, and her dad, Will, stand up from the bleachers and celebrate with the crowd as the players come off the field and enter the dugout. The teams get ready for the next inning, while Will, Boo, and the rest of the crowd sit back in their seats. Boo notices her friends Maddie and Robert running up to the bleachers. Maddie has a hot dog, and Robert is carrying a small cardboard box with an assortment of candy and a drink. Boo says, "Hey, Dad! Here comes Maddie and Robert." Will looks over before going back to his newspaper and says, "Okay, great."

Robert climbs up the bleachers over to Will and Boo and says, "Sounds like we missed something. We can hear the cheers all the way over at the concession stand."

Will replies, "Yup. Sure did. A real close one, but of course the team came together in the heat of the moment. They write books and movie scripts about moments like that."

Robert laughs as he takes a seat close to Boo and starts to sort through his candy. Boo looks at Robert and says, "Can you share with me, Robert?"

"That implies that I will have to give up all my precious candy from my allowance money. Sorry, but I'm on the fence about this."

Boo laughs as Maddie climbs past Robert and sits on the other side of Boo. Boo asks, "All you got was a hot dog, Maddie?"

Maddie answers, "Oh no! I forgot my drink back at the counter!"

Boo replies, "No worries, I have a plan." Boo blinks her pretty blue eyes at her father as Will side-eyes away from his paper saying, "Okay, honey. What do you want?"

Boo answers, "Only your love and your money of course."

Will laughs as he reaches into his pocket for his wallet. "At least your response started with love. I'll take it." Will hands Boo some money and says, "While you're over there, say hi to Mom for me. And please get me a soda as well. And tell your mother to dig for a soda can deep into the cooler. I like my sodas after they chilled under several layers of ice."

Boo gives her father a kiss and says, "Thanks, Daddy. You're the best."

"Of course I am." Will goes back to reading his paper as Maddie starts to eat her hot dog. Robert looks over to Will and asks, "So what's the big story today, sir?"

Will looks up from his reading and turns the front cover article toward Robert. Robert reads: "WOMAN ESCAPES FROM MENTAL HOSPITAL IN NORTHWEST SUBURBS. LEAVES TWO SECURITY GUARDS DEAD. Wow! That sounds downright spooky. When did this happen?"

Will says, "Early last night. The lady is supposed to be old as dirt too. But she got away and is still on the loose."

Robert replies, "Come on! They can't find an old lady? How far could she have gotten?"

Will reads further down in the article and says, "Well, they haven't found her yet. Last reports said she was heading east toward city limits."

✦ ✦ ✦

As Liam waits on deck and takes a few practice swings, a security guard at an airport a few miles to the west gets a phone call at the front desk. The security guard is a retired cop who works the evening shift. The part-time job helps him stay active. More importantly, it's a healthy separation from his nagging wife. She hasn't learned after forty years of marriage that he doesn't want to talk to her during the evening baseball games. Tonight, he's watching the crosstown series. He answers the phone saying, "Security post 2. How can I help you?"

Dispatch answers, "Hey, Glen. Sorry to break you away from the game. This is Alice over at the main office."

Glen replies, "Hey, Alice. Not a problem. The game is moving slowly anyway. How can I help you?"

"I need you to do a security check in your section of taxiways. We got a strange report from the air control tower. They had some pilots report to the tower that something with big with red eyes was resting on top of one of the hangars close to taxiway alpha bravo."

Glen laughs. "Is that right? Something big with red eyes. And it's not even Halloween yet."

Alice laughs. "Hey, don't kill the messenger. That's what I was told."

Glen says, "No worries. They probably saw one of those damn coyotes. They make their way from the forest preserve to the runways through the subway tunnel. That subway tunnel always has animals running in and out of it."

Alice replies, "Can you look at the security camera feed at your desk and tell me if you see anything?"

Glen looks at the different camera feeds for a moment. He finds something on one of the feeds. He uses a control knob and zooms in for a closer look. Something large with pointy ears looks back toward the camera and flashes its red eyes. Glen says, "Well, would you look at that!"

Alice says, "What is it, Glen?"

Glen answers, "Yup. There's something out there. Looks big too. I'll go check it out and report back to you via the portable radio."

"Okay. Be careful. Let me know what you find."

Glen grabs his flashlight and keys off his desk. He takes one last look at the score of the baseball game as he heads out the back door toward the company pickup truck. He fires up his vehicle and activates the yellow and blue caution lights on the roof and rolls down the window. The roar of several jet engines echo and pass throughout the landscape. He drives along taxiway alpha bravo as he approaches the hangar. As he arrives, he sees two glowing red eyes peek over the roof line of the hangar. He stops the truck, exits, and points his flashlight along the roof. The creature suddenly dashes away from the roof line and is out of sight. A mechanic working inside the hangar approaches Glen and says, "Hey! Did you see anything up there? I just called for security to come and check it out. They said you were on your way."

Glen receives a message from Alice over the radio, "Hey, Glen? Are you out there yet? I just got a call from a mechanic that reported something is out there too."

Glen grabs the radio from his utility belt and answers, "Hey, Alice. I'm out here talking to the mechanic now."

The mechanic says, "Yeah, it sounds like its dragging something along the roof of the hangar. It's scratching it's claws around and making a hell of a noise."

Glen continues to walk around, pointing his flashlight along the roof line. He instructs the mechanic to wait inside the hangar. He grabs his radio and says, "Hey, Alice. I think we'll need some help here. Maybe animal control and police."

"Message received, Glen. Have you seen what it is? That way I can give a better description to animal control."

Glen hears a loud whip through the air. The sound quickly drowns out as a jet rolls down a nearby taxiway toward the runway. Glen points his flashlight toward the strange sound. He doesn't see anything. The jet noise travels off into the distance and quickly fades away. The mechanic walks out of the hangar and Glen walks back toward him asking, "Did you see anything out there?"

Glen answers, "I heard something strange. But I didn't see anything else. Whatever it was maybe it flew away and—" Glen stops mid-sentence as he hears the strange whipping sound return. He looks up to see a winged beast quickly descend over him! He screams as the beast lets out a load screech. The red-eyed beast grabs Glen by his shoulders. It digs its long claws under his skin. It flaps its wings as it attempts to lift Glen off the ground.

The mechanic yells, "Holy shit!" and runs back toward the hangar and over to a phone along the wall.

Glen screams out in agonizing pain as blood oozes down along the beast's claws. The beast flaps his wings harder. It's unable to lift Glen off the ground and releases its claws. The beast peers its menacing eyes at the mechanic. The mechanic screams into the phone, "Look! Just send whatever you got over here right now! What? Screw animal control! You're gonna need a team out here with big guns that can take this thing down from the air!" The beast flaps its wings and lifts into the air. It lands on the roof of the hangar, slamming its long claws along the rippled metal material. The mechanic looks back at Glen. Glen is motionless and not breathing. A pool of blood continues to ooze away from Glen's unresponsive body. The beast claims a victim as Glen's nearby radio echoes, "Glen? Glen! Come in, Glen! Damn it!"

Alice runs from her desk over to a phone, which is directly linked to the airport police station. She quickly grabs the phone, raises it to her ear, and dials 0. The line answers, "Airport Police Headquarters. This is Sergeant Dean. How can I direct your call?"

Alice exclaims, "Hello! Please, this is Alice from security! I need you to immediately direct me over to your commander in charge of special weapons and tactics! We have a grave situation over at the hangar along taxiway alpha bravo! I think one of my security guards is down!"

....

CHAPTER 2

BY POLICE ORDER EVERYONE CLEAR THE FIELD NOW!

Sergeant Dean tells Alice, "Okay, ma'am. No problem. I'll direct your call over to Commander McKinley."

Commander McKinley, a seasoned officer with over twenty years of service, is sitting in his office when his phone rings. He picks up the phone saying, "Commander McKinley. Go ahead."

Sergeant Dean says, "Hey, Commander. I got a call from Alice. The lady in charge of security. She's requesting your unit to mount up."

Commander McKinley replies, "Wow! She's never done that before. Send it over."

Alice says, "Hello! Commander! This is Alice! I think one of my security guards is down over at a hangar near taxiway alpha bravo. And one of the mechanics may be in grave danger!"

Commander McKinley asks, "Jesus! What's happening over there?"

"Not too sure, sir! Something is out there! A beast of some kind is flying around and raising hell. Please help!"

Commander McKinley says, "We are on the way! I'll activate my team and we'll be en route ASAP. You stay on the phone with the mechanic, and I'll have one of my sergeants contact EMS."

Commander McKinley presses a button on his phone labeled "P.A." and says, "All tactical officers, report to the armory immediately! I need the pilot to get the bird ready for takeoff!"

He marches down the hallway toward the armory. He's a middle-aged man but in better shape than most of his young tactical officers. His high, tight, and spiked reddish-brown hair and his chiseled jawline matches his tough and rugged face. He enters the armory and sees his team of four other officers donning body armor and inspecting their long rifles.

Chris, one of his younger officers, asks, "Hey, Boss, what do we got?"

Commander McKinley says, "Sounds like an unknown threat has taken out one security guard, and a mechanic may be in danger over at one of our hangars." Commander McKinley grabs his long rifle, heavy vest, and tactical helmet out of his caged locker and says, "Come on! Let's go! Everyone on the helicopter pad in one minute!" He marches down another hallway toward the helicopter pad.

Alice goes back over to the phone still connected with the mechanic and says, "Hello? Hello! Sir? Help is on the way." Alice hears the horrifying sound of screaming on the other end of the line. She exclaims, "Oh, Jesus! Sir! Sir?" Alice hears what she assumes is the mechanic screaming and shouts, "Please! Oh, God! Ahhhh! Someone hel—!" Suddenly, there is silence on the other end of the phone. The beast claims another victim. Alice hangs up the phone. Her heartbeat pounds as her breathing begins to significantly increase. She attempts to contact Glen with her radio while her hands shake from the adrenaline pumping through her panicking body.

Commander McKinley is about to exit the building as his pilot approaches him saying, "Chopper is ready, Commander. Where are we heading?"

Commander McKinley answers, "A hangar near taxiway alpha bravo."

His earpiece attached to his radio echoes, "Commander, we have EMS en route. When you arrive to the scene, let me know where you would like them to stage."

Commander McKinley says, "Message received. On my orders, no EMS is to make entry into the hangar until we secure the area."

The rest of his team runs down the hallway toward the awaiting helicopter. Within seconds, the entire team is aboard the helicopter and ready for takeoff. The helicopter pilot dons his helmet and mic, which connects directly to the air control tower. He says, "This is Airport S.W.A.T. Helo 1 requesting emergency clearance from HQ over to taxiway alpha bravo." Within moments, air control replies, "Message received Helo 1. Clearance is granted. All flights in or out have been redirected to the other side of the airport. You're clear to proceed."

The helicopter lifts off into the evening air. The pilot activates the search light and thermal imaging camera, which are attached below the helicopter cockpit. Within a minute they arrive at their destination. Commander McKinley assesses the area from his open sliding door. Chris hands the commander a tablet and says, "Here, Commander. The tablet has the live feed up from the TIC camera."

Commander McKinley says, "Thank you," as he directs his pilot saying, "Circle the area a few times. Let's get a good assessment of the area before we land."

The pilot says, "Yes, sir" as he circles the hangar several times.

Chris looks over the commander's shoulder to look at the tablet. Chris points out the outline of a body on the pavement. Commander McKinley tells the pilot, "Hover over this area and shine your light straight down."

The pilot directs the search light over the mangled and motionless body of Glen. The pilot says, "I guess that's the security guard."

Commander McKinley replies, "Jesus Christ! The TIC isn't picking up a heat signature. Looks like he's gone. Anyone got eyes on the mechanic?"

The pilot says, "No, sir. Don't see anyone else and no sign of our mystery guest. Wait! What is that?"

Commander McKinley sees something gallop through the entrance of the hangar. It looks up at the helicopter, lets out a loud screech, and opens its wide wings. Commander McKinley says, "Holy shit! What the hell is that? Chris, get your sniper rifle ready!"

As Chris gets into position with his long rifle, the pilot swings around to give Chris a clear line of sight. The beast crouches into a squatting position and begins to flap its massive wings. The beast takes flight before Chris can make a shot. The beast swings past the helicopter and begins to fly away from the airport. Chris says, "Wow! Jesus, Commander, what the hell are we dealing with here?"

Commander McKinley says, "Whatever it is we're not going to let it get away. Let's hunt this bastard and take it down!" Commander McKinley directs his pilot to head east and continue their pursuit. The pilot presses a button that connects him back to the air control tower. He says, "This is Airport S.W.A.T. Helo 1. Be advised, we are continuing pursuit of this thing. It's heading east toward the city."

✦ ✦ ✦

Liam takes his stance along the plate. Ryan is on first base. Liam takes a practice swing as he looks back at the umpire asking, "Sorry, sir. What's my count?"

The umpire answers, "Two balls and two strikes."

Liam nods his head, taps the plate with his bat, and gets ready for the next pitch.

The umpire gets ready and shouts, "Play ball!"

Ryan shouts from first base, "Come on, Liam! Bring me home, dude, and the next round of hot dogs are on me!"

Boo and Robert clap and cheer for Liam.

Will stands up from his seat, claps, and says, "Come on, Son! You got this!"

The pitcher sees his pitch sign and winds up for his next pitch.

✦ ✦ ✦

The helicopter races east in pursuit of the ferocious monster. The beast flaps its gigantic wings as it whips around several vehicles on the road. Commander McKinley talks into his mic and says to his pilot, "Connect me with the Emergency Communications Center (E.C.C.) in the city! And turn this bird on a slight angle so Chris can get a clear shot!"

The pilot slightly turns the helicopter toward Chris's side. Chris is secured to his jump seat looking down at the scope of his long rifle.

Commander McKinley says, "When you have a clean shot, Chris, take it!"

Chris exclaims, "I'm trying, Commander, but with all of this traffic, I can't get a clear shot without possibly hitting someone."

The helicopter pilot says, "Commander, you're online with the E.C.C., sir!"

Commander McKinley says, "Okay. Thanks. Hello, Dispatch. This is Commander McKinley from Airport S.W.A.T. We are currently in pursuit of a large, winged…creature. It looks like some type of mutant bat! It's taken out a security guard and possibly another victim in one of our hangars. We are currently in pursuit of this thing heading east down Lawrence Avenue. Our approximate altitude is one hundred feet off the ground. We just passed through Schiller Park and Rosemont. We are heading over the forest preserve now."

Dispatch from the E.C.C. says, "Message received, Commander. We will make the necessary notifications. Do you think you'll be able to take down this thing before it enters the surrounding neighborhoods?"

The beast speeds on the mighty wings of the wind away from the pursuing helicopter. Suddenly, a dense fog develops along the surrounding forest area. Chris attempts to line up for a shot, as there are no vehicles coming down the road. He fires. *BANG!* He looks through his scope but only sees the misty fog. He turns to Commander McKinley and says, "I don't see him, sir!"

The helicopter flies over the running path along the Des Plaines River. Commander McKinley sees the creature flap its massive wings just under the fog. He exclaims, "Damn it, Chris. You missed it!" The creature reemerges from the dense fog as he exits the forest preserve and heads into a densely population residential area. Commander McKinley switches from crew communications back over to the E.C.C. and says, "That's a negative, E.C.C. We haven't been able to neutralize the threat. It's flying over your jurisdiction and the suburb of Norridge. We are continuing our pursuit." Commander McKinley looks at Chris and exclaims, "Chris! I expect the next shot to be your best shot!"

Chris says, "Yes, sir!"

It's a game of cat and mouse as both combatants continue to head east down Lawrence Avenue.

Liam takes a swing and gets a piece of it. It flies through the air but into foul territory. Ryan turns around and shakes his head and heads back to first base. Will exclaims, "That's it, Son! You got a piece of it. Now work on your timing."

Boo shouts, "Come on, Liam! Knock this one over to the other field!"

Liam nods his head and gets into his ready stance. He waits for the next pitch. In the near distance, there is the sound of several police sirens and a helicopter. The pitcher gets into his stance. He checks Ryan at first base. Robert jokes, "You don't have to worry about him stealing second! He's too fat! He'll never beat the ball."

Ryan shouts, "Shut up, Robert!" The pitcher laughs, which forces him to reset. He gets ready. The sound of the police sirens and the helicopter continue to get louder as they approach the park. The pitcher throws the ball down into Liam's strike zone. It's a fast ball right down the middle. Liam swings and connects, sending the baseball immediately into the opposite direction.

The baseball flies over the center field outfielder. The outfielder runs and tries to catch up with the ball but to no avail. The ball lands several feet past him. The crowd jumps up and cheers as Ryan runs as fast as he can around second base heading toward third base. Liam smiles as he runs past first base on his way to second base. The sound of police sirens and the pursuing helicopter echo off the nearby buildings and homes surrounding the park. Suddenly, there's a loud screech! Everyone on the field pauses their game to see the spectacle in front of them. The winged creature is seen by all as it swoops down toward the baseball fields. People start to scream and run away while they hear the helicopter's loudspeaker shout, "This is the police department. For your safety, please evacuate the field and leave the area!"

Liam looks at the winged beast in awe of its size and speed. It swoops past the baseball fields and past the row of trees along the sidewalk. Liam looks at Boo. Boo is mesmerized by the monster and the events unfolding right in front of her eyes. Will stands up, grabs Boo's hand, and exclaims, "Come on! We are out of here! Robert, Maddie, follow Boo and me back to the concession stand." Will looks at Liam and shouts, "Liam! Come on! Over to the concessions stand to get Mom!" The family and the rest of the onlookers begin to quickly clear the field.

The helicopter rapidly swings low along the baseball field and whips up sand as it continues its pursuit. Liam gets a mouth full of sand as he exits the field. He runs up to his father out of breath. Liam grabs his chest, continuing to gasp for air. His father notices his son's distress and reaches into his pocket for Liam's inhaler. Liam takes a quick puff of his inhaler, holds his breath for a few seconds, and exhales. Will asks, "Are you okay, Son?" Liam nods his head and gives his father a thumbs up. Will looks up when he hears another loud screech from the winged beast as it dashes toward the police helicopter.

Inside the cockpit the pilot shines his light directly in front along the flight path. The pilot exclaims, "Holy shit!" as the creature flies like a missile straight at them! The pilot pulls back the controls to dodge the creature's attack. The helicopter swiftly climbs upward toward the evening sky. The creature runs its massive claws along the searchlight, rendering it inoperable. The beast screams as it slashes its death-dealing claws along the center portion of one of the field lights. Sparks fly out of the metal column of the light post as the lights flicker for a moment before going dead. People scream and scramble while frantically running out of the way. The upper portion of the light post begins to fall inward toward one of the baseball diamonds. It hits the field with a thunderous crash and dozens of lights break simultaneously.

The creature drifts away from the park and begins to head back west toward the forest preserve. Police from the pursuing squad cars exit their vehicles and point their weapons up toward the beast. An order from one of the senior ranking officers exclaims, "Open fire! Take it down!" People fleeing the field scream as they hear and feel the loud piercing pops of gunfire. The helicopter pilot scrambles as he acknowledges his warning lights and turns the chopper around. The beast flies over a nearby golf course and speeds like a rocket back toward the forest preserve. Commander McKinley looks at the tablet. The video feed is gone. He says to his pilot, "Did that thing take out the searchlight and the TIC camera?"

The pilot answers, "Looks that way, Commander. We'll have to head back to HQ. I can't fly this thing without a searchlight."

Commander McKinley looks at Chris and says into his mic, "God damn it! We almost had that thing. Return to base."

The pilot replies, "Yes, sir." He turns the helicopter on a course back to their headquarters.

CHAPTER 3

. . . .

THERE GOES THE NEIGHBOR'S ANNOYING DOG

Sirens pierce through the once peaceful summer evening as most police officers quickly reenter their squad cars and continue their pursuit of the aerial beast. Will runs up to the concession stand with all the kids. Other officers run toward the field to make sure that everyone is okay. The initial panic of the unfolding events begins to fade quickly as parents are anxiously reunited with their children. Timmy, Tommy, and Maddie's mom, Lisa, runs up and intercepts her children as they approach the concession stand. Lisa says to Will, "Thank you, Will. I was just talking to Annie when everything happened."

Will smiles and replies, "No worries, Lisa. I'm just glad no one was hurt. No one is hurt, are they?" Will scans the area and assesses the situation as he's been trained to do with his job.

Annie, Liam and Boo's mom, exits the concession stand and gives both Liam and Boo a hug. Annie says, "Oh, thank God, you're okay. When I heard the screams and all the commotion, I feared the worst." Annie looks up to her husband, Will, and asks, "Is everything okay, honey? What the hell happened?"

Will turns around and answers, "Hard to say, honey. Everything happened so fast. Police were chasing something. Looks like it's gone now. Hopefully they catch it. Whatever it is."

The police sirens fade out into the distance. Lisa looks at Robert and says, "Robert, let's take you home. Just text your parents that you're okay and we'll be bringing you home."

15

Will says, "Yeah, I agree. I don't think anyone will want to continue the games tonight. Looks like everyone is getting in their cars and heading home."

Will looks at Annie. "What do you have to do before you're ready to leave, honey?"

Annie replies, "Oh, just clean up the concession stand. Shouldn't take me too long."

Will replies, "Let's all help you and then we will walk home together."

Boo says, "Yeah, Mom. We can't leave you here with a mess to clean up."

"Okay. I agree. Many hands will help. Let's get to it."

Within no time, the family finishes cleaning the concession stand. Liam's baseball coach, Phil, comes over to check on the family. "Sorry to leave you with all of this to do. I just finished talking to some of the coaches and cleaning up the field. We will continue the game sometime soon. I'll send an email blast out to everyone."

Annie, who is closing and locking up the stand, says, "Oh, it's okay, Phil. We figured this is the least we can do to help."

Phil replies, "Thank you. Hell of a night. And of course, it had to happen right after Liam hit a screamer out to center field. Good game tonight, Liam."

Liam smiles. "Thanks, Coach."

Will says, "Thanks for the update, Coach. Have a good night and get some rest."

Phil replies, "You're welcome. Get home safe."

The family walks down Giddings Street and back toward their home. Liam grabs his backpack with both hands as he readjusts and looks up into the evening sky. He doesn't see anything out of the ordinary—a few stars peeking from behind the cloudy twilight sky, the moon rising, and a few jets on their regular flight pattern toward the local airport. Liam looks up at Will and asks, "Hey, Dad? Do you think the police will catch that thing?"

Will smiles as he looks down at Liam. "I think so. That thing was being chased by the city's finest. I have no doubt."

The family arrives back home and are immediately greeted by their family dog, Lady. Everyone settles in for the night. Boo leans into Liam and says, "If I were you, big brother, I'd take a shower. You smell like smelly socks."

Liam takes a sniff and says, "I think you're right. It's never good when you can smell yourself."

Liam and Boo both laugh as Annie and Will walk into the kitchen. Boo goes upstairs to her bedroom as Liam gets ready for a shower. Will attempts to make a pot of coffee. Annie walks past Will and says, "Don't even think about it."

"What do you mean, honey?"

"You remember what the doctors said after your last checkup. No more coffee in the evening."

Will nods his head. "Sorry. You're right. Old habits and all."

Annie says, "I bought you some of that tea you like. It has a little caffeine but just enough to keep you awake until bedtime."

Will replies, "Thanks, honey. Sounds like a plan."

The family settles into their comfortable spots. Liam gets out of the shower and begins to cough. He starts to have another round a labored breathing and reaches over to the bathroom shelf for his inhaler. He takes in a deep breath and presses down on his inhaler, releasing the medication. After a few steady breaths, Liam's breathing calms down and settles back to normal. After the climatic events inside The Elk's Estate the previous summer, Liam developed a moderate case of asthma.

Liam walks back into his bedroom and tries to decide on what he would like to do before going to bed. He looks at the alarm clock along his nightstand. Liam thinks, *It's not too late. Maybe I can log on to the computer and see if Simon and Reggie are playing something online*. Liam likes this option but then he thinks about the last time he logged on and played with Simon and Reggie. Liam was having such a fun time with his East Coast friends that he lost track of time and stayed up well past midnight. He reconsiders this as he looks at his new fresh stack of comic books near his nightstand. He figures that's a safer bet since reading always helped Liam slowly drift off to sleep.

Liam is lying in bed comfortably as he flips through the pages of this comics. Boo knocks along the threshold of his bedroom door and says, "Evening, big brother. What are you doing?"

Liam moves his comic away from his face. "What does it look like I'm doing. I'm keeping up on my summer reading."

Boo laughs. "That's far from summer reading. I've looked through a few of your comics. Most of them barely have any words."

Liam smiles as he replies, "Very true. That's why I try to find more comic book series from Dad's generation of comics. Those comics had a ton of dialogue and story."

Boo continues to stand in the doorway. "So what do you make of all the stuff that happened tonight?"

Liam puts the book down and looks at his bedroom ceiling for a moment. "Honestly, I didn't panic or scream. My first gut reaction was like, 'Oh, great! Here's we go again!' My second gut reaction was to look over to you. You looked like a knight in one of my games. Standing on a line and ready to do battle. You looked fearless."

Boo laughs and says, "Yeah right." Boo pauses for a moment and then continues, "Honestly, I felt the same way. Like, oh crap! Here we go again."

Liam laughs. "And then we both thought, *Please God.... No.*"

Liam and Boo both laugh. Liam looks serious for a moment and says, "But in all honesty, I don't know what to make of it. I'm just glad no one was hurt or worse."

Boo replies, "Yeah, me too." Boo pauses and then asks, "So it's comics and bed for the rest of your night then?"

Liam answers, "Yeah. Just about." Liam yawns and then continues, "I'm getting tired fast. What about yourself? You're not going to sit in your room all night talking to ghosts, are you?"

Boo laughs. "Shut up, dork! I haven't talked to any ghosts in a while. But if there's one ghost I would like to talk to, it's Misty. I miss her."

Liam smiles and says, "Yeah, I get it. If anything, I would like to say thank you."

Boo answers, "But to answer your question, I think I'm going to follow your lead. Do some summer reading and head to bed."

"You still reading those fantasy books from Dad's bookshelf?"

"Yeah, they're a great read. I haven't been able to read a three-hundred-plus page book so fast in my life."

Liam says, "Have fun with that. Good night."

Boo says, "Good night" to Liam as makes her way down the hallway back to her bedroom. Boo gets ready for bed. She lays comfortably in her bed and enjoys her book as her trusty dog, Lady, enters her room. Lady sniffs with her wet nose alongside Boo's bed and then stares at Boo waiting for her attention. Boo looks away from her book, looks at Lady, and says, "You don't need an invitation, Lady. Come on up and make yourself comfortable." Lady snuggles alongside Boo as she continues to read her fantasy book. Soon, Boo looks out toward the hallway. She sees the reflective light bouncing from Liam's bedroom go dark along the hallway wall. She yawns as she continues to read. She flips through the current chapter of her book and thinks, *I'll get through this chapter and then I'm done for the night."*

Boo hears the neighbor's dog from the other side of the alley bark as it usually does. Boo continues to read and starts to fall asleep as he reaches the end of her chapter. As she finishes, she grabs her bookmark resting along her nightstand, marks her page, turns off her reading light, and gets comfortable in bed. Outside the neighbor's dog continues to bark.

Boo tries to fall asleep. She tosses and turns. The neighbor's annoying little yapping dog isn't helping Boo or the rest of the family with their sleeping schedules. The neighbors were constant night owls. They often forgot about their dog and left it outside for far too long. Will's theory was that the neighbors couldn't stand the dog constantly barking and yapping at every little thing coming up and down the street while inside the house. So, their solution was keeping the dog outside in the backyard.

The dog begins to bark more frequently and loudly. Suddenly, it begins to growl at something. Lady lifts her head off the bed as she begins to hear the consistent growls coming from outside. She jumps off the bed, pounces on the windowsill with her front paws, and investigates the situation. Lady growls very quietly. Boo turns over and looks at Lady. Lady, on the contrary, is a very quiet dog and only growls when something isn't right. Boo gets up. "Lady. What is it, girl? What do you see?" Lady's growls get louder as the fur on her back stands on end!

Boo pets Lady and tries to calm her down as she looks out her window. She scans her backyard. Nothing out the ordinary. She pans her eyes along the alleyway. The yellow light illuminates the deserted and creepy alleyway. She investigates the neighbor's yard.

She sees the little yapping dog facing the neighbor's house, looking upward and viciously barking at something on the roof. Boo pans her eyes up toward the roof and sees two red eyes pierce through the darkness! She gasps while backing up. It's the winged creature! The enormous creature spreads its marvelous wings, opens its mouth, and lets out a ghastly shriek. Lady whimpers and retreats away from the windowsill as the creature plunges toward the neighbor's dog and grabs it with its razor-sharp claws! The dog let's out a horrible death cry as the winged creature flies away with its evening snack forked securely in between its hairy back claws. The creature whips toward Boo's window and pulls up and away within a few feet of the glass. A few small spots of red blood sprinkle along the outside of her window. Boo backs up more and quickly vanishes down the hallway toward Liam's room.

CHAPTER 4

....

LIAM! WAKE UP!

Boo runs so fast down the hallway her socks slip on the hardwood flooring, and she stumbles for a moment. She quickly recovers as her hands reach out to catch her fall. She regains her footing and runs alongside Liam's bed. Liam is fast asleep. Boo shakes Liam's shoulder and says in a quiet but abrupt voice, "Liam! Liam? Please wake up! We have a huge problem!"

Liam turns over and says in a groggy voice, "Wha…! What? What is it, Boo? I'm trying to sleep." Liam quickly gains his focus and sees the desperate and concerned look on Boo's face.

Boo's eyes begin to tear up as she says, "Liam!"

Liam sits up and asks, "What is it Boo? What happened?"

Boo stammers, "Th-th-there's blood on my bedroom window. Something's outside! I don't know where it went."

Liam sits at the edge of his bed and asks, "Did you wake up Mom or Dad?"

Boo answers, "No. I didn't. I came to you first."

Liam replies, "Good. Show me the window and tell me what happened."

Liam stands up and puts on his slippers. He and Boo walk into the upstairs hallway. They walk past their parents' room. The door is closed. Liam pauses, looks back at Boo, and gives her a signal to stop moving. Boo asks in a soft voice, "What are you doing?"

Liam answers in an even softer voice, "Just checking. Yup. Dad is out like a light. Snoring and choking the night away. Come on."

Boo grabs hold of Liam's hand. Liam can feel the nervous tension from his sister's quivering hand. Liam looks back at Boo and says, "It's okay. I'm right here."

They enter Boo's room. The room is dark except for the slight amber light reflecting from the alleyway streetlight and bouncing off the bedroom windows and walls. Liam looks over to Boo's bed and finds Lady hiding underneath Boo's computer desk. Lady whimpers and shakes as Liam looks back at Boo asking, "Let me guess. Lady saw it too?" Boo nods her head as she slowly enters her bedroom. Liam laughs a little and says, "Some watch dog. Every time there's something scary outside a window, she goes off and hides."

Liam looks at Boo's bedroom window. He sees the small red drops and says to himself, "What the hell?" Liam goes over to the window and investigates the drops closely. He then looks outside and scans the backyard and the alleyway. Nothing. There's movement coming out the corner of his eye. He looks over toward the neighbor's backyard on the other side of the alleyway. The neighbor stumbles into his yard and says, "Tippy! Tippy! Tippy? Where you at, girl? Come on! Stop hiding. Time to come in now. Tippy?"

Liam looks at Boo and asks, "Boo, what happened? Did someone do something to that annoying yapper dog?"

Boo approaches Liam and says, "Lady started growling. That's not like her, as you know. I looked outside and saw a giant winged creature on top of the neighbor's roof!"

Liam exclaims, "Holy shit! The same thing that we saw over the park?"

"Yeah. The same thing. It swooped down, grabbed the dog, and flew right past my window and over the house. That's the annoying yapper dog's blood!"

"No way! I guess the police didn't finish the job."

Boo sits on her bed and asks, "What are we gonna do, Liam? Are we gonna tell Mom and Dad?"

Liam continues to look out the window and watch the neighbor desperately search the yard for his dog. Liam turns toward Boo and answers, "Not gonna happen. After the events in Michigan and the events last summer inside the Elk's Estate, Mom and Dad don't need to worry about this unless they absolutely have to."

Boo answers timidly, "Then a monster has literally arrived in our backyard."

Liam sighs. "Yup. Looks that way. God knows if this thing is passing through or its gonna be here to stay."

Boo gives Liam a hug and asks, "Can I sleep in your room tonight? I won't be able to sleep a wink tonight knowing that the only thing separating me from that thing is a cheap piece of glass."

Liam smiles. "Not gonna happen. You sleep in your room tonight, and so will I. Let me grab my pillow and sleeping bag and I'll set up shop on the floor."

Liam walks out of Boo's bedroom and vanishes down the dark hallway toward his room. Boo walks toward the window and takes another look into the backyard. The neighbor across the alleyway continues to look up and down the alleyway from his fence line frantically calling for his dog. He shakes his head, and he turns back toward his house. A woman appears in the backdoor window of the neighbor's house. Boo can't make out the words, but both of the neighbors seem upset and worried. Boo looks over to her computer desk and sees two glowing eyes pierce through the darkness! She gasps as she steps back toward her bed. She trembles and her heart begins to race until she hears a slight whimper. The glowing eyes are radiating from Lady, her not-so-trusty guard dog. Boo says, "Come on, Lady. It's okay. Come back into the bed."

Liam enters the room and asks, "What's up, Boo?"

Boo answers, "It's Lady. She won't come out from under the computer desk."

Liam rolls his eyes. "Okay." He looks in Lady's direction and says, "Come on, Lady. Get out of there. Back to bed."

Lady follows Liam's commands and quickly dashes across the dark room and hops back on top of Boo's bed. Liam spreads out his trusty Scout sleeping bag across the carpeted floor. Boo settles back into bed. "Thanks, big brother. I appreciate it."

Liam replies, "No worries. I'm sure you would do the same thing if the roles were reversed."

Boo laughs. "You can think that if it makes you feel better."

Liam looks through the window to see the neighbors turning off their backyard light and closing the door. He asks, "Anything else happen across the way?"

Boo answers, "Nothing more than the neighbors looking upset that they couldn't find their dog. Poor thing. Yes, it was annoying, but still."

Liam replies, "I hear you."

Boo sits up one last time for the night and asks, "Liam. Honestly what are we gonna do? I have a feeling that more is gonna happen."

Liam answers, "When you, your gut, and that extra keen sense of yours starts saying things aren't right, that's when my stomach starts to turn. Well, hopefully nothing else will happen tonight. We will try to find out more in the morning. I have a feeling too."

Boo asks, "What's that?"

Liam answers, "That I'll have to talk to Ryan and Robert about this, and I'll also have to contact some old friends and family too."

Liam and Boo get settled for the night. They talk briefly to settle both of their nerves. Slowly conversations cease and they both fall asleep.

✦ ✦ ✦

Meanwhile, down in the heart of the city, a pretty young woman parks her car in the parking lot of the Cook County Medical Examiner's Office. She exits the vehicle as her long blonde hair flows through the breeze coming off Lake Michigan. She grabs her purse and her case with a shoulder strap. The case is holding her laptop and a medical file for a current patient. The orange street lights over the woman continue to buzz as she quickly walks through the partially vacant parking lot.

She looks around cautiously and feels uneasy being alone. She's startles only for a moment as an ambulance activates its lights and sirens and dashes down the street past her. She grabs her phone out of her purse and dials a number. The phone rings only for a moment when a voice says, "Cook County Medical Examiner's Office."

The woman says, "Yes. This is Rosanna. One of the county psychologists. I was contacted this evening regarding—"

The voice interjects, "Yeah, yeah, yeah. This is Ms. Ross, right? I was the one who contacted you. This is Rodney. Sorry for calling so late, but I figure you'll want to see this."

Rosanna replies, "It's okay. I was just finishing up some paperwork at the hospital when I got the message. Which door should I go to?"

Rodney answers, "Just head up to the front entrance and I'll be there to buzz you in."

Rosanna walks up the stairs and sees Rodney on the other side of the tall glass windows. Rodney, wearing green medical scrubs and a white jacket, waves and presses a button. Rosanna hears the buzz coming from the entrance doors. She grabs hold of the door and walks through the glass vestibule. She walks up to Rodney who meets her in the lobby entrance. "Thanks again for coming, Ms. Ross. I appreciate your time."

Rosanna replies, "It's not a problem. I was just on my way home anyway."

Rodney fixes his glasses and pushes them back up the bridge of his nose. "You look very young, Ms. Ross. Are you a recent graduate?"

Rosanna answers, "Yes, that's correct, Rodney. I'm sorry, should I be calling you Doctor?"

Rodney smiles and laughs. "No need for all the pleasantries, Ms. Ross. Rodney is just fine. However, I should be asking you the same thing. Should I be calling you Dr. Ross?"

Rosanna smiles and says, "No worries. Rosanna is fine."

Rodney says, "Okay, Rosanna. Please follow me." They walk down a long hallway toward an elevator. Their voices bounce and echo off the tall and vacant halls. Rodney continues, "Have you ever been to the county examiner's office before?"

Rosanna says, "No. This is my first time being here. I was only briefed about the building during my orientation with the county."

Rodney presses a downward arrow button on the elevator panel. "I see. Well, welcome to my home away from home."

Rosanna asks, "How long have you been working for the county, Rodney?"

"Long enough to think I've seen it all. But that was before my guys from the county meat wagon brought me the two security guards from your hospital."

The elevator bell chimes, and the doors slide open. Rodney moves his right arm forward and says, "After you, ma'am."

Rosanna enters the elevator. "Thank you."

Rodney enters the elevator, waves his county medical badge along a scanner, and presses a button for B2. Rosanna looks at Rodney and asks, "When did you receive the bodies?"

Rodney looks up toward the elevator ceiling and says, "Let me think. I think my guys dropped them off about twenty-four hours ago. After the police finished their initial investigation of course. I've been backed up all day doing autopsies. Figure I could at least do my initial assessment on both of them before calling it a night and heading home. After I opened the bags...." Rodney takes a deep breath, pauses for a moment, and continues, "I called your hospital immediately for a follow-up."

Rosanna says, "I see."

Rodney asks, "Were you at the hospital when the incident occurred?"

Rosanna shakes her head. "No. I was already home for the night. The incident and the escape happened during the overnight shift."

Rodney continues, "I see. And have you been briefed about what happened and the state of the bodies?"

Rosanna answers, "I was only briefed about my patient's escape and the two security guards who were killed."

The elevator stops, the bell chimes, and the doors slide open. They both exit the elevator and Rodney says, "Please, follow me. The fridge is just down the hall." They walk along the hallway, which is illuminated by several old florescent lights. Several of the lights blink as they reflect shimmering light off the green tiled walls and brown tiled floors. Rodney says, "Please, don't mind the smell. It's a mixture of heavy cleaners and formaldehyde. Now, are you sure the woman who escaped was the person who killed the security guards?"

Rosanna says, "Yes. That's correct. It's extraordinary really."

Rodney looks at Rosanna as they continue to walk and asks, "Why's that?"

Rosanna answers, "Well. My patient is a relic. One of the oldest patients we have in the county system."

Rodney pauses before they reach set of double doors and replies, "Interesting. So, you mean to tell me that a relic of an old woman did this to two middle-aged men?"

Rosanna answers, "I'm not sure what she did, Rodney. All I know is the aftermath."

Rodney looks at Rosanna and says, "Hmm… Very interesting indeed." Rodney pushes one of the double doors open and continues, "Please come in. Welcome to my office."

Rosanna follows Rodney into the morgue. The morgue is lined with several empty steel gurneys along the back end of the room. To the left is a wall with an observation window, a silver table with rows of surgical tools, and a tape recorder. To the right is a wall filled with rows of small metal doors, each with a lockable handle and a latch. Each of the metal doors has a slot big enough for an index card. The doors house the remains of someone behind them and include an index card with a name and a serial number.

Rodney says, "Okay good. My boys came through and cleaned this place up." Rodney smiles at Rosanna. "You wouldn't believe the mess we had around here to..." Rodney notices Rosanna. She immediately looks uncomfortable with her current situation. Rodney switches gears and says, "I'm sorry. I'm down here so much I forget that this place can be extremely uncomfortable for those who've never been. Would you like me to proceed?"

Rosanna looks around the room and then looks back at Rodney. "It's okay. Thank you for recognizing my comfort level. I made it this far. I'll be fine. Trust me."

"Okay, Rosanna." He slaps his hands together as he walks over to the wall housing the small metal doors. He places both of his fists along his hips and examines the names on the index cards. He walks up and down the row of doors and continues, "Let me see. Let me see. Where did we put those two?" He looks back at Rosanna and says, "Sorry. I hate to ask, but what were the two last names of the guards? I can look it up in my notes if need be."

With her arms crossed, she says, "No problem. I have the file right here." She unfolds her arms, opens her file, looks through her notes, and says, "Got it. Nickel and Salvatore."

Rodney slaps his hands together again, smiles and says, "Thank you! That's it. Okay…Nickel and Salvatore. Where are you guys? All right! Found you. Let me open up Mr. Nickel first." Rodney pulls the curved L-shaped handle and the metal door swings open to the right-hand side. Inside, is a heavy black bag containing a human body. Rodney approaches the metal roll-out tray housing the black bag and grabs hold of it with both hands. He takes a firm grip and walks backward, drawing out the metal tray and black bag along with him.

Rodney walks along the right side of the metal tray and gestures for Rosanna to approach. She approaches slowly and walks up to the foot of the metal tray. Rodney hands her a set of rubber gloves. Next, he reaches into his white coat pocket and pulls out a small canister and hands it to Rosanna. She takes hold of the canister and asks, "What's this?"

Rodney answers, "Just a vapor rub. Helps with the smell, and this one was...unique."

Rosanna applies a small amount of vapor rub underneath her nose and puts on the pair of rubber gloves. Rodney says, "It's okay. And if you need to leave after I open this bag, you can leave. No worries."

Rosanna takes a deep breath and nods.

Rodney grabs the zipper and says, "Okay, Dr. Ross. Here's Mr. Nickel." Rodney unzips the heavy black bag revealing the remains of Mr. Nickel. Inside is an extremely skinny, almost skeleton, body with gray skin wearing a hospital gown.

Rosanna gasps as she steps back and exclaims, "Oh, my God! How is…?"

Rodney answers, "Exactly, Dr. Ross. Exactly. How is it possible that a relic old lady turns a middle-aged man into a corpse who looks like it's in long-term decomposition?"

Rosanna approaches the metal tray again and asks, "Have you ever seen anything like this, Rodney?"

Rodney nods his head. "I've had a fair share of old bodies make their way through here from time to time. Usually, one of those missing person cases where authorities find the remains after long a while."

Rosanna asks, "From your expertise, what is your estimate on the length of time it would take to cause this amount of deterioration?"

Rodney answers, "I included my findings during my recorded assessment, Dr. Ross. Mr. Nickel, who's only been dead less than twenty-four hours, has decomposition similar to bodies who died over a year ago. I handed you a vapor rub which is standard procedure to anyone in the morgue. But you may notice the lack of smell. Which makes this particular investigation very unique."

Rosanna asks, "And what about Mr. Salvatore? The other guard. Does he look similar to Mr. Nickel?"

"That's the second reason I contacted your hospital and asked for a follow-up. Mr. Salvatore looks exactly like Mr. Nickel. Two bodies less than twenty-four hours old look like they died over a year ago."

CHAPTER 5

GOOD MORNING

Liam wakes up to Boo looking out the window as the hot morning sun shines and rises. Liam rubs his eyes and gives a loud yawn. "What do you see, Boo?"

Boo turns her head toward Liam and answers, "Cops in the alley."

Liam stands up and walks over to Boo to investigate.

They see two police officers and a police SUV in the alley. One officer is talking to the neighbors on the other side of the alley. As the neighbors respond to the officer, the officer is seen taking down notes on his notepad. The other officer walks back and forth and periodically shines his bright pocket light on the dark pavement.

Boo says, "Looks like the neighbor's wife is really upset."

Liam replies, "Well, yeah! Don't you think we would react the same way if something happened to Lady?"

Boo says, "True."

Liam asks, "How long have the cops been there?"

"They just pulled up a few minutes ago. When I woke up the neighbors were in their yard looking around. The husband was walking up and down the alley and calling for his dog. He saw something on the ground and then I saw him on his phone."

Liam and Boo continue to watch the activity in the alley as Annie pours herself a cup of coffee downstairs in the kitchen. After Annie adds her cream and sugar to her coffee, she opens the kitchen window blinds, which overlook the backyard. She notices the activity in the alley as she sips on her steaming cup of coffee.

She sees Tim, her next-door neighbor, walking in his bathrobe toward the rear fence line of his backyard. He has one hand in his bathrobe pocket. The other hand holds a glass mason jar filled with his cold brew coffee. Annie looks down at her cell phone on the kitchen counter as it buzzes from a text message from Will. Annie looks at her phone. Will, who's already at work, informs Annie that he'll be at training all morning and will be away from his phone. Annie puts her phone into her pants pocket and decides to walk out to the backyard.

Liam and Boo notice their mom walking in the backyard toward the alley. Boo says, "I guess Mom's as curious as we are. I wonder why Dad hasn't gone out to investigate."

"That's because Dad's already at work, silly. He leaves before the crack of dawn. Probably didn't notice anything out of the ordinary when he left for work. Plus, if he was off, we would still hear him snoring the morning away."

Boo laughs. "Oh, yeah. I forgot he works today."

Annie walks closer to the fence separating the backyard from the alley. She sees Tim talking to one of the police officers as the other officer continues to talk to the neighbors. The officer talking to Tim is holding a small, clear evidence bag. Annie sees a small broken dog collar and stains of red blood smeared along the inside of the bag. Tim turns around, notices Annie, and says, "Morning, neighbor. How are things? Will at work?"

Annie answers, "Things are fine, Tim. Yeah, Will's at work today. What's going on?"

Tim looks back at the officer. "Thanks for the heads up, man. I appreciate it."

The officer replies as he begins to walk toward his partner, "No problem, sir." Radio chatter from the officers' radios echoes through the alley.

Annie hears the radio dispatch say, "1635 Bravo, what's your status? We have another assignment for you when you're ready."

The officer talking to the neighbors replies into the radio mic on his shoulder saying, "1635 Bravo to dispatch. We'll be finishing our investigation in a few minutes. You can put the new assignment on the computer and we'll let you know when we're en route."

Dispatch replies, "Message received, 1635 Bravo."

Annie looks at Tim as he takes a large gulp of his cold brew and asks, "So what's going on, Tim?"

Tim answers, "Pretty wild actually. I was in my kitchen having my coffee and saw the police in the alley. I thought someone broke into my garage, so I came out right away. I asked the officer what's going on. He said something happened to the neighbor's dog last night."

Annie looks at the neighbors across the alley. The wife is visibly upset with tears streaming down her face. Her husband tries to comfort her as they both look at Annie. Annie says, "Sorry to hear about your dog!"

The husband waves as the couple turns and heads back to their house. Annie looks back at Tim and says, "I feel bad. They've been living at that house for years, but I never introduced myself."

Tim laughs and says, "Don't feel bad. I haven't introduced myself until today. The only thing I knew about them was their annoying dog and its constant barking."

Annie asks, "Did you find out anything else from the officer?"

Tim answers, "Yeah, apparently someone, or something, took their dog last night. Doesn't look too good. The husband was looking for her this morning. He checked the alley and found its broken collar and a small trail of blood running through the alley toward our houses."

Annie replies, "Oh, God! That's horrible!"

Tim says, "Yeah, it looks pretty grim for the dog. The police think maybe a coyote got a hold of it. There's been a few spotted in the area. When I talked to the cop he thinks a coyote was clever enough to climb on top of the garage and escape with the dog down the alley. They haven't found the poor thing yet."

One of the officers enters his police cruiser as the other finishes some documentation. Tim looks at him and says, "Excuse me, Officer. One last question."

The officer rolls his eyes and says under his breath, "There's one on every block." The officer walks over to Tim and says, "Yes, sir. What can I help you with?"

Tim asks, "So, what's was the deal with all of the commotion, police sirens, and helicopters last night?"

Annie looks at Tim and says, "There was some kind of winged creature being chased by a police helicopter. It flew over Liam's baseball game. Gave everyone a hell of a scare."

The officer looks at Annie and asks, "You were at the field last night, ma'am?"

Annie answers, "Yes, but I was in the concession stand. I didn't see much amongst all of the chaos."

Tim chuckles. "Are you kidding me! The police were chasing a flying monster! That's insane!"

The officer replies, "Yes, it's true. I wasn't working last night. But the overnight shift was talking about it when I walked into the police station this morning. The evening shift said the airport S.W.A.T. team was chasing something that was spotted over the flight path. Apparently, it attacked a few workers and a security guard last night."

Tim replies, "That's unreal, man! Did they catch it?"

The officer answers, "Unfortunately, they lost it when it entered the Robinson Woods a few miles west of here."

The officer inside the police cruiser lifts his head over the roof and exclaims, "Hey, Paul! We have another assignment. Come on!"

The officer nods his head, looks back at Annie and Tim, and says, "Have a good day, folks. If anything, I would keep an eye on your dogs. Don't leave them in the backyard unsupervised until we find out more."

Paul enters the police cruiser as his partner fastens his seat belt and presses a few buttons on the mobile computer. Paul asks, "Hey, Jeremy. What do we got?"

Jeremy answers, "Looks like there was an attack this morning in the forest preserve."

Paul fastens his seat belt. "Which one?"

Jeremy puts the car in drive and drives out of the alley. "Robinson Woods."

Paul turns the computer screen toward him and reads the description of the incident. He says, "Assist on-shift detective with DOA investigation and removal. Multi-jurisdiction response. Cook County Sheriff and forest preserve PD requested. What the hell?"

Jeremy turns on the sirens as they enter the main road and turns west toward the forest preserve. He replies, "Yup. Sounds like it's going to be a long shift."

Police sirens echo off nearby buildings and fade into the distance. Tim and Annie finish their conversation as they both make their way back into their houses. Liam and Boo turn away from the bedroom window and walk downstairs toward the kitchen. Lady is scratching at the back door as Annie opens it. Annie lets Lady outside and closes the gate behind her. Annie sees Liam first through the open side window and says, "Morning, honey. Do me a favor? Stand outside and watch Lady. Until we find out more about what's going on, Lady is not allowed to be outside unsupervised."

Liam says, "No problem, Mom. I got her."

Annie says, "Thanks, honey. I appreciate it. I'll work on breakfast."

Liam looks back at his mom before he exits through the back door. "Bacon and eggs?"

Annie smiles and says, "Deal."

Annie pulls out the bacon and eggs from the refrigerator as Boo pours herself a cup of chocolate milk. Annie says, "Morning, honey. How did you sleep?"

Boo turns around while drinking her chocolate milk and gives Annie a thumbs up. Boo puts the cup on the counter and asks, "Why do you ask?"

Annie, who's busy putting bacon on the frying pan, replies, "Before your father left for work, he peeked his head into your room and saw Liam sleeping on the floor under his sleeping bag. He mentioned it to me before he said goodbye this morning. Figured I would ask if you had a bad dream or something."

Boo scrambles for a good answer. "No bad dreams. With all of the crazy stuff that happened last night, I asked Liam to sleep in my room. I felt more comfortable with him close by."

Annie smiles.

Boo asks, "Why are you smiling?"

Annie answers, "You've always leaned on your brother for protection. He's been your safety blanket for a long time."

Annie flips the bacon and cracks a few eggs into another frying pan. The wonderful smell of a home-cooked breakfast fills the house. Annie looks at Boo and asks, "Do you remember when you and your brother both slept in the same room?"

"Vaguely. I remember the bunk beds."

"Yup. That's correct. You and your brother had the bunk beds."

Boo asks, "The same bunk beds that were up at the lake house in Michigan?"

"Correct. The very same."

Boo replies, "Why do you ask?"

"Well, when you were little, no older than three years old, you would wake up in the middle of the night and I would hear you whimper and cry. A mother's ears are never off duty. Your father's … that's another story. But anyway, I figured you had a bad dream. I would wake up and make my way to your room. By the time I would open the door and check on you, you had already climbed up the stairs to the upper bunk and snuggled up next to your brother. You would fall right back to sleep every time. In a way, seems like some things stay the same."

Boo says, "Cute story, Mom. Thanks for sharing. How's breakfast coming?"

Annie looks at the bacon and eggs. "It should be done in a few minutes."

Liam walks back toward the back door with Lady. He opens the door and Lady scrambles up the stairs. Lady sniffs the air and puts her paws on the counter looking for some finished bacon. Annie turns around and exclaims, "Off the counter! No, Lady, you're not getting any bacon! Daddy is not here!"

Liam walks up the stairs and says, "Smells good, Mom."

Annie replies, "Thanks for taking care of Lady, honey. It should be done in a few minutes."

Liam says, "Thanks, Mom. I'm pretty hungry this morning."

"That's why I'm making extra. I'm sure you're plenty hungry after playing your game last night."

Liam grabs the chocolate milk out of the refrigerator and walks over to the kitchen cabinet to get a glass. "Hey, Mom. Have you heard anything from my coaches? Are we gonna be able to finish the rest of the game?"

The bacon sizzles as Annie removes slices from the frying pan onto a plate lined with paper towels. Annie shakes her head as he says, "Nope. Nothing honey. Figure they'll figure it out when they can. I'm sure they have to do some clean-up after the chaos last night. If I hear anything, I'll let you know."

Liam says, "No worries, Mom."

Annie continues to scramble the eggs in the pan as she asks, "Any plans for today, honey?"

Liam answers, "Not sure. I'll probably hang out with the crew later today. Take a bike ride somewhere."

"That's fine, honey. As long as you stay with the group. With all of the goofy things happening in the neighborhood, all that I ask is that you stick together and make sure you bring your phone with you."

Liam takes a sip of his chocolate milk, smiles, and says, "Deal."

Liam walks over to the dining room table where Boo is already sitting. Boo is watching a show on her tablet while she enjoys her chocolate milk. A few minutes later, Annie walks into the dining room with two plates for Liam and Boo. Liam and Boo both say, "thank you" as Annie walks back into the kitchen to make her plate. When she reenters the dining room, she says, "Okay. So free time today. Enjoy it. Tomorrow you'll be going to Grandmom's house to help clean out of the garage and the attic."

Liam and Boo roll their eyes. Boo asks, "Do we have to?"

Liam says, "Yeah, really Mom? Have you seen how much crap is in her garage?"

Annie gives both of her kids a death glare as she replies, "Yes I have. That's why both of you are going to help your father. All hands will be on deck to sort through all of the stuff left behind from your grandfather. Damn it! I forgot my silverware. I'll be right back."

Annie walks back into the kitchen. Boo looks at Liam and says in a low voice, "So, what's the plan? Are you gonna talk to the crew about what we saw?"

Liam whispers, "Yeah. That's the plan. But first, I think we need to talk to some of our friends back in Philly. Follow me upstairs after breakfast."

....

CHAPTER 6

HEY, MONSTER SLAYER! HOW'S LIFE IN THE SECOND CITY?

Liam and Boo finish their breakfast and take their empty plates back into the kitchen. Annie, who is still finishing her breakfast while she reads a book from her tablet says, "Thanks for picking up your plates. Just leave everything on the counter and I'll take care of it in a few minutes." Liam and Boo make their way up to Liam's bedroom. Liam grabs his cell phone off his work desk.

Boo asks, "What do you want to do first?"

Liam answers, "I'll text Simon, Reggie, and Ellie and see if they are available to do some screen time. They're an hour ahead of us. They should be awake by now."

Boo replies, "I doubt it. Knowing Simon and Reggie the way I know them, they probably spent half the night or more playing video games online."

After the events at the Elk's Estate, Liam and Boo continued to stay in close contact with most of the Philly group. Especially their cousin Ellie and her friends Simon and Reggie. Simon and Reggie would invite Liam to play online video games with them. Simon, Ellie's boyfriend, would periodically send Liam his current ghostly investigation footage and ask for Liam's feedback. Neil wasn't involved in most of their interactions. This is partly due to Neil's extremely busy summer internship, work schedule, and his continuously bad habit of ghosting the group when he didn't feel like talking to anyone.

Liam texts: "Hey, guys! Something weird is happening here! It's hitting way too close to home. Call me when you get a chance."

After a few minutes, Ellie is the first to respond saying: "No worries. I'll head over to Simon's house right away and wake him up. Reggie slept over at Simon's house last night. When we're ready to do some screen time, I'll text you."

As Liam and Boo patiently wait for the group to assemble, a small private jet lands at the airport a few miles to the west. The jet successfully glides over to a far taxiway where a black SUV is parked and ready for pickup. As the jet's engines throttle down and the front passenger exit door begins to open and deploy its folding stairs down to the ground, two men exit the SUV. Both men are dressed in the traditional black uniforms with the white collars of Catholic priests. A younger adult man exits the jet carrying several large bags slung over his shoulder. The man is wearing a gray clergy alb with a stitched silver cross in the middle of the chest line. The man climbs down the stairs as the two priests walk toward him. Each priest bows their head. One of the priests, Father Russ, warmly says, "Thank you for making the long journey all the way from the Vatican, Bishop."

The man bows his head and replies with a European accent, "Thank you, Father."

The other priest, Father Luke, says, "Please, Bishop. Let us help you with your belongings."

The man smiles and says, "Thank you. Yes, please. But be careful."

Father Russ grabs some of the bags except for the large rectangular bag. As Father Russ reaches for this bag, the younger man, Bishop Michael, interjects saying, "Not that one, Father! Sorry. This bag must stay by my side at all times."

Father Russ smiles, bows his head, and replies, "Yes, of course, sir."

As Father Russ carefully places the bags into the rear hatch of the SUV, Father Luke opens the back passenger door for the Bishop and says, "After you, Bishop."

Bishop Michael smiles and enters the vehicle. Within minutes everyone is seated and the SUV drives toward the security post and away from the taxiway.

Father Luke is seated next to Bishop Michael while Father Russ rides in the front seat. The driver shows his credentials to the guard at the security gate. The guard nods his head and runs over to the guard post to quickly open the gate. The SUV enters the main road and then turns east toward Liam and Boo's neighborhood. Father Luke looks over at Bishop Michael and down at the long rectangular bag sitting on his lap. Bishop Michael looks over to Father Luke and asks, "You are curious, Father?"

Father Luke smiles. "Of course. It's like when you're a kid and you hear folklore stories and legends. And then one day, you ask yourself if the legends are true."

Bishop Michael replies, "I'm sure there's a lot of stories and legends of the men from my order."

Father Russ turns his head to face Bishop Michael and asks, "Bishop? Would you be so kind as to tell us why you were summoned here?"

Bishop Michael looks at both Father Luke and Father Russ and asks, "Did the archdiocese not inform you of the case?"

Father Luke smiles and chuckles for a brief moment, then replies, "No. Of course not. All I got was a phone call early this morning from the cardinal of our archdiocese saying that a bishop from the Order of the Silver Cross will be arriving early today via private jet. Father Russ and I were told to await a transport that will pick you up. The only other instructions we received were to escort you back to our rectory."

Bishop Michael looks ahead and sees a newspaper folded next to the driver's seat. He asks, "Please, sir. May I see your newspaper?"

The driver grabs the newspaper and says, "Yes, of course, Bishop. Help yourself. It's today's issue."

Bishop Michael grabs the newspaper and says, "Thank you, my son. God bless you." He looks down and the front-page article, smiles, and turns the article toward the two priests saying, "This is why I'm here, gentlemen."

The front page has a blurry image of a winged creature flying over a baseball park. The article headline reads: CHAOS, HELICOPTERS AND GUNSHOTS SPILL INTO A PEACEFUL SUMMER NIGHT AS POLICE SEARCH FOR ANSWERS.

After a short wait, Liam finally receives a text from Ellie saying: "Sorry for the delay. These two were out cold. Had to make a quick run to the coffee shop to help them wake up. We're ready."

Liam replies: "Awesome. Thanks. No worries. Signing on now."

Liam looks at Boo who's looks bored while she was waiting and says, "They are good to go. Going online."

Boo says, "Finally. That only took forever and a day."

Liam sits down at his computer desk and says, "Stop. It wasn't that bad. Plus, we're talking about Simon and Reggie. What else do you expect?"

Boo laughs as she says, "True story, big brother."

The screen comes to life as Liam and Boo are excitedly greeted by Ellie, Simon, and Reggie.

Ellie is sitting in the middle of the screen while Simon and Reggie lean over her from either side. Ellie smiles and Simon shouts, "Hey, monster slayers! How's life in the Second City treating you?"

Liam says, "Hey, everyone! Nice to see all of you. Especially Simon and Reggie. Good job getting them awake, Ellie."

Simon says, "It was difficult waking up at this ungodly hour, but when you have the most beautiful girlfriend in the world banging at your front door, you don't—"

Reggie interjects saying, "Oh, shut up, man! Yeah, we all know Ellie is your girlfriend. It's been that way for about a year now. Get over it. We have!"

Simon laughs. "Never. I'm still head over heels for her."

Ellie rolls her eyes. "Never mind him, Liam. He's a pain in my ass most days."

Simon says, "So, Liam and Boo! What's this I hear about some strange stuff happening in your neck of the woods?"

Liam and Boo give the group a brief synopsis of the previous night's events and the encounter with the winged creature and the neighbor's dog.

Reggie says, "Dude, are you serious?"

Simon says, "Wicked!"

Ellie says, "You mean to tell us that there was a flying monster over your backyard?"

Boo says, "That's what I'm saying! I can take a picture of the small drops of blood on our bedroom window and send it to you if you want proof."

Simon says, "Yeah, Boo. Please do! Dude, that's so awesome."

Ellie elbows Simon in his side. "Simon. We are working on your manners, remember?"

Simon fake smiles and he grimaces in pain. "Oh yeah! Sorry. That's rude. Sorry to hear about the dog, I guess."

Liam and Boo and the rest of the group laugh at Simon as Liam interjects, "Let me see if I can find something from the local news." Liam does a quick search and finds a few articles relating to the incidents around his neighborhood and the surrounding area. Liam sends the articles over to the Philly group. They all read the articles from the screen.

Boo does some quick research from her phone. "I'll send this article to Ellie's phone. My dad was reading about it the evening that the monster flew over Liam's baseball game."

Simon asks, "What was your dad reading, Boo?"

Boo answers, "Something about an old woman escaping from a mental hospital in the nearby suburbs. Apparently, the police can't find her, and she's the reason two security guards were taken out of the mental hospital in body bags. I'm sure the two incidents aren't related, but still, it's crazy how all of this stuff is happening all at once."

Simon says, "God, I miss you guys! Life here in Doylestown, PA, isn't nearly as exciting without you too hanging around. What we should do is take a little road trip out to Liam and Boo's area and—"

Ellie interjects, "Don't even think about it. My parents will never sign off on me taking a road trip with my idiot boyfriend."

Simon laughs, puts his arm around Reggie, and says, "Not only your idiot boyfriend but his best friend in the whole wide world will be along for the ride."

Reggie says, "Thanks, man. But Ellie is right."

Simon replies, "You're right. Well, monster slayer and she-who-speaks-to-ghosts, how can we be of service to you?"

Liam says, "Boo and I are planning to possibly meet up with our crew later today and discuss everything that happened. In the meantime, I figure the Philly team can do a little bit more research, and Simon and Reggie can work their magic online and find out if there's any way to connect the dots and to find out if there's any folklore about a flying monster in the Midwest."

Simon says, "I'm glad to see my talents are noticed by others. Thank you, monster slayer."

Liam says, "Thank you. Let me know what you find out."

The group says their goodbyes and everyone signs off.

Boo looks at Liam and says, "Okay, that portion of our detective work is underway. What's next, big brother?"

Liam pulls up the article, which is the same article Bishop Michael was reading on the front page of the local newspaper.

Liam reads aloud: "The unknown creature is being blamed for the ghoulish and untimely deaths of two on-duty airport employees. One being a security guard and the other a maintenance worker. Presently, the names of the victims have not been released by local police. The identities will be released after police confirm notification to their next of kin." Liam skim reads as he glances over the reported sighting and the subsequent damage at the park. He begins to read aloud again saying, "The pursuing S.W.A.T. team from the local airport police lost visual contact of the creature as it approached the Robinson Woods. Please stay tuned as this story continues to develop." Liam looks at Boo and says, "After we meet up with the crew, that's our next move."

Boo asks, "What's our next move? Going to Robinson Woods?"

Liam says, "Exactly."

CHAPTER 7

....

INVESTIGATION IN THE ROBINSON WOODS

Boo looks at her brother and says, "Robinson Woods is a bit of a hike for us, don't you think?"

Liam shakes his head. "I don't think so. It's only a few miles from our neighborhood. We can ride our bikes straight down Foster Avenue to get there. The sidewalk runs from our neighborhood all the way to the forest preserve."

Boo replies, "How do you know all of that?"

Liam answers, "Dad used to live near the Robinson Woods before he and Mom got married. Before his knees started to give him trouble, he used to still run all the way out to Robinson Woods from home."

Liam looks at the clock. The morning continues to move on quickly. He grabs his phone and texts the crew from their group thread: "Hey, everyone. I want to meet up and maybe take a bike ride out to Robinson Woods. Who's with me?"

Ryan is the first one to text back: "I'm game as long as someone buys me lunch. I'm starving."

Robert texts: "You're always starving big guy!"

Ryan answers, "Shut up!"

Tommy texts back: "Timmy and Maddie have a doctor's appointment. My mom is taking them. I was planning to hang out with Robert and Ryan anyway. I'm game, but I agree with Ryan. We should plan to eat before we go."

Robert replies: "Why don't all of you plan to meet up at my house within the hour. My dad cooked his famous pizzas last night. Plenty of leftovers here!"

Ryan texts: "Your dad's pizza has been part of this equation the entire time! Why didn't you say something earlier. Let's do it!"

Tommy replies: "Sounds like a plan. See everyone soon. I got my allowance today! I'll spring for ice cream at that shop on Harlem Avenue on the way home."

Ryan replies: "Now I know why Liam brought you into our group. You're one of the good ones, Tommy. See you then."

Liam smiles and says to Boo, "Looks like we're in business. Before we leave, let's go and tell Mom we're planning to go over to Robert's house and maybe take a bike ride. And of course, we'll promise to be home before dinner."

Boo says, "I don't feel comfortable lying to Mom. And you're supposed to be the responsible one, Mr. Boy Scout."

Liam laughs and says, "Now think about what I just said. Nothing that I said is lying. I'm simply omitting information. Learned that trick from Dad."

Boo smiles and says, "You know what, you're right. Good thinking, Liam."

Liam replies, "Good thinking, Dad!"

The two police officers, Jeremy and Paul, reach the intersection of Lawrence and East River Road with lights and sirens activated. Jeremy stops at the intersection and takes control of traffic before he proceeds north along the eastern edge of the Robinson Woods. As he makes the turn onto East River Road, he sees several police cruisers a half a mile ahead along the western side of the road. Paul shakes his head and says, "Yeah, it looks like it's going to be a long shift. These multi-jurisdictional deals are a big pain in the ass. Everyone stepping on each other's toes."

Jeremy replies, "It's all the same to me. Either be here or be somewhere else. The only thing that's gonna suck is being out in the heat."

Paul laughs and he says, "And the smell of the body too."

Jeremy replies, "Thanks for reminding me."

Jeremy turns off the sirens as he reaches the destination and parks the cruiser along the side of the road with the others. Jeremy and Paul take notice of all of the activity happening at once. Other city police cruisers block a lane of traffic while dozens of onlookers observe and record all of the activity on their phones from the other side of the street. The propelling sound of an approaching helicopter echoes throughout the air. Paul looks up into the golden blue sky and sees a police helicopter zip across the forest preserve as two other news channel helicopters hover over the forest at a slightly higher altitude.

Jeremy looks at Paul and says, "Smile. You'll definitely be on TV or someone's social media post today."

Paul laughs and says, "That's part of the job nowadays; that doesn't even phase me anymore. Hey, do you think those news helicopters have permission to hover along this area? Aren't they in the flight path for one of the airport runways?"

Jeremy answers as he and Paul continue to walk toward the entrance of the forest preserve, "Police probably requested the airport to use another runway and flight path so they can conduct their investigations from the air. Of course the media is taking advantage of the opportunity."

Paul says, "You're pretty clever, young man. Keep that up and you'll be leading investigations like this in no time."

Paul and Jeremy walk past several cruisers from different representing jurisdictions including Illinois State Police, Cook County Sheriffs, and Cook County Forest Preserve Police. Paul asks Jeremy, "Why do you think state police are here?"

Jeremy answers, "The Des Plaines River is probably the reason. Illinois State Police has jurisdiction along any major waterways."

Paul smiles and says, "You see. Clever. Keep studying, young man."

Paul and Jeremy are met by their supervising shift sergeant. Paul says, "Morning, Sarge, how's everything going?"

Jeremy shakes the sergeant's hand and says, "Jesus! They have you out here too? Anyone else showing up?"

Sarge answers, "As a matter of fact. Yes. I'm waiting here for the Cook County Medical Examiner's van to show up. Maybe they're stuck in traffic."

Paul asks, "So what do you need from us, Sarge?"

Sarge replies, "I want you to go over to an apartment building down the street from here and do a welfare check on a young lady named Amy. She could possibly be the reason all of these fine people are gathered here today."

Paul replies, "What do you mean possibly?"

Jeremy says, "Yeah, really. And who's in charge of this investigation? City, county, or state?"

Sarge looks at both Jeremy and Paul and says, "Okay. Looks like I got time to kill. Come with me, gentlemen. Seeing is easier than trying to explain it." Sarge walks over and lifts the yellow police tape wrapped along the entrance of the forest preserve and says, "Please, gentlemen, allow me." Paul and Jeremy follow Sarge into the forest preserve. They walk along the wide trail surrounded by thick oak trees, wide wild bushes, and tall prairie grass. As they walk, Sarge begins to explain, "Okay. So, to answer your question, Jeremy, The Cook County Forest Preserve Forensic Team will be leading the investigation. State police are here but they'll be leaving soon. They just wanted to make sure it wasn't a body in the river. If so, the investigation would fall on their shoulders. The lead investigator seems like a very smart and distinguished older gentleman named Detective Steve Cunningham. He'll be the one with the silver hair and a matching mustache and glasses. And believe me when I tell you, he's got an interesting case on his hands."

As they continue to walk farther up the trail, Paul asks, "What do you mean, Sarge? Damn! It's getting hot out here."

Sarge laughs a little and says, "So get this. Some poor bastard who's way into personal fitness goes out into the morning sun for a lovely run along the trail. When he starts to head north along the Des Plaines River Trail, he notices something lying on the ground a few yards away. He takes a closer look and finds out it's a female corpse and calls 911. Cook County Forest Preserve Police show up first. They meet the guy at the entrance of the trail, and the guy shows the cops where the corpse is located. They find a trail pack, an ID, and a cell phone flung a few yards away from the body. The cops look at the phone. There's dozens of missed calls from some guy named Jacob. The phone starts ringing and the cops answer it. Turns out, the poor guy on the other end of the phone is the young lady's boyfriend. He's frantic and says he hasn't been able to reach his girlfriend all night. He figures something is wrong but didn't know what to do."

Sarge, Paul, and Jeremy reach the crime scene where they see several officers walking around and Detective Cunningham examining some evidence before it's sealed in a plastic bag. Jeremy wipes the layer of sweat off his face and says, "Sounds pretty normal stuff in our line of work. What's the catch?"

Sarge smiles. "Haven't you noticed anything yet, gentlemen?"

Paul asks, "What's that?"

Sarge answers, "The sun is boiling down on this area, and none of us are gagging for fresh air." Sarge looks at Paul and says, "Paul, you're a senior officer. Ever been to a crime scene where the body doesn't smell to high heaven?"

Paul answers, "Once or twice. And that's because the body was way old and already completely decomposed."

Sarge says, "Exactly. Now Paul, take our partner over to Detective Cunningham a take a look at that body."

Paul and Jeremy walk toward the detective. Detective Cunningham turns and says, "Good morning, Officers. How can I help you?"

Sarge interjects, "It's okay, Steve. They're my guys. I just wanted them to take a look."

Detective Cunningham says, "Okay. Go ahead." Detective Cunningham looks at Sarge and asks, "Hey, Sarge! Has the medical examiner's office shown up yet?"

Sarge answers, "No, sir. I'll walk my guys out in a minute and take another look."

Jeremy and Paul look at the body. "The body is a pale white corpse with long brown hair showing complete decomposition and deterioration of muscle and tissue."

Paul and Jeremy start walking back to Sarge. Paul says, "You mean to tell me that the body over there was alive and well twenty-four hours ago? That doesn't make any sense!"

Sarge replies, "That's exactly correct, gentlemen. In fact, less than twenty-four hours ago according to initial reports with the storyline we received from the boyfriend. That's why I need you to go to her apartment, do a welfare check, and report back. If no one answers, break the damn door down if necessary. I wish I could give you some keys to her unit, but no keys were found at the scene. But we need to find out if that body over there is the same Amy who was alive and well yesterday."

✦ ✦ ✦

Liam and Boo leave their house and ride their bikes down to the end of the block. They stop at the corner. Boo says, "Okay, big brother. Which way do you want to go?"

Liam looks down the street and then across the street. He points and says, "Let's go down this way and bike across the park. I want to see if they are making any repairs."

Liam and Boo bike down Giddings Street and turn toward the bike path that goes right through the park. They see a city crew cleaning up the downed field lights and removing the majority of the debris into a large blue dump truck. As they bike further east along the bike path, Liam sees one of his coaches, Phil, prepping the baseball field by driving an ATV up and along the baseball diamond while dragging a large piece of chain-linked fence along its back end. Phil takes notice of Liam and Boo, smiles, and waves at them. Liam and Boo stop along the dugout as Phil approaches them.

Phil turns off the engine and says, "Hey, Liam! Hey, Boo! Where you off to?"

Liam answers, "Hey, Coach! Off to a friend's house for the afternoon. Maybe take a bike ride."

Phil responds, "You picked a nice day for it. Not supposed to get any rain for a few days. Definitely helps me and the other coaches keep the fields ready for the upcoming games."

Liam asks, "Any idea if we'll be able to resume and finish the game from last night?"

Phil answers, "No clue. I'll have to wait and see how long it will take the city crew to complete the repairs. I should know more by tonight. I'll be sure to text the team when I find out more. Enjoy your day and be careful out there."

Liam and Boo both say "thank you" as they continue heading east along the bike path toward Robert's house.

As they arrive at Robert's house, they see Ryan's and Tommy's bike resting along the side of the house next to their side entrance. Liam and Boo rest their bikes next to their friends' and knock on the door. Liam and Boo can smell the beautiful and sweet aroma of Mr. Kragel's pizza warming up in the oven when the door opens and Robert greets them. He says, "Perfect timing! Come on in. Pizza will be ready in a few minutes."

The group enjoys their lunch together while they discuss and recap the events of the previous evening. Liam and Boo also recap the incident with the neighbor's dog and Boo's up-close encounter with the creature. Liam explains why he wants to check out Robinson Woods. The group, now fully aware of the reason Liam wants to check out the forest preserve, is now less than enthusiastic about the bike ride. Especially Robert and Ryan.

Ryan says, "Dude! Didn't you learn your lesson back a couple of years ago when most of us, excluding Tommy, were almost killed by a big scary werewolf at your grandparents' lake house?"

Robert says, "Yeah, really. My parents will probably never let me go away with your family again after that disaster."

Ryan looks at Liam and says, "Exactly. And need I remind you that you and your whole household was almost taken out last summer by some type of crazy pissed-off shadow ghost?"

Robert interjects, "Yeah, dude. Especially your dad. He crossed over and came back. You're talking about a different level of risky business."

Ryan looks at Tommy and says, "Tommy! Any thoughts on the matter?"

Tommy answers, "Not really. I've spent the last two summers hearing about these wild stories from the group. You're the ones with the firsthand experience. I guess that includes me now after the events of last night. I'm with whatever Liam decides."

Ryan looks at Liam and says, "And need I remind you in each situation both last summer and two summers ago, there were a handful of people who never made it home."

Boo interjects, "Ryan! Stop it! In either case, both last summer and the summer before, it's not Liam's fault. Especially last summer. That whole thing was an elaborate trap. We were just the unfortunate ones who fell into it."

Liam responds, "But we were the lucky ones because we all made it home safe. Look, I know it sounds crazy, but my gut instinct is telling me that a lot of the crazy things happening around our neighborhood are linked together. And my gut is telling me that the

Robinson Woods is the bridge keeping those links together." Liam looks at Ryan and says, "And need I remind you that people have already been affected. Haven't you heard or listened to the news recently? There are bodies being found left and right. And if nobody stops it, it will continue."

Ryan chuckles. "Oh okay, monster slayer, as your friends on the East Coast like to call you. What exactly are you gonna do to stop this thing? Hit it with your baseball bat?"

Robert interjects, "Look! I have my concerns and a little bit of post-traumatic stress cruising through my mind right now. But all that Liam wants to do is look around and then head home. Right?"

Liam nods his head. "Exactly. Check some things out. Let our experience from previous events help us solve this mystery. Especially now. This time, it's in our backyard. Like literally in our backyard. Now, I'm going out there alone if I have to, but I'm leaving. Anyone coming along?"

Liam makes his way outside. Boo follows right behind him. Tommy is the next one outside along with Robert. They each put on their helmets and mount their bikes. Liam starts riding toward the end of the driveway. He looks back and asks Robert, "Do you think we should wait for Ryan?"

Robert says, "Screw him! Big mouth likes to talk a lot of shit. Let's go."

Ryan exits the house and makes his way over to his bike. "Yeah, I know I have a big mouth, Robert, thanks for that. I also have excellent hearing and a weak bladder. Give me a break. I needed to use the bathroom. I'm with you guys. If I chicken out, I'll never hear the end of it."

The friends mount their bikes and make their way north along Austin Avenue and then turn west as they reach Foster Avenue. They slowly make their way toward Robinson Woods.

CHAPTER 8

. . . .

BLOOD IS LEFT ON A BRANCH

The crew are close to Robinson Woods. They wait for the traffic light to change at the corner of Foster and Cumberland. Ryan points to the gas station on the corner and says, "I don't know about you guys, but I'm stopping over there to get a pop. Who's with me?"

Robert replies, "Sounds like a good idea! I can go for that and maybe some gum and a bag of chips."

Ryan says, "Good thinking. Maybe I'll get a chocolate and peanut butter candy bar too. One needs sugar and protein when they are exercising."

Liam looks at the group and says, "Sounds good. Let's take a break and get some pops. We're actually making really good time."

The light turns green and the group bikes across the street to the gas station. Everyone parks their bikes along the sidewalk lining the edge of the convenience store. Ryan runs inside. Robert and Boo follow after. Liam looks at Tommy who's still on his bike and asks, "You coming in, Tommy?"

Tommy takes off his baseball cap and whips the sweat away from his forehead. "Not just yet. Figure someone should stay back and watch the bikes. Some of us didn't bring our locks and chains."

Liam replies, "Good thinking." Liam peeks around the corner of the convenience store and looks back at Tommy saying, "Tell you what. I'll be back in a minute. I thought I saw a police car going down the street. Gonna see if the coast is clear."

Tommy replies, "Sounds good, dude. Be careful."

51

Liam mounts his bike and peddles down the parking lot toward the sidewalk. As he peddles down the sidewalk, he notices a police cruiser parked along the side of the road with the engine running and the bright blue-and-white lights flashing. He slows down his bike for a moment as he sees two police officers exit their vehicle and walk up to a three-story apartment building where a young man at the building entrance is pacing anxiously back and forth. Liam takes notice of the two officers. The younger officer takes notice of Liam and waves at him saying, "Hey, buddy."

Liam waves back and thinks, *Those are the two officers who were outside my house in the alley this morning. I wonder what they are doing here.*

The two officers meet the young man waiting by the apartment entrance. Liam starts to peddle past the apartment building slowly as he overhears the conversation. He hears the young man say, "Yes! That's correct. I'm Jacob. Amy is my girlfriend. Have you found out anything? Please tell me she's okay!"

Liam peddles past the building and sees a crowd of onlookers gathered at the corner. He looks both ways out toward the road before he peddles out to the street. He peddles to the end of the block and observes the situation. He sees several police vehicles and a van from the Cook County Morgue idling. Two men exit the van, both of which are wearing dark blue coveralls. One of the men opens the back door and removes a stretcher and a body bag.

Liam looks up and sees a police helicopter hovering over an area about a half a mile west of the forest preserve entrance. He looks up to the north along the eastern stretch of the forest preserve and notices no activity at the northern entrance along Bryn Mawr Avenue. He turns his bike around and quickly peddles toward the convenience store. As he reaches the convenience store, he sees the crew waiting by their bikes and enjoying their snacks. As Liam pops his kick stand down to the ground, Boo throws Liam a soda pop and bag of chips. She smiles and says, "You can thank me later and treat me to snacks at the next ball game."

Ryan says, "You were gone for a hot minute or two. Not complaining though. We don't mind the break from this hot summer day."

Tommy looks at Liam and asks, "Did you find out anything?"

Liam answers, "Looks like something happened over at the forest preserve. They got a decent number of police cars down there and a van from Cook County Morgue."

Robert says, "Are you serious?"

Liam answers, "I wouldn't lie to you about something like that. Looks like they have that whole area cordoned off while they do some type of investigation."

Robert asks, "What's the plan then? Just head home? Ain't no way we are gonna be able to get in there."

Liam smiles and says, "Actually, I think I came up with a Plan B."

Boo asks, "What do you mean?"

Liam points north along Cumberland Avenue and says, "There's no cops at the forest preserve entrance along Bryn Mawr. Let's take Cumberland up to Bryn Mawr, bike down the corporate center area, and quickly make our way across the street."

As he chews on his candy bar, Ryan says, "Great! More biking. I should have gotten two candy bars."

Tommy says, "Dude! Just chill. I'm still game for ice cream after we finish our tasks. We came this far. Let's finish it."

Ryan finishes his candy bar, puts his hands in the air, and says, "Fine! I've always known Tommy as a man of his word. I'll hold you to it. Let's ride!"

The group bikes along their alternate route and quickly reach the intersection along Bryn Mawr and East River Road. The group waits for the light to change before crossing the street. As the light turns green, Liam looks to the south. He looks back at the group and says, "Looks like the coast is clear. Come on!"

The group crosses the street and immediately begins riding down the bike path into the forest preserve. They continue riding for about a quarter of a mile before Liam hits the breaks. The rest of the group follows suit. Boo asks, "What are thinking, big brother? Do you see anything?"

Liam gives the quiet hand signal over his mouth as he points to a picnic clearing just past the tree line. Liam pantomimes "Cops over there!" The group looks just past the tree line and sees a police cruiser making its way along the parking lot and out toward East River Road. Liam signals for the group to move away from the trail and deeper into the forest.

They all follow Liam and ride their bikes into a ditch area just off the bike trail. Liam, in a quiet but immediate tone, says, "Quiet! Come on! Right over here!" The group finds spots to hide along the vast selection of bushes and trees. Liam lifts his head out of the ditch to look for the cops. The police cruiser pauses for a brief moment and then enters the main road just past the forest preserve. Liam stands up and tells the group, "Come on. The coast is clear."

Ryan stands up from behind a large bush and says, "Yeah, until it's not. Just how close do you want to get to the cops before we all get caught and possibly get in trouble?"

Tommy walks around the tree from which he was hiding behind and says, "Man! I don't think I've ever hid from the cops before. I hate to admit it, but it is kind of exciting."

Robert interjects, "Yeah, if you're gonna continue to hang with us get used to an occasional run-in with the cops."

Tommy smiles. "Are you serious?"

Boo answers, "Unfortunately, he's not, Tommy. Ryan and Robert were with us during a high-speed police pursuit back in Michigan."

Tommy exclaims, "No way!"

Ryan says, "Oh, yes way!"

Robert interjects, "Oh, indeed. I was right next to the big guy here. He let out a nervous fart so bad that I thought he shit his pants."

Ryan exclaims, "Shut up, Robert!"

The group laughs and Liam says, "Hey! Keep it down. Did you hear that?"

Tommy asks, "Hear what, dude?"

Ryan says, "He's right. I have the ears of a rabbit. Something is coming this way."

Liam says, "Quick! Everyone, hide!"

The group crouches down and runs back to their hiding spots. Off in the distance they hear what sounds like several people running through low-hanging branches and bushes just to their west and heading in their direction! Liam can hear Ryan's breathing continue to increase and become shallow as he feels his own heartbeat thump rapidly from his chest up to his neck. Liam looks up from the row of small bushes he's hiding behind. He sees what's coming toward them. It's a family of deer. The family of deer dash past the group without giving them any attention. The deer continue to run out to the clearing along the picnic area and back into the southern part of the woods. The group looks toward the south and sees the police helicopter travel away from the area and back toward the city.

Liam lifts his head more. He scans and searches the surrounding area. No more movement. He says, "Hey, Boo, Tommy…Guys. Coast is clear again. Come on let's go."

The group gets up and brings their bikes back onto the trail. Robert says, "Okay! Well, that really sucked. Haven't been that scared since Iron River. What do you think that was about?"

Liam answers, "I don't know. It's hard to say. Come on. Let's go just a little bit further."

Liam points ahead toward the end of the trail where it branches off in different directions. He says, "Just up there is the Des Plaines River. That's basically where that police chopper was hovering. Let's go check that out and we'll get out of here."

Ryan shakes his head. "I don't like it, monster slayer. You want us to go in the direction where the animals were running away from as if their lives depended on it?"

Robert asks, "What's the matter, Ryan? Are you getting nervous and gonna crap your pants again?"

Ryan exclaims, "Shut up, wimp! Fine, I'll go but under protest. I have to find new friends in the fall."

The group makes it to the end of the trail where it branches into different directions along the Des Plaines River. Liam signals the group to wait around the bend while he checks to see if there's any activity nearby. He looks down both sides of the trail. No activity. He looks over toward the river. The murky bluish-green river water ripples and slowly moves down in a calm southern stream. He looks upstream toward a large storm drain, which runs underneath the nearby highway to the other side of the forest preserve. A cool breeze flows in from the west and crosses the banks of the river toward Liam. Liam is thankful for the cool breeze on this now blistery summer afternoon until he catches a whiff of the smell flowing through the wind. Liam coughs and chokes for a moment. He recognizes that smell, and it sends a shiver down his spine. It's inescapable. It's the smell of death.

He uses his natural senses to help detect where the smell is coming from and then he sees it. He's amazed as what he sees just a few yards off the western bank of the river. He walks back toward the group and signals them to come toward him. Boo is the first arrive. She asks, "What is it, Liam?" Boo inhales deeply through her nose and says, "Oh, God! What is that smell? Is that what I think it is?"

Liam nods his head and points to the other side of the river. The group gathers at the eastern bank of the river along the bike trail while they cover their noses. They see the fresh remains of a whole family of deer who look like they were ripped apart by some large animal!

Robert says through his covered nose, "Jesus! That's disgusting! What could have done that?"

Ryan coughs as he takes a big inhale through his mouth. He backs away and says, "That's it! I'm out! I'm gonna be sick!" Ryan coughs some more while he collects himself next to a nearby bush.

Tommy says, "Jesus, guys! Do you think our mystery guest did that?"

Boo says, "Looks that way." Boo stands up. She starts to look around and begins to have a look of concern over her face.

Liam turns around and asks, "What is it, Boo?"

"Liam, I think it's time we get out of here. Something dark and evil is nearby and it's watching us."

Tommy says, "How do you know that? Are you sure?"

Liam stands up and signals for the rest of the group to follow. "Yes, she's sure. When Boo's other sense starts to kick in, then you know something is up. Okay, let's get out of here."

Just then, a police officer appears along the bike trail just a hundred yards south off their location. The officer sees the group and exclaims, "Hey! What are you kids doing back here? The preserve is closed by police order!" The group runs toward their bikes and mounts them as quickly as possible. Liam stumbles and scrapes his leg along a sharp low-hanging branch. He cuts himself and blood instantly starts oozing from the cut down to his sock.

Boo looks back as she gets on her bike and asks, "Liam, are you okay?"

Liam looks down at the cut. "Yeah, I'll be fine, but I'll have to clean it when I have a chance. Come on!" The group quickly rides down the path back toward the exit along East River Road.

The police officer walks briskly toward the area where he spotted the group. He looks down and sees a small drop of blood where Liam cut himself. He begins to run toward the other end of the trail. He looks down toward the far end of the trail as he sees the group leave the forest preserve. He says to himself, "God damn, kids. None of them listen or follow directions. Not worth the effort."

The officer's radio mic speaker echoes, "Hey, Rich! Where did you run off to?"

The officer presses the push-to-talk button. "I'm just along the trail a bit to the north. Saw some kids. Scared them off. They're out of here. Making my way back to the crime scene."

The man on the radio replies, "Sounds good. Looks like the forensic team is finishing up, but the detective wants all hands on deck, so head back."

Rich says, "Message received."

Rich gets a whiff of the smell coming from the other side of the river. He scans the area and notices the family of deer. Rich thinks, *Jesus! I'll have to let the detective know about this!*

Behind Rich, a young female voice says, "Afternoon, Officer. What seems to be all the trouble?"

The officer spins around to look at the woman. His jaw drops when he sees a gorgeous young woman with long black hair and strikingly beautiful eyes wearing a tight and revealing running outfit. Rich stammers, "There's be-been an incident along the trail, ma'am. The preserve has been closed by police order. I'm afraid I'll ha-have to escort…"

The woman looks deep into the officer's eyes as she moves closer to him. Her eyes transform from a deep brown color to a glowing blood red as she says to him, "No need for that…Officer. I can find my own way out."

The officer is silent, in a trance and lost in her eyes. She points to the rotting family of deer on the other side of the river and continues, "And don't worry about calling in those leftovers over there. My pet will be hungry before sunset. He'll take care of the rest of that."

Rich's radio echoes, "Hey, Rich! Where you at? Come on! The detective is waiting!"

The officer doesn't answer. He continues to look into the woman's glowing red eyes as she says, "Now, run along back to your buddies. Have a good day, handsome, and remember you never saw me." Her eyes turn back to dark brown and she quickly walks away from the officer.

Rich turns and walks back toward the crime scene. He continues to stumble and shake his head as he makes his way out of sight. The woman inhales deeply through her nostrils. She follows her nose down to the ground where she finds small drops of blood. She says, "Well, well, well. What do we have here? That smells familiar." The woman bends down and starts to crawl on the ground. She lifts her head and says, "There's more of it over there." She gets to her feet and follows the trail back to the tree branch where Liam cut himself. She yanks the branch off the tree and brings the branch right up to her nose. She inhales and immediately grabs her hand, which still holds the permanent scar where Jacek struck home. Astonishingly, she says, "It can't be! I know that bloodline anywhere! That's the blood of Mikolaj's family and that little shit son of his, Jacek!"

CHAPTER 9

....

WHAT HAPPENED TO AMY?

Angelica walks back to the large storm drain that runs parallel to the river. The endless stream of traffic echoes through the corridor from the continuously congested expressway above. Angelica swings the blood-stained tree branch back and forth in her hand. As she approaches the storm drain, two glowing red eyes flash back at her. The storm drain is dark and damp. The moist concrete floor is stained with various layers of green algae. The walls are covered with colorful and vibrant letters left behind from dozens of graffiti artists. The constant sounds of cars driving along the nearby expressway and water dripping from a leaky pipe continuously rattle in the background. A pair of river rats scurry along the edge of the wall as a mother brown bat flies into the storm drain carrying food for her remaining pup.

She walks over to witness the mother brown bat feeding her remaining pup and says, "That's a good mother. Thank you for letting me borrow one of your pups. I promise to be a good mother…I miss being a mother. He will be a vital part of my family." The beast growls at Angelica as she walks through the storm drain. She says, "Yes, yes I know, Pet. I know you're getting hungry." Angelica walks alongside Pet who frighteningly towers over Angelica. She extends her outstretched arm and slowly pets the giant monster under his long blood-covered chin and says, "I promise you can have dinner as soon as the sun goes down, my dear. You just have to be patient. Too many of those modern-day knights running around out there.

But I'm sure they'll be leaving soon." Pet breathes a sigh of relief and purrs like a kitten as she continues to rub his chin.

Angelica flashes her radiantly glowing red eyes at Pet and says, "Now, my sweet angel. I have a job for you tonight. First, smell this branch." Pet brings his long mouth and nose down to Angelica's outstretched hand and smells the blood saturated branch. As he growls Angelica says, "Yes, my lovely. That's a bad smell. It's the scent of our enemies. I want you to follow your nose and use your mighty wings to locate them for me. Could you be my eyes tonight?" Pet bows his head as he understands his instructions. Angelica smiles and she says, "Good, my dear. And after you're finished, I have a surprise for you. We are moving, my sweet, to somewhere close to here. At the very least, it will be less damp and smell less like deer and human piss. I'm taking you to our new home so you can meet the rest of the family."

A few hundred yards south of the storm drain, Detective Cunningham directs Officer Rich and some other officers to pack up the rest of the equipment. Detective Cunningham is greeted by two members of the Cook County Medical Examiner's Office who are pulling along a stretcher and an empty black body bag. Detective Cunningham recognizes one of the members and says, "Good afternoon, Mitch. How are things?"

Mitch says, "Yes, sir. Doing just fine, Detective. Sorry it took so long to get here. Traffic coming in from downtown is just...."

Mitch shakes his head as Detective Cunningham interjects, "It's not a problem, Mitch. I figured as much. Plus, I figured you'd be busy. Especially over these last couple of days."

Mitch replies, "Yes, sir. It's been too busy. If this keeps up, we'll run out of room in our freezer." Mitch looks down at the decaying body and says, "Jesus! How long has that thing been here? It looks like she's been dead for a while."

Detective Cunningham answers, "Good question. In fact..." Detective Cunningham sees Sarge and motions for him to approach.

Sarge takes the cap off his head and wipes the sweat from his forehead with a handkerchief from his back pocket. Sarge sarcastically asks, "Yes, Detective. What else can we do for you on this fine day?"

Detective Cunningham answers, "Sarge. Have your officers made contact with the girl's boyfriend? Have they made entry into the apartment yet?"

Sarge replies, "Not sure. Let me find out."

As Sarge moves away from the detective in order to talk on his radio, Detective Cunningham motions to Mitch and his partner to start loading the body into the body bag. Sarge begins to talk into his radio saying, "1632S to 1635 Bravo."

After a few seconds the radio echoes, "1635 Bravo go ahead, Sarge."

Sarge answers while holding down the push-to-talk button on his radio, "1635 Bravo, have you made entry into the apartment yet?"

The officer on the radio replies, "Not just yet. We were looking for an easy way in, but it looks like we will have to force entry into the unit. The boyfriend doesn't have a key."

Sarge asks, "Any signs of someone not being home for a couple of days?"

The officer answers, "There's some mail and some delivery packages addressed to the possible victim sitting in the foyer. Talked to one of the neighbors. Last time they saw her was last night when the victim went out the courtyard toward the running trail. Interesting thing, the neighbor lives below her. She said there was a lot banging and smashing in the victim's apartment last night."

Sarge listens, nods his head, and says, "Message received. Force entry and let me know what you find."

Paul looks at Jeremy and says, "Sarge said to force entry, so why don't you grab the ram out of the trunk and let's get this thing done."

Jeremy says, "Sounds good. I'll be right back."

As Jeremy returns with the door ram, Jacob asks, "Hey, do you mind if I come up with you?"

Paul answers, "It's best if you wait down here and we will come get you after we search the apartment."

Jacob rolls his eyes and shakes his head as he walks away from the officers in frustration. Paul and Jeremy walk up the stairs to the third floor.

Paul, slightly out of breath, says, "Why are all of these calls on the top floor? We never get calls for the people living on the ground floor."

Jeremy replies, "I figure the higher units are like the back of the school bus. Those are where all the cool kids hang out and in turn cause more trouble."

Paul laughs and then catches his breath. "Interesting comparison, young man. Now if you will please do the honors."

Jeremy gets ready to force entry through the door when the neighbor below Amy's apartment comes out to the hallway stairs. The older woman with a European accent exclaims, "I knew that young girl was going to be a problem since the day she moved into this building! Always playing her workout music too loud and running that washer and dryer in her unit until the late-night hours." She puts her hands over her head and says, "And you should have heard all of the racket she was making last night. Oh, my God! I banged my broomstick on the ceiling for over an hour and then I sent my husband up there to talk to her, and she wouldn't even answer the door. I almost called the police last night and then it finally stopped."

Paul looks down at the woman as Jeremy rolls his eyes. Paul asks, "I forgot to ask you before, ma'am. What time did the noise stop?"

The neighbor answers, "I remember it was past my bedtime. She carried on doing God-knows-what until well after 10 p.m."

Paul says, "Thank you, ma'am."

The neighbor interjects, "You're not going to break down the door, are you? Oh, my God! The cost of a new door! It comes right out of the association. I know these things because I'm on the association board and I—"

Paul interrupts, "Sorry, ma'am. We have to. So please let us do our job."

She waves her hands in disgust as she reenters her apartment and slams the door.

Jeremy shakes his head. "I think every apartment building in this city has at least one old lady who's a pain in the a—"

Paul interjects, "Yes, and they're the first ones to call 911 and also complain to the city if the responding unit was rude and/or didn't resolve the issue, so if you please." Paul points to the door and Jeremy reaches back and throws the ram into the door. The wooden door flies open as the wooden frame splinters and creates a loud thump, which echoes off the walls in the hallway.

Paul enters the apartment as he draws his weapon from his holster. He yells, "Hello! Police department! Anyone here?"

Jeremy drops the ram onto the hallway landing, draws his weapon, and quickly enters the apartment. Jeremy sees Paul standing in the middle of the ransacked living room coughing and with his left hand over his nose and mouth. Jeremy takes in a deep breath and begins to cough and gag asking, "Jesus, Paul! What the hell is that smell?"

Paul continues to cough. "I don't know. Smells like a dead wild animal in here."

Jeremy scans the living room and continues to walk through the apartment, trying to regain his composure. Jeremy looks back at Paul who is standing in front of a sliding glass door that leads out to an outdoor balcony. He says, "Hey, Paul. Any signs of forced entry on the door behind you?"

Paul looks up and down the glass door and examines the lock. "Nope. Looks secure to me."

Jeremy replies, "Well then do me a favor. Open it so we can air out this place."

Paul nods his head. "Good idea."

Paul fully opens the glass door, and Jeremy continues to walk through the apartment across the dining room and into the kitchen. The kitchen is more ransacked than the living room. Both the refrigerator and freezer doors are left wide open. Water drips from the freezer as a slight sounding temperature alarm continues to chime from the refrigerator. Half-eaten raw meat is left to rot as flies and maggots crawl along its surface. Most of the cabinet doors are left open. Pots and pans are scattered around the counters and floor.

Jeremy covers his nose and mouth. "Hopefully I found the source of the smell, Paul."

Paul, who is now regaining his composure, says, "Great! Have you checked the back door yet?"

Jeremy walks toward the rear entry door as he replies, "Not yet. I was just about to do that." Jeremy scans the door, lock, and jam.

Nothing out of the ordinary. No signs of forced entry. He opens the door that leads to the back hallway and stairs. He scans the hallway. Nothing out of sort. As he walks back into the kitchen, he sees Paul standing along the threshold from the dining room into the kitchen.

Paul asks, "Anything out of the ordinary?"

Jeremy replies, "Nope. In fact, the doors are the only things that are not screwed up in this apartment."

Paul looks down at the dining room table and notices some mail. He picks up a few pieces of mail and says, "Well, here's some good news. We got the right apartment. All of these letters are addressed to our girl."

Jeremy replies, "Well, that's good."

Paul chuckles. "Sure is. Bosses get pissed when we force entry into the wrong place. A lot of paperwork for everyone. And the place is starting to smell better."

Jeremy stops to listen for a moment.

Paul asks, "What is it, partner?"

Jeremy asks, "Have you checked the bathroom yet? I hear running water."

Paul answers, "I haven't searched the back part of the unit yet. I'm getting old, kid. I didn't even hear any running water."

Jeremy walks back to the main hallway, which separates the unit from the living area into the bedrooms. He sees a closed door with light illuminating the floor and threshold from a light inside the bathroom. Paul points his weapon as Jeremy approaches the door. Jeremy quickly scans the hallway. He looks down and notices something on the floor. He says, "Paul! Look!" Paul looks down to where Jeremy is pointing his gun. Paul notices a few small drops of blood. Paul and Jeremy both begin to breath heavier as their heart rates dramatically increase. Jeremy steps alongside the door on the right side as Paul approaches the door from the left side.

Paul looks at Jeremy, nods, and begins to pound on the door with his fist saying, "Hello! Police department! Come out now!"

No response.

Paul looks at Jeremy who turns and points his weapon toward the door. Paul says, "I'll open the door. You make entry."

Jeremy nods his head as he flips the safety switch off his weapon. Jeremy says, "I'm ready. Go!"

Paul turns the door knob and pushes the door open. Jeremy bursts into the bathroom. He does a quick scan. He breathes heavily as he rapidly slides the shower curtain open only to reveal an empty shower and bathroom. Jeremy turns off the water and notices more blood along the tiles on the walls and along the far bottom of the bathtub. He looks down and sees some dirty and tattered hospital gowns lying on the floor near the bathroom counter. The counter is a mess with all of the hygiene and beauty products scattered and thrown around.

Paul enters. "What do you have, kid?"

Jeremy shakes his head. "Nobody in here. But it looks like a lot of evidence collection."

Paul says, "Okay. Sounds good. Looks like we have two more rooms to check. I'll check the room behind us, and you check the other room."

Jeremy says, "Okay. I'm on it."

As Jeremy and Paul complete their search, they both meet back in the main hallway. Jeremy asks, "Anything in there?"

Paul answers, "Nope. This room looks like it was untouched. It's an office. Neat and clean. What about yourself?"

Jeremy says, "It's the woman's bedroom. Someone left it all messed up. Dresser drawers left open, clothes thrown all over the place, and someone pulled down some travel luggage off the top shelf and peeled through that as well."

Paul says, "Jesus, Jeremy! What do you think happened here?"

Jeremy says, "I don't know. Maybe we should ask that boyfriend to come upstairs."

Paul replies, "Good thinking."

Paul, Jeremy, and Jacob climb back up the stairs toward the entrance of Amy's apartment. Jacob asks, "Did you find anything, Officers? Please, tell me something."

Jeremy says, "No one was found inside. Have you been inside her apartment before, sir?"

Jacob answers, "Yes. More than a few times. Why do you ask?"

Paul interjects, "Now, Jacob. All we want you to do is look inside the apartment from the hallway and let us know if this is the way Amy usually kept her place. We can't let you inside unfortunately. That will contaminate the scene."

Jacob says, "Contaminate the scene? That doesn't sound good."

Jeremy opens the apartment door. As Jacob looks inside, Paul asks, "Is there any chance Amy would have left her place like this?"

Jacob gasps. "Good God! No, sir! Amy would never leave her place like this. I mean honestly, who could live like this."

Jeremy smiles and he interjects, "You'd be surprised."

Paul says, "That's good for now, Jacob. Thank you, young man." Paul signals for the group to head downstairs as Jeremy closes the door. Paul looks back at Jeremy and says, "Why don't you hang out here as I walk out our gentleman and asks a few questions."

Jeremy replies, "Sounds good. I'll do just that."

Paul walks Jacob outside as he presses the push-to-talk button on his radio saying, "1635 Bravo to dispatch."

After a brief pause, dispatch replies, "Go ahead 1635."

Paul answers, "Dispatch, 1635 Bravo will be sitting on this location to keep it secure. We are requesting an evidence collection team and our shift sergeant to the scene please."

Dispatch said, "Message received, 1635. We'll let you know when they're en route and their ETA."

Jacob shakes his head and asks, "What the hell is going on, Officer?"

Paul replies, "That's our job. We are trying to figure that out. I have your contact information, and I'll let you know when we know more. Now, before I let you go, is there anything else that you can remember about last night?"

✦ ✦ ✦

The previous evening, Amy arrives home to her apartment as the hot summer sun begins to set over the tree line along the forest preserve across from her apartment. She kicks off her shoes and throws her purse over to the couch. She says to herself, "Jesus! What a long day. Finally, I'm home. I don't mind working a longer shift. More money in my pocket, but then I have to put up with the extra traffic."

She checks the thermostat in the hallway and thinks, *It's getting a little hot in here.* She walks over to the wall-mounted air conditioning unit and increases the circulation. Her cell phone begins to chime from inside her purse. She walks over and looks at her phone. It's Jacob. She answers and says, "Hey, babe. What's going on?"

Jacob answers, "Nothing much. How was work?"

Amy answers, "Long as per usual. Glad to be home."

Jacob replies, "Glad you're home. Are we still on for tomorrow? The afternoon baseball game and a movie in the evening?"

Amy replies, "I'm hoping, so as long as you're paying for it. I'm broke."

Jacob laughs and says, "Of course. It's totally my treat. I'm looking forward to seeing you. Any plans for tonight?"

Amy continues to talk to Jacob as she opens her sliding glass door and walks out to her balcony. "I still have time to run on the forest trail before sunset. I'm thinking of going out for a few miles, come home, make some dinner, and hopefully relax for the rest of the night."

Jacob replies, "God bless you for wanting to run in this heat."

Amy laughs and she replies, "It's starting to cool off. Plus, a long run and a good audiobook help me relax after a long day."

Jacob replies, "Enjoy it and call me later."

Amy smiles and says, "Will do."

Amy gets dressed into her running gear and grabs her small trail pack. She places her wallet, house keys, and a cold bottled water from the refrigerator into her pack. She puts on her headphones, closes and locks the front door, and runs down the steps toward the front entrance. Her neighbor peeks out of her apartment door and exclaims, "Hey! No running down the stairs! You're making too much noise!" Amy smiles as she tries to ignore her annoying neighbor and begins to run through the courtyard toward the forest preserve.

As the sun continues to disappear along the western sky, Amy continues to run along the trail. She enjoys her audiobook as she passes a few fellow runners and bikers making their way out of the trail for the evening. She arrives to the trail marker, which splits the path along the eastern side of the Des Plaines River. She takes off her trail pack and takes a quick sip of her crisp, cool water. She looks at her phone and notices the time. She thinks, *I should be able to make another mile before it gets dark in here.* The sun has vanished along the western sky, and the brilliant summer sky colors of pink, orange, and purple have transformed into a dark foggy blue. She thinks, *I just need another twenty minutes or so, and then I'll reach my goal. Let's get to it.*

She runs along the northbound trail toward the large storm drain under the expressway. As she runs past, a pair of glowing red eyes flash from inside the dark cavern. As she hits her goal of 1.5 miles, she turns around and starts to head back to main entrance of the trail. She thinks, *Awesome! Hit the halfway mark and now it's time to head home.*

As she passes the storm drain on the way back home, she hears a loud growl over her audiobook headphones. She pauses in pure fright as she rips the headphones off and spins around in an attempt to locate the terrifying sound. She whips her head so fast she makes herself dizzy. She scans her immediate area. No one is in sight. She yells, "Hello! Anyone there? Who is it?" She scans with her eyes as she hears another growl coming from inside the storm drain. She screams in pure panic as Pet lifts his head from underneath the cavern and reveals his monstrous head under the twilight sky. Amy turns around and attempts to run away. She's immediately greeted by an older woman wearing a hospital gown. The woman's skin looks pale, and she has incredibly dark circles around her eyes. Amy meets Angelica!

Angelica says, "I'm sorry for scaring you, my dear. I'm a patient from a nearby hospital and I've lost my way. Could you help me?"

Amy screams as Angelica laughs. Amy starts to run past Angelica. Pet flaps his mighty wings and flies into the air. He lands right in front of Amy. Amy stops so fast she falls flat on her back. Angelica continues to laugh as she says, "There's no use screaming or running, young lady. No one can hear you. Trust me. I know a deserted forest when I see one."

Amy starts to cry. "What do you want? Just let me go!"

Angelica moves closer to Amy and bends down close to her. She inhales deeply through her nostrils and says, "There's nothing like the smell of fear and youth mixed together. It's a sweet-and-salty smell." Angelica lifts a small twig off the ground and says, "I don't want much. Just the sweet taste of youth again."

Angelica rubs her hand along the stick as a brilliant display of glowing purple sparkles form on its surface. Amy attempts to back up and make her way back up to her feet. Angelica sighs as she says, "I already told you it's pointless. Now, stop moving, little girl." Angelica whips and points the stick toward Amy as a flash of light and purple mist encircle her. She screams painfully only for a moment and then silence. The purple mist moves away from Amy and encircles Angelica as she inhales the mist through her nose. She immediately transforms into a much younger and beautiful woman.

Amy lies motionless in the absence of life on the ground. Angelica inhales deeply and says to Pet, "Ahh! The smell of youth. I feel like my old self again. Do I look more pleasing to the eye?" Pet nods its head. Angelica says, "Good! I'm pleased. I haven't felt this good in a long time." Angelica looks down and sees Amy's trail pack. She bends down, grabs the pack, and says to Pet, "Now, let's see what our useless idiot was carrying around in her pack. Obviously, she won't be needing it anymore." Angelica laughs and pulls out the contents. She examines Amy's ID and grabs the keys. She looks back at Pet saying, "Now, Pet. Why don't you run along and find something tasty for dinner. I'm going to take a quick peek into our dearly departed friend's place and help myself to a few things. Now, be a good boy and I'll be back later." Pet bows his head, kneels slightly in a bouncing position, and begins to flap his large ghastly wings. He lifts off into the air and looks back to see Angelica walk out of the forest preserve toward the rows of apartments across the street.

....

CHAPTER 10

TOMORROW IS GRANDMOM'S HOUSE

The crew makes their way home after the long journey on their bikes from the forest preserve. The trip to the ice cream stand was unfortunately delayed due to Liam's injury. As Liam and Boo arrive back home, the rest of the crew ride up to their driveway. Liam and Boo turn around as the rest of the crew slows down. Ryan is the first to shout, "I haven't rode on my bike that much in my entire life. If we ride over to get ice cream, I'm getting triple scoops. I believe I've earned it."

The crew laughs.

Tommy says to Liam and Boo, "Hey! Do you want us to wait for you or just head out?"

Liam looks at his cut, which is now dried and no longer oozing down his leg. "Unless Boo wants to go with you, I'm done for today. Not only did I bleed all over my socks, but I got some dry blood on my shoe. And I sweated through my shirt. As soon as I hit the air conditioning, I know I won't want to go back out."

Robert looks at Liam and replies, "Fair enough. I get it. What do you say, Boo? You up for ice cream?"

Boo looks back at Liam and then answers Robert saying, "No thanks. I'm with my brother on this one. I'm done for the day. Thanks for the invite though."

Robert says, "No worries."

The crew waves goodbye and continues riding down the street. Liam and Boo walk their bikes up the driveway toward the garage. They see the open garage door and their mother, Annie, walking out of the garage. Liam says, "Hey, Mom! What are you up to?"

Annie answers, "Just finished watering all of my flowers and the garden. This damn heat is too much! When is it going to rain around here? I can use the break from the heat and so can the grass and flowers." Annie looks at her watch and says, "You two were gone for a while. Did you enjoy your bike ride?"

Liam shrugs his shoulders.

Annie looks down at Liam's bloodied leg and asks, "What happened to your leg?"

Liam smiles while Boo laughs. Liam answers, "Cut it on a tree branch. No big deal."

Annie replies, "It will be a big deal if you get blood all over my carpet. Go in through the side door and straight downstairs into the laundry room and pick out some new clothes out from the dryer."

Boo interjects, "Took Mom all of thirty seconds to know you hurt yourself, worry about her carpets, and figure out how to mitigate the situation."

Liam laughs as Annie looks at Boo asking, "And how are you, Daughter? Do you have any new cuts, bumps, or bruises I should be aware of?"

Boo smiles, "No, Mom. I was a perfect little girl as per usual."

Annie sarcastically says, "Doubt that! Now, why don't you two freshen up and cool off for a bit. God knows how your father is doing in this heat. I swear the man goes through a dozen T-shirts at work on days like this."

After Liam takes a shower and cleans his leg, he leaves the bathroom and finds a laundry basket waiting for him in the hallway. Annie, who's in the kitchen, is starting to make dinner. "Just put all of your smelly, sweaty, and bloody clothes in the basket including your shoes! I can try to wash them off in the slop sink after I'm done making dinner."

Liam replies, "Okay. Thanks, Mom."

Boo walks into the kitchen to get a glass of water. Annie looks at Boo and says, "It looks like you got some sun today, Boo. Did you spend most of the time around Robert's house, or did you end up taking a longer bike ride?"

Boo answers, "We took a bike ride out to the woods."

Immediately, Boo realizes she's made a mistake by saying too much.

Annie asks, "Woods? What woods?"

Boo turns around, knowing she's probably in trouble. She thinks, *No use trying to make up a story. Moms, especially my mom, know when we're lying. Just tell her most of the truth. And do it quickly.*

Annie says, "Don't make me repeat myself! What woods?"

Boo answers, "The Robinson Woods. Out near East River Road."

Liam, who was on his way up from the laundry room, overhears the conversation. Annie glares at Boo. "You and your brother biked all the way out to the Robinson Woods?"

Liam interjects, "Yeah, Mom. It's the woods that are right next to Dad's old—"

Annie turns toward Liam and interjects, "Yes. Where your father and I lived when we first got married. That's several miles away from home. I'm very familiar." Annie looks back at Boo and continues, "And it's also where all of that police activity has been happening recently."

Liam asks, "You heard about that?"

Annie turns to Liam and says, "Yes, Son. I heard what happened over there. It's been on all the local news outlets and radio stations."

Liam says, "Sorry, Mom. It's not Boo's fault. It was my idea."

Boo interjects, "And the crew wanted to take a ride today. Honestly."

Annie looks back at Liam and asks, "Is that true?"

Liam looks at Boo as Boo winks back at him. Liam answers, "Yeah, Mom. When we got there we could only get on the bike trail for a few hundred yards. The police cordoned off the rest. Sorry."

Annie takes a deep breath and calmly says, "It's okay. With everything that has happened in this family and with all of the strange things happening in and around the neighborhood, I just want to make sure you're safe. At the very least, you were with your friends."

Within the hour, the family sits down for dinner. The aroma of stir-fry chicken and vegetables fills the house. Liam comes into the kitchen to make his plate. Annie is ready to serve him his food. Liam says, "Smells great, Mom. Chicken stir fry. One of my favorites."

Annie smiles as she replies, "Thanks. One of my favorites too. A nice and light meal for hot summer months, and it's easy to make."

Boo makes her plate and the family sits down for dinner. Annie leads the family in grace and gives thanks for her family's protection and the continuous blessings along the way. Liam says, "Amen" and grabs hold of his silver cross, which is hanging on a silver necklace chain tucked underneath his T-shirt. Annie says to Liam, "I received an email from your baseball coach. Looks like they can make up the rest of the game between you and that other team tomorrow evening before your regular team practice. The plan is to have your game at 6 p.m., finish it, and then have a short practice afterward. The coaches definitely want to have everyone back home before it gets dark."

Liam says, "Sounds good, Mom. Thank you. Have they said anything else about that flying creature and the repairs needed at the park?"

Annie finishes chewing her food and answers, "All they said is the police have an active investigation. The police advised the baseball league to finish all practices and games thirty minutes before dark. I let your father know the updated time. You and your sister are going to help your father tomorrow at Grandmom's house with cleaning out some things."

Boo sarcastically interjects, "That's sound like a great time… spending a scorching summer day in an old garage and attic. Actually, it sounds hot, miserable, and disgusting."

Annie looks at Boo and says, "That's the plan. And before you get all 'boohoo,' remember that your father is coming off work all sweaty and tired. He plans to come home in the morning and rest for about an hour and then head straight down to Grandmom's. He wants to clean out the attic first before the heat of the day sets in." Annie looks at Liam and says, "And don't worry. Dad will have you home with plenty of time to get to the field. Plus, I talked to Grandmom this afternoon on the phone. She's looking forward to seeing you two. So please, be on your best behavior."

The family finishes their dinner. Liam and Boo help Annie clean up the kitchen. Annie asks, "Anyone up for a movie night? Popcorn, soda, and maybe some ice cream?"

Liam says, "That sounds like a good idea."

Boo adds, "As long as I get to pick the movie."

Annie smiles and says, "Deal."

The family settles into their cool finished basement for a fun family movie for the rest of the evening. At the end of the movie, Annie says, "Good choice, Boo. It's been a long time since I saw that one. What did you think, Liam?"

Liam answers, "It's a good movie. Not one of my favorites, but it was still good."

Annie grabs the empty popcorn and ice cream bowls and says, "I'll take care of the bowls. Boo, grab the empty soda cans. Liam, could you let Lady outside and take out the trash please?"

Liam sees his dog as she waits by the side entrance door. "Give me a second, Lady. Just let me grab the trash."

The side entrance door flies open, and Lady runs out toward the backyard with Liam close behind with the white trash bag full of garbage. The brilliant summer colors of orange, pink, and red drift off and fade as the sun has set beyond the western horizon. A dark blueish-purple fills the evening sky. The wind blows a cool breeze out of the west and passes along Liam's back as he walks over to his garage to deposit the trash into the bin. Liam waits for Lady while she sniffs and paces back and forth. Liam thinks about leaving Lady outside for a little bit but then he looks across the alley and into his neighbor's empty backyard. He patiently waits for Lady. When she finishes, Liam says, "Come on, Lady! Time to go inside. Let's go!" Lady prances back to Liam, and they run toward the side entrance. As Liam looks down at Lady, he hears a large swoop go through the air. He looks up. Doesn't see anything. Lady starts to growl as she points her body back toward the backyard alley. Liam says, "What was that?" Lady continues to growl. Liam continues to scan the backyard and the sky above. Nothing is out of sort. Lady looks up at Liam and starts to whimper. Liam looks down at Lady and says, "I think it's time to go inside, Lady. I don't see anything. Come on, let's go."

Annie finishes putting everything away in the kitchen, begins to make a cup of tea, and picks up her book. Liam walks past his mom. Annie says, "Thank you, honey."

Liam replies, "No problem, Mom. You gonna do your usual?"

Annie sits down on the living room couch. "Yup. That's the plan. Gonna read my book for a bit and then I'm off to bed. What about you?"

Liam answers, "Planning the same. Going to stretch out in my room, put the ball game on the radio, and read my comics."

Annie replies, "Sounds like a plan. Boo is already in her room. Have a good night, honey. Love you."

Liam replies as he walks up the stairs, "Love you too, Mom."

As Liam enters his room, he turns on his nightstand lamp. The illuminated room is seen perfectly by Pet who is watching Liam and Boo as he peeks around the roof from the far side of the family's detached garage. The piercing red eyes glow as Pet growls and licks his disgusting teeth.

Back at the forest preserve tunnel, Angelica gathers the items required to complete her cast. She takes a kitchen stove grate out of a bag, which she stole from Amy's house, and places it on the damp concrete floor. She then grabs a handful of dried grass and kindling and places it in the center of the grate. Next, she takes a medium-size pot with a long handle out of the bag and fills it full of water from the river. Angelica sniffs the water and says, "Dirty, river water. Smells like algae and rotten eggs. I love that smell. Death is a similar fragrance." She places the pot onto the grate. She grabs the stick used to stop Amy in her tracks and rubs her other hand along the shaft. "I need a little spark to get this party started." The tip of the wooden stick glows fire red. A small burst of radiant red energy flies off the end of it as she points it toward the kindling. The kindling bursts into an open flame and begins to heat the dirty river water. She looks into the pot and begins to see a vision of Liam and Boo's backyard as Pet observes from his vantage point. She says, "Excellent work, Pet. So, this is where the bastard family of Mikolaj and Jacek live. Interesting, definitely a far reach from the long halls and high towers of their fortress back home."

Pet understands and hears everything Angelica is saying to him. Angelica sees the two upstairs bedrooms. She sees movement as Liam and Boo move about their rooms. Angelica says, "Now, my dear. Please go in for a closer look. I want to get a good look at the family. But be careful not to be seen."

Pet nods his ugly head and begins to crawl along the roof of the garage. Pet hits his head on a low-hanging tree branch along the garage as he moves. It startles a squirrel who has been keeping still since Pet's arrival. The squirrel attempts to dash along the tree branch, but Pet spots it immediately. Pet quickly grabs the squirrel and swallows it in one bite. Angelica interjects, "Pet! Please. This isn't the time for snacks. I promise to feed you when you come home. Focus on the task at hand, please." Pet scans the immediate area. No one is seen outside. He flaps his large wings and ascends into the air briefly and lands quietly on the roof of the home.

Pet bends over the edge of roof and peeks inside Liam's room! He sees Liam next to his office desk turning a dial on his radio. The red eyes continue to watch Liam as he grabs a few comic books off his shelf before he walks back toward his bed. Liam is completely unaware that the only thing separating him from immediate peril is a piece of glass! Before Liam settles into bed, he takes the silver cross out from under his shirt and pulls it over his head. The light from the silver cross reflects off Pet on the other side of the window. Pet growls and lifts his head above the roof line as the light from the cross reflects back at him. Angelica sees the cross through the reflective boiling water. She spits at the sight of the Holy Cross and says, "The family may not have their high towers and long passages anymore, but they still have the Almighty on their side. That cross has some type of divine power to it. I can feel it!"

Liam hears some scratching on the roof and wonders what's making the noise. Angelica says to Pet, "I know, my dear. Just the sight of that symbol makes me enraged as well. Go take a peek into the other room and see what we have in there, if you please."

Pet cautiously makes his way along the roof toward Boo's room. Boo hears it, too, as she takes a break from playing a game on her tablet and listening to music on the radio. She stands up from her bed. She looks up toward the ceiling. Pet sees her from the window.

Angelica can see Boo from her reflected images in the water. She says, "Would you look at that. A little girl. How cute! And I thought that this family only produced a healthy stream of boys. How the times have changed! Wait...what the hell is this?" Angelica looks back and witnesses the unimaginable begin to happen in Boo's room.

Inside Boo's room, the lights begin to dim and fade, and the radio starts to change stations and play old jazz music. A vibrant blue glow fills the closet on the opposite side of Boo's outside window. Boo walks toward the closet door and nervously says, "What the hell is this? Is that who I think it is?" Before Boo is able to turn the handle, the doorknob begins to turn on its own! As the door opens, Boo takes in a sigh of relief as she sees Misty coming up to her and giving her a hug. Boo says, "Oh my God! Misty! Where have you been? I haven't seen you since…the estate."

Misty says, "I've missed you too, Boo. Now, please listen! I've been sent here to help you. Don't go near the window, and please get your brother."

Boo asks as she turns toward the window, "Why do you want me to not go near the window, Mis—" Boo trembles as she sees Pet's piercing red eyes glow back toward her. Pet growls.

Liam runs into the room. "Boo, there's something making noise on the roof. I don't know—"

Boo interjects, "Liam! Shut the door!"

CHAPTER 11

....

ANGELICA'S NEW COVEN

Liam looks at Boo and notices how scared she is as she looks back toward the bedroom window. Liam pans over to the window to see Pet's radiant red eyes piercing back at him! Angelica sees Liam, Boo, and Misty and says, "This can't be! The little girl has the gift! She can see spirits from beyond the grave just like...." Angelica pauses in mid-thought and grabs her mouth. She regains composure and exclaims to Pet, "Pet! Hurry back home now! We have work to do!" Pet growls, looks up toward the night sky, and launches itself off the roof. Liam runs over and grabs hold of his little sister. In a stammer Liam says, "It-it-it's okay, Boo. I go-got you. I won't let that thing hurt you."

Liam shivers. Boo smiles and says, "Thanks, big brother. Got a cold chill I see."

Liam says, "Sure did. I don't know why? Am I scared, yes. But this is different."

Boo giggles. "That's because you're standing on top of Misty."

Liam takes a big step back. "Oh! Sorry, Misty. If I only could see her. I didn't mean to."

Boo replies, "It's okay. She was holding on to me too."

Liam cautiously walks over to the bedroom window. He looks back at Boo as Boo begins to talk to Misty. Liam asks, "What's Misty saying, Boo?"

"Misty says, 'There's nothing to worry about at the moment. The monster is gone.'"

78

Liam nods his head and continues to walk over to the window to get a second look. As he peers into the backyard, he scans the area. All is quiet. The only movement is the tree branches at the end of his backyard as the evening wind continues to gust through a line of trees.

Boo lets out a little giggle. "You can take Misty's word for it. She's only saved our lives once already."

Liam smiles as he turns around and replies, "I'm sorry, Misty. Thanks again for everything last summer. I never got a chance to thank you."

Boo eyes drift to the left. She concentrates for a moment and then says, "She says it was the least she could do. And she says you're very welcome." Boo eyes drift to her left again.

After a few moments, Liam asks, "What is she saying, Boo?"

Boo looks back at Liam and answers, "She says she's sorry she hasn't seen us since last summer. Says it's all very complicated. Especially after the crossover." Boo listens to Misty for another brief moment and says, "Got it. Misty was sent here on a special mission. They wanted to send a friendly face." Boo laughs as she continues, "And they were getting tired of her constantly asking if and when she could see me and play. She was given two sets of instructions. First, not to let you or myself go next to the window. Second, when we are over at Grandmom's house tomorrow to look for an old wooden chest somewhere. And an old coffee can that has a lot of keys inside. Look for an old brass key. That will open the chest."

Liam asks, "Wha-what's this all about? And does she know what the hell the thing with glowing red eyes was doing just outside your window?"

Boo listens to Misty. She nods her head as she answers, "She doesn't know any other details for now. That was all she was told to pass along."

Liam asks, "Pass along from whom exactly?"

Boo listens, smiles, and then answers, "She was approached by our grandfather. She says those were the orders she was given, and he couldn't tell her anything else for now. But he said she had to get here immediately."

Liam replies, "I'd say. Timing couldn't have been better. Thanks again, Misty."

Boo says, "She said she's happy to help. She would like to talk to me for a while and maybe play with some of my dolls."

Liam laughs. "Then I'll leave you to it. Have a good night you too. Try to not stay up too late."

"Don't worry. Misty has to get back soon. Have a good night, Liam."

Liam smiles as he shuts the door.

The night continues as a Cook County Forest Preserve Police cruiser idles in the parking lot along the far northern stretch of the Robinson Woods. An officer inside the police cruiser enjoys his late-night dinner out of his brown paper bag. Dispatch contacts him saying, "Dispatch to unit 16."

The officer rolls his eyes and says to himself, "It never fails. As soon as I try to eat my meal in peace. It's like they know." Dispatch repeats their message. The officer reluctantly grabs the mic, presses the push-to-talk button, and says, "Yeah this unit 16. Go ahead, Dispatch."

Dispatch replies, "Unit 16, command wants to know if you secured the area around Robinson Woods."

The officer answers, "That is affirmative, Dispatch. Walked the trail before sunset and circled the parking lot. All is quiet around here."

Dispatch replies, "Message received, 16. Command is requesting you stay on the property for the rest of the shift unless otherwise instructed."

The officer answers, "Message received, Dispatch. I'm prepared to stand by."

The officer finishes his meal as a thick misty fog begins to form from the cooling waters off the Des Plaines River. The officer looks at his watch and says to himself, "Damn, I'm already tired and I've only started this shift a few hours ago. If I'm gonna sit here all night and look at the trees, I'm gonna need some pick-me-up. That donut shop down the street is still open for a bit. If I'm nice to them, they'll make a fresh pot of coffee and give me some of the old donuts for free." The officer looks around and says, "Hey, what command doesn't know won't hurt them. I'll be back in a bit."

The officer drives past the parking lot gate, exits the vehicle, and closes the gate behind him with a lock and chain. He gets back into the cruiser and drives out of sight down East River Road.

Across the street from the forest preserve, a man exits a car and opens the trunk. The hooded figure looks around and scans the area. No one is around. He throws a leather satchel around his upper body. The satchel has a silver cross embroidered on the opening flap. The man then wraps a leather scabbard around his waist. Lastly, he inspects his silver sword as it reflects a shimmering light from the streetlights and moonlight above. The figure looks up as Pet swoops its massive wings across the dark sky and quickly drifts down below the tree line inside the Robinson Woods. Bishop Michael smiles, places his sword into the scabbard, and says, "It's time to work in the gray."

Bishop Michael drifts behind a tree as a large cargo truck drives down the vacant road. When the truck drives past him, he looks both ways. The coast is clear. He dashes across the street and runs into the woods. He kneels down and pans the area until his eyes adapt to the dark forest around him. The only movement are the branches carrying to warm summer wind and the increasing misty fog from the river. When his eyes adjust to the darkness, he begins to move to where he saw the creature drift below the tree line. Bishop Michael grabs the silver cross necklace from under his gray shroud. Moonlight shimmers off the silver cross as Bishop Michael begins to pray saying, "Heavenly Father. I ask that you continue to guide my judgment and actions. Let me be brave where there is fear and doubt. Let me be your divine servant and draw the creatures who hide in the shadows into the light and drive them from this Earth. Bring your divine light and guide me to the field of battle." Within moments, a slight glimmering light begins to illuminate off the left arm of the holy cross. Bishop Michael smiles and says, "Looks like I'm heading west. Thank you, my Lord." Bishop Michael heads down the western trail toward Angelica and Pet.

Pet swoops down under the storm drain and crawls over to Angelica. Pet bows and closes his radiant red eyes as Angelica slowly strokes the top of his head. Angelica continues to embrace Pet as she says, "Thank you, my dear. You did so well. We've learned so much tonight. Now we know that the offspring of Mikolaj and his pain in the ass son, Jacek, can be useful after all. Especially that little girl. Who would think that SHE, the descendant of our enemies, has the same gifts that I possessed at her age! The master will want to keep her and help build our new coven. Tonight, we head to where our master sleeps, my pet. Unless of course, his grave has been disturbed after all of these years."

Angelica lifts her head and inhales the warm summer breeze through her nose. She is startled as Pet begins to growl. Angelica turns toward the scent and says, "I know that horrible smell anywhere. Chrism, holy water, garlic, and silver. There's a bastard soldier of the Almighty here, Pet. We must leave now!" Angelica opens her palm as the large tree branch levitates toward her hand. She quickly grabs some essential items and throws them into one of Amy's old travel bags. She looks up and sees a small glimmering light shine off the murky surface of the river and a shadowy silhouette of a hooded figure. She gasps as Bishop Michael shouts, "Angelica! The Bishops of the Silver Cross sentence you to death!" Pet turns, snarls at Bishop Michael, and gets ready to pounce on Angelica's command.

Angelica pushes Pet out of the way and says, "They've been sentencing to banishment, imprisonment, and death for a long time, Priest!"

Bishop Michael walks quickly toward Angelica and draws his silver sword out of his leather scabbard. "Your time is over, Angelica! It's time you meet the devil who owns your soul."

Angelica drops the travel bag and extends her hand toward several small sharp branches. The branches begin to levitate and turn their pointy ends toward Bishop Michael. She flings the branches at Bishop Michael and says, "I have a better idea, Priest. Why don't you meet your Almighty first."

The branches fly through the air as quick as a loose arrow toward Bishop Michael. Bishop Michael draws his non-dominant arm toward his face. The branches bounce off Bishop Michael as they hit the silver chain mail hidden underneath his gray shroud. He reaches into his satchel and removes two small glass spheres that are full of a clear liquid. He throws them toward Angelica and says, "Sip on some of this, Witch!" Angelica raises the long tree branch to block the incoming projectiles. They both break on impact and splash tiny droplets onto Angelica. Angelica screams out in pain as droplets of holy water hit her body. She taps Pet on the arm and exclaims in agonizing pain, "Pet! We are leaving!"

Angelica grabs the bag and mounts her long tree branch as Pet extends his wings. They dash out of the storm drain and above the foggy evening sky. Bishop Michael runs toward the monstrous duo only to see them vanish above the thick soupy layer of fog. He holsters his silver sword, smiles, and says, "I'll find you again, Witch! All I have is time!"

Angelica and Pet fly east above Foster Avenue as the many homes and businesses quickly pass below them. They continue to fly a few miles before Angelica points down toward another forest preserve along Foster Avenue and Cicero. They descend below the tree line and quietly glide safely back to the ground. Angelica looks at Pet as he growls. She says, "I know, my darling. I hate those pesky priests as much as the next person. Don't you worry about him. He's just a foot soldier of his church. A glorified errand boy with a cross and a sword. We, on the other hand, have a commanding general of darkness. All we need to do is wake him from his long slumber. Come with me." Pet walks behind Angelica through the marshy forest area until they reach the mouth of an ill-maintained trail. Pet raises his ears when he hears something ahead of them. Angelica gives Pet a signal to stop and hide for a moment. Angelica raises her nose into the air. She inhales and looks back at Pet asking, "You hear something don't you, my dear? I'm starting to hear it too. Horrible shitty music. More potently, I can *smell* them. They smell awful! Chemically enhanced perfume, the sweet smell of alcohol, and the remains of some type of tobacco smoke. I smell young people, my dear. Let's go in for a closer look."

They carefully and quietly sneak along the outer lining of the trail, and Angelica sees an old rusty black iron gate that is left open. She peers inside and breathes a sigh of relief. "Thank our lord, Pet! The cemetery still remains! Looks like no one has maintained the land for a long time. Let's take a better look at our visitors."

Angelica and Pet see three teenage girls hanging out in a semicircle in the abandoned cemetery. Most of the tombstones are broken and in ill repair. A few broken pieces of cement from old gravestones litter the ground along with old rotten party paraphernalia left from other previous gatherings on the site. One of the girls with blonde hair is on her phone and changes a song before taking another sip from the clear bottle of alcohol next to her. Another girl with red hair is relighting some candles that went out after a quick gust of wind. The last girl with brunette hair and glasses stands up from resting along an ivy-covered tomb. She takes another cigarette out of her handbag and taps on the shoulder of the girl with the lighter. As one of the girls hands the lighter to the other, Angelica looks at Pet and asks, "My dear, how do I look? Have the marks from the holy water healed?" Pet inspects Angelica with his glowing red eyes. He nods his ghastly head. Angelica smiles and says, "Now I have an idea, my darling. These teenagers, just like all teenagers, can be useful idiots with our plans. I'll go talk to them. You stay in the shadows and find something to eat. I'll call for you later." Pet nods its head and quickly glides off into the forest searching for his next meal.

Angelica's glowing red eyes shift to dark brown as she straightens out her outfit and her hair to look more appealing. She walks across the threshold of the cemetery. "There's no place like home." The girls turn and are shocked to see Angelica walking in the cemetery toward them. One girl tries to hide the bottle of alcohol. The other puts her cigarette out on a long narrow tombstone, and last girl next to the candles jumps up as she exclaims, "Oh, shit! The cops are here!"

Angelica laughs. Her smile shimmers off the radiant light from the candles on the ground. The girls appear nervous at first. Angelica continues to laugh. "Not to worry about, my dear. I'm not the police. Far from it actually. So, who are you and what are you doing here?"

The girl with blonde hair answers, "We weren't doing anything. Honest. Just blowing off some steam."

Angelica smiles and looks at the girl with brunette hair. "Can I trouble you for a smoke? I haven't had one in such a long time."

The girl with brunette hair hands her a cigarette and a lighter.

Angelica smiles as she takes the cigarette from her. "Just the cigarette, my dear. I have my own light."

Angelica reaches down to the ground and grabs a small twig. She waves the twig, and a small flame engulfs the far end. Angelica lights up, and the girls stand in awe of what they just witnessed.

The girl with the brunette hair asks, "How the hell do you do that?"

Angelica smiles as she takes a long drag off her cigarette. "I'll tell you more in good time. First, you tell me who you are."

The girl with the brunette hair says, "I'm Blair."

Angelica turns to the girl with blonde hair, as she says, "I'm Chloe."

Angelica replies, "Nice to meet you both."

She then looks at the girl with red hair, and says, "And last but certainly not least."

The girl replies, "Lilith."

Angelica nods her head, smiles, and says, "Lilith. Such a pretty name."

Lilith says, "How did you do that?"

"I'm sure you would like to know." Angelica looks around at all of the girls as she continues, "So what were you young ladies up to? I'm sure it's more than escaping home and society for a little bit. You came into the cemetery for a reason, didn't you?"

Lilith answers for Chloe and Blair. "We wanted to try out some stuff we saw online. Talk to spirits."

Angelica nods her head. "And just how old are you girls?"

Blair interjects, "Seventeen!"

Angelica looks at Blair and replies, "Seventeen years old. To be young like that again. I remember being seventeen. Wandering around cemeteries and craving the answers from what awaits us beyond the grave."

Chloe laughs. "You don't look too old to me. You look like you're in your early thirties if I were to guess."

Angelica smiles, and inhales a long drag off her cigarette. "Thank you, my dear. I'm afraid I'm far older than that."

Lilith smiles as she examines Angelica from head to toe. "Well, whatever you're doing, you look good for your age."

Angelica approaches Lilith and sits down along the lit candles. She gestures for Lilith, Chloe, and Blair to sit in a circle around her.

Chloe and Blair wait to see what Lilith does before they proceed. Angelica raises her hands with her palms raised toward the air. As she lifts her hands, the fire dancing along the melted wicks of the candles begin to grow and climb high into the air. The light reflecting off the growing flames illuminate the astonishment on the young girls' faces. Lilith sits down across from Angelica. Chloe and Blair follow suit. They make a circle around the candles. Angelica says, "As you can see, ladies, there's a lot I can do. But this is only a drop in the bucket of my abilities." The girls smile. Angelica continues, "You already have a curiosity for the dark arts. And, I feel, you are already searching for guidance. If you'll allow me, I'll be your teacher. What do you say?"

....

CHAPTER 12

GRANDMOM'S HOUSE

Liam begins his day by waking up to his dog, Lady, licking his face. Liam wipes away Lady's drool and exclaims, "Lady! Leave me alone, will ya. It's summer. Summer means staying up late, reading comics and sleeping past my regular wake-up time." Lady jumps onto the bed, curls up, and lays on top of Liam. Liam sighs and pets Lady as he begins to smell the sweet-and-salty aroma of bacon and eggs cooking downstairs.

Boo peeks into Liam's room with a smile and says, "Looks like your dog found you."

"Indeed. Can't you take her for a walk this morning?"

"No way! She doesn't want anything to do with me after Misty came over for a visit last night. Even good ghosts freak out our fearless guard dog. Plus, you know what she's wants. A brisk run around the park a few times. That's your department."

Liam laughs. "Yeah, that's not a bad idea. Better to get it done now before the heat of the day sets in. It smells like Dad is downstairs doing his usual."

Boo replies, "Yup! He's down there cooking up a storm. Which is customary after a busy day at work."

Liam asks, "Does Dad look tired?" Boo shakes her head as she answers, "Nope! I went down to be his taste tester. He seems to be a good mood. Maybe he got some sleep for once. He said we're leaving in about an hour to go down to Grandmom's house. He wants to hit the attic area over the garage before it gets too hot."

Liam gets out of bed and grabs his baseball hat, headphones, and running shoes. Lady starts to stretch and jump up and down in excitement. Liam smiles and says, "Okay, Lady! Yes, we're going out for a run. Let's go and get back in time for breakfast." Lady flies past Liam, bolts down the stairs toward the side door, and waits impatiently for Liam.

Will looks at Lady waiting by the back door, smiles, and says, "I guess Liam is awake."

Liam walks down the stairs and enters the kitchen. "Morning, Dad. How was your night?"

Will answers, "Not bad, kid. I went to bed around midnight. Slept until my relief time." Will opens the oven to check the food. Liam clips a pink leash around Lady, turns toward Will, and asks, "What are you making, Dad?"

Will closes the oven and answers, "I'm making hash browns, bacon, and eggs. The hash browns should be finished by the time you're back from taking Lady for a run around the park. After breakfast, please get ready for Grandmom's house."

Liam opens the door, leash in hand, and says, "No problem, Dad. Sounds good."

It's cooler this morning than the previous sweltering days. Liam looks up at the white puffy clouds moving from west to east. A cool breeze hits his face. He looks down at Lady, who starts to pull on the leash. Liam puts on his headphones, looks down at Lady, and says, "Okay. Let's go! Just two times around the park. I want to be home in time for food."

Liam runs down Narragansett Street toward Dunham Park. As he runs to the park side of the street, he sees a few older couples playing tennis on the court. He waves at them as he and Lady continue down the sidewalk. Liam turns toward the trail that leads to the baseball diamonds, the concession stand, and the indoor gymnasium. He slows down as he approaches the baseball diamonds where he sees his coach, Phil, getting the field ready for the games and practices later that evening. Phil waves at Liam. Liam waves back and says, "Hey, Coach! Getting an early start to the field?"

Phil smiles and takes a break from the raking the sand. He walks over to Liam and shakes his hand. Lady sits down next to

Phil and rolls over so he can rub her belly. Phil says, "Of course! I always have time for Lady. How are you, girl? You look happy this morning."

Liam says, "Of course she's happy. She's doing one of her favorite things. Running around the park and trying to chase the squirrels up the trees."

Phil laughs. "Yeah, I'm getting a head start. With all of the craziness the last few days, I've, unfortunately, been neglecting my duties."

"I don't blame you, Coach."

"Yeah, I have the day off from work. Figure I'll get the infield ready, paint the lines, and then cut the grass. Well, the day is marching on. You enjoy your run. See you tonight."

Liam answers, "Yeah. See you tonight, Coach. Looking forward to finally completing that game."

Phil replies, "If you play the same way you did right before all hell broke loose, we are sure to win. Have a good day."

Liam runs two times around Dunham Park and then makes his way back home. Within the hour, Liam, Boo, and Will are on the road and heading to Grandmom's house. They drive south along Interstate 294. Will gets into the exit lane for Interstate 55 toward Joliet and eventually uses an exit ramp toward the City of Darien. Darien is small but cozy suburban area southwest of Chicago. Darien is where Will, his mother, Bethany, and father, Bill, moved after Will's father retired from the fire department. This is where Will spent his middle school and high school years before going off to college.

They drive down the quiet and windy road of Will's old block until they reach their destination. Will pulls the van into the driveway where he sees Bethany (Grandmom) already at work in the garage. In the driveway, there's a large trash dumpster, which was dropped off by a private waste management company earlier that day. Bethany waves at her family. Liam and Boo exit the van and run up to Bethany. Bethany smiles and says, "Hey, kids! Good to see you. Now, do you want to start off by helping your dad with his father's mess or making your way into the kitchen and having some homemade cookies and juice?"

Liam and Boo smile. Boo says, "I like the homemade cookies and juice idea first."

Liam nods his head. "Yeah, me too."

Bethany walks past the row-upon-row of old boxes and bins, hugs her son, and says, "Only if that's okay with your dad, of course. How are you doing, Son?"

Will smiles. "Doing fine, Mom. No worries. I actually got some rest last night. And, yes, that's fine. I can use a few minutes alone in the garage to sort out a few things."

Bethany shakes her head. "Sorry to make you go through all of this stuff. But it's time to get rid of it."

Will laughs and says, "It's okay, Mom. I understand. I don't want you lifting all of these heavy boxes and bins all by yourself. That's why you have us. Looks like the company dropped off the dumpster without a problem."

Bethany turns toward the dumpster and she says, "Yup. They arrived yesterday evening with it. They said to throw in as much stuff as it will hold. No worries. Just no paint or compressed cans. They said to put that stuff off to the side and they will take it to the city waste management office to get it disposed properly."

Will looks around the garage, examines the several rows of boxes, and says, "Is this everything? I thought I told you not to lift and move anything from the garage attic."

Bethany rolls her eyes. "Son, this is only the stuff your father kept in the garage. I haven't even touched the attic. That's up to you to sort out."

Will takes a deep breath, starts to feel overwhelmed, and replies, "Okay. Sounds good. Well, let me start with the stuff in the garage for now." Will looks at Liam and Boo and continues, "Why don't you two enjoy your treat and I'll see you in a little bit."

Liam and Boo smile and walk with Bethany back into the air-conditioned house toward the kitchen.

After Liam and Boo have over their fair share of treats and beverages, they slowly make their way back to the garage. They open the garage door to see Will already hard at work, throwing stuff away or moving it outside. Liam and Boo walk over to Will. Liam asks, "So what's the plan, Dad?" Will lifts a large box over the inside of the dumpster and drops it. There's a loud crash as glass breaks on impact and metallic items scatter across the floor.

Will takes a small handkerchief out of his back pocket, wipes the sweat off his forehead, and answers, "This isn't my first rodeo when it comes to this sort of job. Figure the best thing is to separate this stuff into three categories. Category 1 will include stuff that Grandmom wants to keep. That stuff will stay in the garage. Category 2 will be stuff Grandmom doesn't mind donating to a local charity. That stuff will go into the van and we will deliver it to Goodwill on our way home. Category 3 will be garbage. That goes straight into the dumpster."

Boo nods her head as Liam says, "Okay. Got it. Let's get to work."

The family works together for over an hour, continuing to bring items over to Grandmom. Bethany has final say as to which items are saved or thrown away. They take the time to go through each box. Most of the boxes include old junk, which Bethany thought her husband threw away years ago. Will looking into other boxes is as though he is discovering past treasures for the first time in a long time. When Will opens another box, he smiles from ear to ear as he exclaims, "Hah! I can't believe it! I thought Dad threw this stuff away years ago."

Bethany asks, "What's that, honey?"

Will answers, "It's my old baseball card binders and some of my old comic books!"

Liam takes a break and looks at his father's lost treasure. Liam exclaims, "Wow, Dad! It looks like a lot of old rookie and draft pick cards in these binders. And these are some great vintage comics too."

Bethany smiles. "Yeah, your grandfather would buy his son the complete set of baseball cards every year for Christmas. Your father always looked forward to looking through them all and sorting them out by teams. But that didn't stop him from hitting me up for extra money at the drugstore so he could buy more cards and comics." Will smiles as Bethany continues, "See, it's worth coming over and looking through all of this stuff."

Will replies, "Sure is."

Will reaches down and lifts an old coffee can with a sealed plastic lid. As he opens it, Bethany asks, "What's in there, honey?"

Will replies, "It's full of old keys and some loose change. Interesting."

Suddenly, Boo remembers her conversation with Misty and says, "Hey, Dad! Let us take a look at that while you sort through the rest of the box."

Liam interjects, "Yeah. I've been starting up an old coin collection. Maybe there's some rare coins in there."

Will chuckles as he hands Boo the can and says, "Sure! Sounds good. But let Grandmom have the rest of the spare change. She can always take it to the bank to get sorted."

Bethany interjects, "Let me find some plastic gloves, kids! I have some under the bathroom sink. You don't want to get all of the old metallic material on your hands."

While Bethany gets gloves for Liam and Boo, they begin looking through the old coffee can. Liam whispers to Boo, "How do you want to do this, Sis?"

Boo looks around and grabs a large cloth grocery bag off one of the shelves. She whispers back, "You look through the coins. I'll look through the old keys. If we find anything that resembles what Misty told us, just follow my lead."

Liam winks at Boo and says, "Got it."

After a few minutes of sorting, Boo taps Liam on the arm and whispers, "I found a couple of old keys."

Liam whispers back, "Let me take a look at them." Liam inspects Boo's findings and says, "Yup. They look like old brass keys to me."

Boo puts the keys in the grocery bag, winks at Liam, turns toward Will, and says, "Hey, Dad! Is it okay if we check out the attic?"

Will pauses from his treasure hunt, looks at Bethany, and asks, "I don't know. What do you think, Mom?"

Bethany turns toward Liam and Boo and asks, "Why do you want to go up there, honey?"

Boo answers with a smile, "Just curiosity I guess. Never been up there before."

Liam interjects, "Nope. Me neither."

Bethany replies, "I guess it's okay. I would just be careful. Lord knows what your grandfather left up there for us to sort out."

Will replies, "Okay. Sounds good. But be careful. And remember something, you two."

Boo asks, "What's that, Dad?"

Will answers with a laugh, "Only walk on the plywood. Not on drywall in between the support beams. Otherwise, I'll be seeing you faster that you can think. And bring a flashlight. I don't think we even have a working light bulb up there."

Liam and Boo laugh as Will continues, "Go ahead. And be careful."

Liam pulls down the attic ladder and peers up to the dark void above. He walks over to a light switch along the garage floor wall and turns it on. Boo looks up into the attic. Liam asks, "Any light?"

Boo answers, "Nope."

Liam walks over to a nearby utility shelf and grabs a flashlight. Liam hands Boo the flashlight and says, "Okay. Flashlight it is."

Boo answers, "If we can make our way around the Elk's Estate during a thunderstorm in the middle of the night with only a flashlight, I think we'll be fine."

Liam laughs uncomfortably and says, "Yeah. Don't remind me."

Liam and Boo climb up the wooden collapsible ladder up to the attic. Boo turns on her flashlight as she reaches the top. She pans around and scans the area and then climbs to the floor above. Liam climbing up the ladder asks, "What you got up there, Sis?"

Boo looks down toward Liam. She puts her finger to her lips and quietly says, "All kinds of stuff. Come on."

Liam looks back and sees Will talking to Bethany and discussing whether she should keep some antiques Will found in another box.

As Liam climbs to the top, Boo says, "Be careful. You're the taller one. You might have to bend down a bit so you don't hit the rafters."

Liam looks around as Boo pans the flashlight back and forth. Liam exclaims in a low voice, "Wow! Look at all of this stuff. I can't believe Dad nor Grandmom know anything about the stuff up here."

Boo says, "Yeah. Apparently, Papa was really strict about anyone touching or going anywhere near his stuff. He basically forbade Dad or Grandmom from coming up here."

Liam asks, "Papa has been dead for years. Why didn't he make time to come up here and take a look around?"

Boo answers, "I remember Dad talking to Mom one time about cleaning up Grandmom's house after Papa passed away. Apparently, he was up to his ears in old junk he had to throw away from the crawl space and a storage room in the basement."

Liam replies, "I guess he was just tired and didn't even want to start cleaning this stuff out at the time."

Boo walks in front along a narrow passageway and pans the flashlight back and forth as she walks with Liam. They walk through the dark and musty attic. Boo wipes away old spider webs and Liam begins to cough as they continue to kick up layers of dust off the floor. Boo looks back at Liam and asks, "Are you okay? Do you need your medicine?"

Liam reaches into his shorts pocket, nods his head, and says, "Yeah. I think I do." Liam takes a dose off his inhaler, and Boo continues to look up and down the long passageway. Liam sees old model train setups and boxes labeled MODELS. Liam says, "I guess this was Papa's. I remember Dad saying something about his father really being into trains and building model planes when he was a kid."

Boo pans her light along a stack of boxes labeled PHOTO LAB SUPPLIES and asks, "What do you make of this, Liam?"

Liam looks toward the light as Boo continues to point. "I think this is some of our great-grandfather's stuff. Dad mentioned that his grandfather used to have a photography lab set up in his basement. Apparently, he was some type of amateur photographer."

Boo replies, "That's pretty cool. It's stepping back into our family history up here."

Liam looks at a box and says, "You want to talk about family history, look at this, Boo!"

Boo pans her light toward Liam and asks, "What's that, Liam?"

Liam opens a box labeled MILITARY.

Boo asks, "What's in there, Liam?"

Liam pulls out some old camouflage uniforms and some black-and-white photos and exclaims, "Wow! These are some original pictures from Papa serving in Vietnam and some other pictures of his father in World War II."

Boo carefully walks over next to Liam, shines her light, and looks at the items inside of box. "Wait till Dad takes a look at this stuff! He loves finding things about our family's service." Boo turns around and shines her light in the opposite corner. There she sees an old wooden chest with a brass lock in the center. Boo taps Liam on the shoulder.

Liam turns around and asks, "What do you have, Boo?"

Boo continues to shine her light in the opposite corner and begins to move closer to the wooden chest. "I think I found what Misty was talking about."

Liam walks behind Boo. Boo begins to crawl on the floor as she gets closer to the edge of the room. Liam bends down as well. Boo hands Liam the flashlight and says, "Here! Hold this while I check these keys."

Liam holds the light steady on the wooden chest as Boo wipes a thick layer of dust off the top of it. The swept-away dust reveals a family crest on top of it. Liam coughs slightly. Boo turns and says, "Sorry. Didn't mean to make it worse for you."

Liam replies with a puzzling look, "It's okay."

"Did you know that our family had a family crest?"

Liam shakes his head. Boo reaches for the set of old keys. She tries a few keys but to no avail. Boo is down to her last key. She turns to her brother and says, "Fingers crossed." Liam crosses his fingers as Boo tries the final key. She turns the key and the old rusty lock breaks open! Boo removes the lock, turns to Liam, and says, "Jackpot! Misty was right!"

Liam smiles and gives Boo a thumbs up. Boo turns back to the chest and opens the hatch. The hatch creaks like an old coffin in a classic vampire movie. Boo asks Liam for the flashlight. Liam hands it over as Boo begins to examine the contents inside the chest.

Boo finds several items that are wrapped in old brown clothes. She hands one to Liam, and Boo grabs another. They begin to unroll the cloth. Liam unrolls his item and finds what appears to be an old weapon of some type with a metallic pick end and a wooden handle. Boo unrolls her item and finds an old journal. She turns to Liam and asks, "What did you find?"

Liam twists the object around in his hand. "I'm not sure. Looks like some old piercing tool or maybe a weapon of some type. What about yourself?"

Boo lifts up an old brown leather journal about the size of a traditional hard cover book. Liam says, "Now *that* looks interesting. What's inside it?"

Boo opens the book as she approaches Liam. She combs through the weathered brown pages and reveals old diagrams, maps, drawings, pictures, and narratives written in English and another language. Boo beams the light at one of the pictures in the beginning of the journal. It's a black-and-white photo of a family inside a large hall with a family crest behind them. Boo points out a young man in the photo and says, "Now *that's* spooky."

Liam asks, "What's that, Boo?"

Boo answers, "Look at the young man in this photo, Liam. He looks a lot like you."

Liam examines the photo. "Wow! Boo! This must be the journal from our great-great grandfather."

"Wow! That's incredible!"

Liam asks, "Anything else in that chest?"

Boo crawls back over to the chest, combs through the contents, and says, "Yeah! There's a lot of old clothes. Some chain mail and an old wooden bow! And...what's this?"

Liam asks, "What's what, Boo?"

Boo slowly crawls back over to Liam with a brown leather pouch and reveals the contents to Liam saying, "These are arrowheads with some markings on them."

Liam examines the arrowheads and says, "With our own personal history, I think I can recognize silver when I see it. These look like silver arrowheads, Boo!" Liam examines the wooden/metal tipped weapon and continues, "And the pointy end of whatever this thing is....is silver."

Boo asks, "What do you make of all of this, Liam?"

Liam thinks for a minute.

✦ ✦ ✦

At that moment, Will looks at his watch and says to Bethany, "Those kids have been up for a while haven't they?"

Bethany answers jokingly, "They sure have but they're still alive. I can hear them crawling around up there."

Will laughs. "Gee…thanks, Mom. That's really comforting." Will walks over to the attic ladder, looks up to the dark open hatch, and exclaims, "Hey! You kids okay up there? Find anything good? Why don't you come down and take a break!"

Liam looks back at the light illuminating from the open hatch an exclaims, "Thanks, Dad! There's a couple of cool things up here. We'll fill you in when we come down." Liam looks back at Boo, places the wooden object he found into the grocery bag, and says in a low voice, "Put the journal and the stuff into the bag. We'll grab a few things we found on the way out and show Dad and Grandmom. We'll take a better look at the stuff from the chest later. I think we have to do some family research, Boo. Time to call some friends."

CHAPTER 13

....

THAT IS INTERESTING, ISN'T IT?

Liam and Boo continue to assist Will and Bethany for another hour before Bethany says, "Boy! It's getting hot out here. Why don't we take a break?"

Will looks at his watch and says, "That sounds like a good idea, Mom. After that, we will have to start cleaning up and hit the road."

Will, Liam, and Boo follow Bethany into the house. The warm and sweet aroma of something cooking in the kitchen hit their noses. Will says, "Ah! Smells like home. What are you cooking, Mom?"

Bethany walks ahead of everyone toward the kitchen and answers, "Well, come on in. I've been making Polish sausage and sauerkraut in the Crock Pot. Figure it will be a nice lunch for all of us, and it can cook while I'm helping you with the garage. I have hot dog buns and chips as well."

Liam asks, "Grandmom, do you have any cold soda?"

Bethany says, "Of course I do, sweetheart. Sorry, I forgot to tell you. It's in the garage refrigerator. Can you get one for me please? Diet?"

Will turns to Liam and asks, "Can you get me one too, buddy?"

Liam says, "Sure, no problem, Dad." Liam looks at Boo and asks with a wink, "Do you want one, Boo?"

She winks back and says, "Sure, I'll take a regular soda. Thank you."

Liam walks through the hallway foyer and into the garage. Before he goes to the refrigerator, he grabs the cloth grocery bag concealing the wooden chest items and carries it over to the van.

He opens the sliding door and shoves the bag underneath Boo's seat. He walks quickly back to the garage, grabs the sodas, and walks back into the house. The air-conditioned air hits Liam's face like a cool wind blowing through a hot baseball field. He overhears Bethany saying to Boo, "Since when do you not like my Polish sausage?"

Boo awkwardly replies, "It's not that, Grandmom. I like your food, but it's a bit too heavy of a meal for me to eat on a hot day."

Will says, "That's fine, honey." Will laughs and jokingly continues, "More for me I guess. See if Grandmom has peanut butter and jelly."

Bethany says, "Of course I have peanut butter and jelly. I eat it for lunch a few times a week. The bread and peanut butter are in the cupboard, and I'll get the jelly for you."

Liam taps Boo on the shoulder and whispers in her ear, "All set. The bag in under your seat." Boo nods her head and winks back at Liam.

The family enjoys the rest of their late lunch. They sit for a while to let their food settle before Will looks at the kitchen clock and says, "Well, this was fun, Grandmom. Thank you for a wonderful lunch. But we have to start cleaning up and heading out. We have to drop some stuff off at Goodwill, and Liam has a baseball game starting early tonight."

Grandmom replies, "It was my pleasure. You know how much I love cooking for the family."

Will, Liam, and Boo start picking up their dirty plates and Bethany interjects, "Stop! Leave it. I'll take care of it."

Will asks, "Are you sure, Mom?"

Bethany answers, "I'm sure, honey. It's getting too hot out there for me anyway. I'll clean up the kitchen. You take care of the garage."

Will, Liam, and Boo finish packing up the van and close up the garage for the day. Before they leave, they walk back inside the house to say goodbye to Bethany. Will is greeted with a bag of leftover food in plastic containers. Bethany says, "This is some food for Annie. Don't want her to feel like she was forgotten."

Will smiles as he takes the bag from Bethany. With a hug and a kiss, Will says, "Or a late-night snack for me. Thanks, Mom. We'll see you tomorrow. And we will try to finish the garage and then tackle the attic."

Liam and Boo give each other a shifty-eyed look. Bethany looks at Boo, gives her a hug, and says, "Hopefully you enjoyed your sandwich, sweetheart. Thank you for helping me with your grandfather's junk."

Boo replies, "It's okay. He's sorry he didn't take care of it himself."

Bethany looks puzzled. "What do you mean, Boo?"

Will and Liam look at Boo as Boo answers, "Sorry. I meant to say, *I'm sure* he wishes he took care of it before he passed away."

Liam gives Bethany a hug as Will gives Boo a thumbs up and pantomimes, "Good recovery, honey."

The three make their way over to Goodwill, drop off the donation items, and head home before the late-afternoon traffic begins on the highway. Will thanks Liam and Boo for their help on the ride home. Will asks, "So what kind of stuff did Papa have in the attic? And more importantly, how much stuff are we talking?"

Liam answers, "Not too much stuff, Dad. Definitely worth taking the time to go through tomorrow. A lot of stuff from Papa and his father. And some family history stuff."

Will replies, "Family history stuff. That sounds interesting."

Boo whispers, "If Dad only knew the half of it."

Will looks into his rear-view mirror at Boo and asks, "What's that, honey?"

Boo interjects, "Nothing, Dad. Just thinking out loud."

Meanwhile in an old masonry municipal building on the northwest side of the city, a large box fan loudly spins in the window next to Detective Cunningham's desk. The phones from nearby desks echo through the hallway and vibrate along the glass separating his office from the general administrative area. Detective Cunningham continues to work on his computer when the phone on his office desk begins to ring. He takes the handkerchief out of his shirt pocket, wipes the sweat off his forehead, and then answers the phone saying, "Detective Cunningham. Go ahead."

Cindy, the Cook County Forest Preserve administrative assistant, is on the other end of the phone. She says, "Good afternoon, Detective. How are you today?"

Detective Cunningham answers, "I'd be doing better if that damn air conditioning was back up and running. When is that thing gonna get repaired?"

Cindy replies, "I've been on a phone with the HVAC guys all morning. They are backed up fixing the air conditioning at the medical examiner's office. That took priority. I think you can agree with that."

Detective Cunningham laughs and says, "Yeah. I can definitely agree with that."

Cindy continues, "Speaking of the medical examiner's office, that's the reason for my call. Someone from their office just left a message. He asked to talk to the detective in charge of the investigation regarding the young lady from the Robinson Woods."

Detective Cunningham replies, "Sounds good. In fact, I need to follow up with them. It will help with my case. What's his name?"

Cindy answers, "His name is Dr. Rodney. I'll try to use the county extension and connect you directly if that's okay?"

Detective Cunningham answers, "Yeah, that's fine Cindy. Thank you."

After a brief hold, Detective Cunningham hears a ringtone on the other end of the phone. After a phone rings a couple of times, Dr. Rodney answers, "Cook County Medical Examiner's Office. This is Dr. Rodney."

Detective Cunningham replies, "Yes, Dr. Rodney. This is Detective Steve Cunningham. I'm in charge of the case regarding the young lady in Robinson Woods."

Dr. Rodney says, "Yeah, thanks for the call back. Sorry it took me a minute. We almost had a legit emergency around here with the air conditioning going out."

Steve laughs. "I heard. You up and running?"

Dr. Rodney answers, "Yup. We sure are. Thank God!"

Steve continues, "That's good. So, what can you tell me about Amy, the young lady from Robinson Woods? Have you determined a cause of death and how much time has passed since she died?"

Dr. Rodney pauses for a moment and says, "Yeah… About that."

Steve asks, "What's the matter?"

Dr. Rodney answers, "Yeah. We can't figure out a cause of death, and the level of deterioration to the corpse suggests the time of death could be over a year ago."

Steve replies, "That doesn't make any sense. Why can't you determine a cause of death?"

Dr. Rodney says, "From the remains we gathered, we can determine that Amy seemed like a very healthy young lady. We cannot find any signs of trauma, and her lab reports came back. And shockingly, the lab report shows, with all due respect, that Amy was very healthy."

Steve bangs his fist into his desk, shakes his head, and says, "Well, that's great! I was hoping that your office would be able to shed some light into what happened to this young lady. But instead, I'm left with more questions than answers."

Dr. Rodney nods his head and shifts his glasses. "Yeah, I'm sorry, Detective. Truly. But I'm going to give you a number of another employee from the county. Do you remember the recent story about the old lady escaping the mental ward in the northwest suburbs that left two security guards in my tender loving care?"

Steve thinks for a moment and replies, "Yes, I do. They still haven't found that old lady have they?"

Dr. Rodney answers, "Nope, they sure haven't. And the two security guards who died look just like the young lady from Robinson Woods."

Detective Cunningham readjusts his position in his chair and says, "Now, that *is* interesting isn't it?"

Dr. Rodney adds, "Yup. The old lady was under the psychiatric care of Dr. Ross. A nice young woman who started working at the facility recently."

Dr. Rodney gives Detective Cunningham her contact information. Within moments, Steve is attempting to contact Dr. Ross at her office. The phone rings a few times. The line opens up and a voice says, "This is Dr. Ross. How can I help you?"

Detective Cunningham replies, "Yes, Dr. Ross. We haven't met but my name is Detective Cunningham from the Cook County Forest Preserve Police Office."

Dr. Ross asks, "Okay? How can I help you, Detective?"

Detective Cunningham answers, "I'm the lead detective in a case involving the untimely death of a young lady from Robinson Woods. You may recall hearing about on the local news outlets."

Dr. Ross answers, "I do recall that case. Sad news. Makes me worry about my own safety when I'm out and about."

Steve continues, "I'm sure. Well, the reason for my call is that I've been in contact with the Cook County Medical Examiner's Office. A doctor over there mentioned the body that was recovered in Robinson Woods looks very similar to the bodies of the two security guards from your facility. And the only thing that could possibly tie these three deaths together is the old lady who escaped who was under your care. Is that correct, Dr. Ross?"

Dr. Ross pauses for a moment and then answers, "I can tell you that the woman who escaped from our facility was under my care. However, I'm afraid that I can't tell you anything further about her or her medical care without it being a direct violation of patient privacy."

Detective Cunningham chuckles. "You are correct, Dr. Ross. That is normally the case. Unless that information is important to the continuation of her medical care or during criminal investigations. Now, if you would like me to get a subpoena from one of my judges I can. If that makes you feel better?"

Dr. Ross replies, "That won't be necessary, Detective. I try to be a good advocate for my patients is all. Unfortunately, I don't have a great deal of information. I can give you her name, but her file doesn't have an active address, next of kin, or any advanced medical directives. Under the narratives, it states that the patient is a ward of the state. She was transferred to our facility about twenty years ago after the previous facility closed. She has been known to attack orderlies and doesn't respond to any individual or group therapy sessions. Under previous medical orders, she's been chemically restrained due to a history of violence."

Detective Cunningham listens to the narrative while he takes a few notes on his notepad. He responds, "That seems interesting. Which facility did she belong to previously?"

Dr. Ross pauses for a moment as she flips the page in the patient file. "Let me see, Detective. It says she was transferred here from the old Northwest Sanitarium when it closed its doors in 2004."

Detective Cunningham continues to write down notes as he asks, "I wonder who, if anyone, would still have any of the files from that facility. If I remember correctly, that facility was operated by Cook County."

Dr. Ross adds, "I think so. Sorry." She laughs slightly as she continues, "That was way before my time."

Steve laughs slightly too and says, "See. Now I'm showing my age over the phone. Dr. Ross, would you mind meeting me tomorrow at the Cook County Records Office in the city?"

Dr. Ross pauses and looks at her schedule. "I have a few patients in the morning, and then I'll be free by lunch. If that's okay?"

Steve nods his head. "That will be fine. The records archive in the basement of the facility has really helped me crack a few cold cases over the years. Maybe we can find out more about your patient."

Dr. Ross answers, "That will be fine, Detective. I'll be happy to assist you with the investigation in any way I can."

Detective Cunningham ends the conversation.

CHAPTER 14

....

CONFERENCE CALL WITH THE PHILLY CREW

The evening fast approaches by the time Liam, Boo, and Will arrive back home. Will carries his newly discovered childhood treasures into the house. Liam runs ahead and says, "Here, Dad! Let me get the door for you."

"Thanks, Son. I appreciate it." Will stops, turns back to Boo, and says, "Hey, honey! Would you mind taking care of the gate and the dog?"

Boo with a thumbs up answers, "No problem, Dad. I'll take care of Lady."

Liam opens the door and is immediately greeted by Lady and Annie. Lady jumps up and intends to give Will a hug. Her force almost knocks the plastic bin out of Will's hands. Will exclaims, "Lady! Not now! Go in the backyard with Boo!"

Boo walks over to the gate and says, "Come here, Lady!"

Lady follows Boo's commands and greets Boo with a slobbery kiss. Boo bends down to greet her dog. Annie sees Will walking in with the plastic bin and asks, "So, what else are you bringing into MY house."

Will exclaims, "Remember, it's OUR house. And I'm bringing some lost treasure from my parents' house."

Annie rolls her eyes and says, "Hopefully not too much stuff. We already have a whole basement full of stuff to sort through."

Will takes the bin downstairs into the basement and replies, "Not to worry, honey. I promise it's nothing more than the amount of stuff your parents dropped off here after we moved into this house."

Annie shakes her head. "Fine. Whatever." She looks at Liam and asks, "So how was Grandmom's house, honey?"

As Liam begins to answer, Boo walks inside with the cloth grocery bag hanging from her left shoulder. Boo sees Annie and attempts to walk briskly past her mother as she says with a smile, "Hey, Mom! How was your day?"

Annie peeks her head around the corner and replies, "Just fine, honey. And what did you find at Grandmom's house?"

Boo pauses from climbing up the stairs toward her bedroom and answers, "Just some lost treasure."

Frustrated, Annie says, "Great! More things coming into the house."

Annie looks at Liam as he attempts to distract his mother by saying, "It was a good visit, Mom. Really. Grandmom really appreciated us coming over and helping."

Annie is satisfied with that answer and gives Liam a hug. She walks away from Liam and toward the kitchen counter. "That's great, honey. I'm glad she finally wants to go through all of your grandfather's things. That's always so hard after someone passes away."

Liam looks at the counter and notices Annie preparing vegetables and chicken. She places the food items into a large glass bowl and pours a bottle of marinade into the bowl. Liam asks, "So, what are you planning to make for dinner, Mom?"

Annie turns toward Liam with a smile and answers, "I'm planning to make some chicken shish-kebabs on the grill outside and serve it with some potato chips."

Liam licks his lips when the tangy marinade aroma hits his nose. "That sounds delicious."

Annie says, "Yeah, I figure it will be better not to turn on the oven and heat up the house." Annie looks at the clock and continues, "If you're not busy, honey, I could use some help putting the veggies and the meat onto the skewers. That way it will be done before your game tonight."

Liam, who's always happy to help cook, says, "Sure thing, Mom." He washes his hands and gets ready to help Annie.

Will continues to look through his lost treasure in the basement, Annie and Liam continue preparing dinner, and Boo takes the moment to look through the leather journal that was found in the attic. She rubs the front cover of the brown leather journal. The cover feels dry and wrinkly. She opens the pages. The opening page of the journal has a picture of a family crest. The pages are stained yellow with age and emit a slight odor of decay. She is able to read most of it. However, some of the opening entries in the journal are written in Polish. Boo is fascinated by some of the entries but wonders who she can turn to find out more.

After a few minutes, she has a thought and texts Ellie in Pennsylvania. Ellie texts back: "Hey, Boo! I'm actually hanging out with Simon and Reggie right now."

Boo replies: "Are you guys free to do a video call? Liam and I found some really cool stuff inside Grandmom's attic?"

After a minute, Ellie texts: "Sure! I was working on a few songs from band camp, and Simon and Reggie were just finishing up a video game."

Boo receives a video call on her computer from Ellie. She answers and is happily greeted by the Philly crew. They all say, "Hi, Boo!"

Reggie says, "We miss you, Boo!"

Simon shoves Reggie aside and asks, "Hey, Boo! How are you doing, other monster slayer?" He gives a shifty-eyed look and continues, "Hey! See any ghosts or poltergeists lately? I still want to do an interview with you. It will be great for my research and maybe help increase my followers."

Boo laughs. "Sure thing! Anytime. Hey, everyone! I miss you too. Yeah about that…. Misty visited me."

Ellie replies, "No way."

Reggie, wide-eyed, interjects, "No shit?"

Simon replies, "Wicked! What did she say, Boo?"

Boo answers, "I'll fill you in more later. Right now, I'm wondering if you can find out more about this." Boo pulls up the drawing of the family crest from the journal and continues, "This is from an old family journal Liam and I found in our grandmother's attic."

Reggie says, "Damn! Is that legit? Is your family like royalty or something?"

Ellie answers, "No way! That's our family crest? Didn't even know we had a family crest…that's pretty cool."

Simon says, "Wicked! Maybe you're from a long line of beautiful princesses or something. That would explain your immense beauty."

Ellie pushes Simon as she interjects with a blushing smile, "Shut up, nerd!"

Simon looks at the camera and continues, "You see, Boo? You see how your cousin treats her boyfriend?"

Boo laughs. "Yet, you still are going out with her."

Ellie replies, "Yeah. He knows he can't do much better. I will admit he is cuter when he can figure out stuff like this." Ellie turns to Simon. "Any thoughts, Simon?"

Simon paces back and forth for a moment while he scratches his chin. He suddenly interjects, "I got it! There's a place that specializes in family legacy stuff like family crests and their history. In fact, it's not too far from here."

Ellie asks, "Which place are you thinking?"

Simon answers, "Peddler's Village off Route 202 and Street Road."

Reggie interjects, "The place that looks like a small village out of a hobbit fantasy novel and always decorated really cool for the holidays?"

Simon replies, "Yup, the very one. There's a small shop in there that can look up last names, their family crests, and everything."

Reggie asks, "How the hell do you know that, dude?"

Simon smiles. "Look who you're asking. I went there with my mom a few years ago. She wanted to get a family history gift for my dad for the holidays." Simon pauses in mid-thought for a brief moment and continues, "Tell you what, Boo. Send Ellie some pictures from the journal, and we can take a ride over there tomorrow."

Boo thanks the Philly crew for their help. They talk amongst themselves for a few more minutes before finishing their conversation.

✦✦✦

The family enjoys their delicious summer meal together in the backyard before heading over to the park for Liam's baseball game. The sun continues to set and leaves a blanket of red-and-pink clouds before it vanishes from the horizon. The lights illuminate the baseball diamond as the players compete and attempt to finish their game, which was strangely interrupted a few evenings before. The sound of families conversing and bats hitting baseballs into the evening sky echo up and down Giddings Street. A police cruiser drives slowly around the park and observes the area. Several parents smile and wave at the officers as they drive past. Some feel a mixture of relief to see the police cruiser circling the park. Others feel anxious as they turn their attention away from the game and wonder if and when the mysterious flying monster will reappear and hopefully get captured by authorities.

....

CHAPTER 15

THE LIVE BAIT TRAP IS SET

As the evening continues, a group of three young ladies gather in a forest preserve a few miles to the east. They use the flashlights on their phones to maneuver their way through the dark forest back to the abandoned cemetery. The sounds of crickets and frogs echo slightly through the grass and trees. Lightning bugs flicker past them and gently flash their glowing yellow-green tails. Blair says to Lilith, "Hey! What time did this Angelica lady say to meet her back here?"

Lilith turns to Blair and asks, "Why?"

Blair answers, "I'm just curious. That's all."

Chloe asks Blair, "You not getting cold feet are you? It's clear that this lady has some talents and can do some wild shit."

Blair turns to Chloe and asks, "Aren't you just a little curious when she said to take a bus to the nearest stop and just walk the rest of the way?"

Lilith, who's beginning to get frustrated with Blair, responds, "God, Blair. I already asked her that before we left the other night. She said the cops have been on extra patrols recently. She doesn't want them to see a car parked in the forest lot and wonder if the owners are still wandering the forest at night. Just relax."

Chloe, Blair and Lilith arrive to the deserted cemetery. Chloe uses her flashlight on her phone and scans the area. She says, "Doesn't look like anyone is home. At least, not yet anyway."

Chloe looks at Lilith and says, "Hey! Don't forget to text the parents and tell them we made it over to Blair's house for the night."

Lilith smiles. "Oh, yeah. I almost forgot. My parents are such a pain in the ass. If I didn't let them know my whereabouts at least six times a day, they would send out search parties."

Chloe laughs as she says, "Yeah. Mine too. It's like they don't trust us or something." Chloe looks at Blair who is still struggling to light her cigarette with the lighter. Sparks continue to flicker off the end of the lighter as Blair attempts to make a flame. Chloe jokingly asks, "What's the matter, Blair? First time using a child-safe lighter?"

Chloe and Lilith laugh as Blair holds up the lighter to the light on the end of her phone. Blair replies, "Shut up! I use this lighter all the time. The problem isn't failed usage. The problem is that I'm out of fuel. Shit!"

Suddenly, a flickering orange-and-yellow light illuminates from a corner of a nearby crypt. Blair, Lilith, and Chloe turn toward the light as they hear Angelica laugh. Angelica rests the right side of her body along a gray stone crypt, which is covered in overgrown green-and-yellow vines and brown moss. She holds up a small stick with her left hand. The stick helps to illuminate her face and the surrounding area as the small flame dances off the end of it. Angelica says, "Nice to see you, girls. Are you in need of a light, my dear? Please, let me help you."

Blair cautiously moves toward Angelica. Angelica extends her hand to bring the flame closer the Blair. Blair only takes her eyes off Angelica for a brief moment as she lights her cigarette.

Angelica smiles at the girls as she begins to light several candles along the outside of the crypt. She says, "I'm so glad you decided to come back." Angelica looks at each of the girls as she continues, "Did you follow my instructions?"

Chloe nods her head and Lilith answers, "Yeah. We did what you asked. Walked over here from the bus stop."

Blair turns away from Angelica and shakes her head. Through the shimmering light, Angelica notices the slight doubt bouncing off Blair's face. Angelica walks over to Blair and places her hand on Blair's shoulder. Blair is startled by the icy-cold hand being placed on her shoulder. She jumps slightly when she notices the large scar on Angelica's hand. Angelica asks, "What's the matter, my dear? You seem nervous."

Blair trembles. "I'm okay. I'm just a little wigged out by everything right now. And your hand. It's so...so cold."

Angelica looks at her hand and says, "I'm sorry, my dear. My circulation isn't what it used to be." Angelica smiles at Blair and turns to Lilith and Chloe. "I can understand some of your doubts." Angelica inhales deeply through her nose, turns back toward Blair, and continues, "But I sense less doubt and more fear from you, my dear. Why is that?"

Blair responds quickly, "I'm not scared."

Angelica replies, "Oh, yes you are, my dear. I can sense such things."

Lilith interjects, "Blair is our mother hen and the nervous Nellie of the group." Lilith pauses for a brief moment and then continues, "She was picked on a lot at school. That's why she started hanging out with me and Chloe."

Angelica smiles as she bends down to light some more candles, which are placed in a straight line along the entrance to the crypt. Angelica looks up to Blair. "Is that so, my dear? Why did they pick on you?"

Blair nervously answers, "Because I'm usually very quiet around people, and I used to be much heavier. I used to be a nervous eater."

Angelica replies, "I see. Hence, the continuous desire to smoke. I understand, my dear. Believe me I do...now please, all of you have a seat and form a circle around me."

Blair, Chloe, and Lilith do as they are asked. When they sit down Lilith asks, "Were you picked on when you were in school too?"

Angelica answers, "Yes I was. It seems like ages ago but I do remember. I was a young and beautiful teenager when I joined the convent. The other girls in training weren't that nice to me. They thought I was...different."

Chloe asks, "Wait! You were a nun?"

Angelica answers, "A sister in training, you could say. I was forced to begin my training by my parents. Both of them were deeply religious. They wanted their child to serve their church. They didn't care what my hopes and dreams were. The other girls treated me like their little bitch because I didn't take my studies and practice in their faith seriously. But...that all changed when I met a wonderful man who currently rests in this crypt behind me."

Blair, as she finishes her cigarette, asks, "You know the person inside this crypt?"

Angelica smiles. "Oh, yes! And tonight you will help perform something truly incredible. Something I attempted years ago but unfortunately I was rudely interrupted."

Chloe asks, "So who was this man?"

Angelica answers, "He was my teacher and my true love. He taught me things that I'm willing to teach you too. If you'll allow it of course. Under my tutelage, I will teach you how to be just as powerful as me one day. How does that sound?" Angelica looks at each of the girls. Lilith and Chloe quickly smile and nod their heads. Blair has her head down and doesn't acknowledge the question.

Chloe says, "Blair! Come on! We are your friends."

Lilith says, "Yeah, come on, Blair. Remember who's been there for you when all of the pretty and popular bitches all laughed at you and called you every horrible thing under the sun. Angelica will give us the power to fight back against all of those assholes."

Angelica looks at Blair and demands, "Blair. Blair! Look at me!" Blair slowly looks up at Angelica. Angelica says, "After tonight, I can promise you one thing. You'll never have to worry about being overweight ever again. I will help keep you thin and beautiful for a long time."

Blair draws a slight smile and nods her head. "Okay. What do we need to do?"

Angelica smiles as she answers, "All I need you girls to do is concentrate all of your thoughts onto one of the dancing flames from the candles. That's it. And I'll take care of the rest. Now, are each of you ready to begin? Excellent."

Angelica walks over to the crypt and lifts a small black leather book off the stone step. Lilith asks, "Is that like your spell book or something?"

Angelica answers, "Something like that. It's a part of my soul that was taking from me a long time ago. But, thankfully, I've been reunited with it." Angelica looks down to see a small opossum crawl along the ground next to her. She grabs a small stick off the ground, rubs it up and down with her hand, points the stick at the opossum, and fires a green spark of energy toward the defenseless animal. The animal jumps slightly and is stunned as it rolls over onto it's back. Chloe, Blair, and Lilith are startled by what Angelica did to the animal.

Chloe asks, "What the hell are you doing?"

Angelica smiles and laughs slightly. "It's something I need to begin the ceremony. I simply love opossums. So, fitting for such a ceremony—an animal that acts dead when it's really alive and just waiting to continue with its life." Angelica flicks her hand to open her spell book. She grabs a small black metallic key from its tightly secured space inside her book and places it inside her pocket. She looks up and sees the crescent moon appear behind a patch of silvery clouds. She says, "It's time. Now please, young ladies, I need you concentrate on the flame and not worry about the things around you. Consider this a test and"—she pauses briefly and winks at the girls—"your…initiation."

Angelica stands up and flicks her wooden stick toward the crypt door. The door immediately begins to illuminate a bright red color. She then reaches into her pocket, grabs the key, and places it into the lock. She turns the lock, and the double doors open to reveal an old brass casket lying upon a small rise off the stone floor. She lifts the lid off the top to reveal the remains of a skeletal figure wrapped in a long burgundy robe and a wizard cap lying preciously next to it. Angelica bends down and kisses the top of the decayed skeleton's skull. She trembles as she says, "Hello, my love. You've been asleep for far too long. Tonight you rise and we can be whole again."

Blair takes her attention away from the flickering candles for a brief moment and stares at Angelica inside the crypt. She shakes her head in disbelief. Lilith breaks away from the flames and exclaims, "Blair. Just do what you're told!" Blair nods her head and continues to concentrate into the dancing flames on the end of the candle.

Angelica steps down from the crypt, bends down, and grabs her black leather book. She looks up to the crescent moon as it slowly drifts behind white silvery clouds. She opens to a page and begins to cast the spell saying,

"Crescent moon on the star-filled sky
hear the words of your dark servant cry
solutions, chemicals, and earthen oils
help resurrect my love as the cauldron boils."

She flicks her stick toward the stunned opossum. A burst of energy flies toward the opossum, and a slight squeal is heard as a small mist forms around the animal. Angelica waves her stick from the encircling mist back toward the crypt. The mist flows away from the now decayed opossum and follows Angelica's stick. It quickly flows into the crypt and inside the coffin. Suddenly, there's a loud groan from the coffin as the mists begins to form around the skeletal remains. The mist fills the crypt like an uncontrolled fire inside a house. Angelica impatiently waits for the mist to clear. As the mist begins to clear, a skeletal figure appears standing along the threshold. It slowly places its wizard's cap on top of his skull.

Angelica says, "Welcome back, my love."

Blair breaks away from the candle and sees the figure standing in the doorway of the crypt. She immediately screams, stands up, and backs away as quickly as she can. The other girls break away from the candles and look at the living skeleton as it begins to slowly walk outside the crypt toward Angelica. Blair exclaims, "Lilith! Chloe! Let's get the hell out of here! Screw this! I'm done!" Blair runs as fast as she can out of the cemetery.

Angelica smiles as she shouts, "Oh! You think you can leave just like that? Not so fast! We need you to complete the ceremony, my dear!"

As Blair attempts to leave the cemetery and dash into the woods, she hears a loud and quick swoop of air. She looks up and sees two red eyes glowing as Pet dives toward the ground to stop her escape. Blair screams in horror as Pet lands right in front of her. He extends his massive wings and growls, showing his ugly and mangled teeth. Angelica laughs while Chloe and Lilith scream and cry for help as they try to escape another way. Blair looks back only to see Chloe and Lilith run away. Blair cries out, "Chloe! Lilith! Oh, God please help me!"

Angelica waves her stick in the form of a circle around the ground. A large volume of circular mist begins to form. Angelica commands to Pet, "Pet! Bring me the fat one first. Then the others."

Pet immediately flaps his wings, lifts off the ground, and grabs Blair with his massive clawed feet. Blair screams in terror as she is lifted up into the air and back toward Angelica. Angelica exclaims, "Drop her right into the mist, Pet, and then get the one with the blonde hair." Pet descends toward the ground and drops Blair into encircling mist. Blair screams out in crying horror as she lands into the center of the mist. There's a quick squeal of pain from the bottom of the mist and then silence. Angelica looks toward the skeletal figure and says, "Just wait here, my love. I'll be back with the others in a minute."

Chloe and Lilith run for their lives through the dark forest toward the sound of cars driving on a nearby road. Chloe exclaims to Lilith, "Jesus Christ! What the hell is going on? And what about Blair?" Chloe falls onto the ground as she trips over a tree branch. Lilith runs back and picks Chloe up off the ground.

Lilith looks toward the line of headlights out in the distance and says, "Screw Blair! We need to save ourselves. We just need to make it to those lights and—"

Suddenly, Chloe is lifted off the ground as Pet grabs her with his giant claws. Chloe cries and screams out for help to no avail as Pet takes her back toward the cemetery.

Lilith screams out, "Chloe! Oh, God no! Please help us!" Chloe attempts to collect her thoughts before her final scream for help as Pet drops her into the circulating mist as well.

Lilith turns around and sees Angelica flying through the air on a long tree branch toward her. She screams as Angelica beams her glowing red eyes at Lilith. Lilith screams, "Please! Someone help me!" Angelica flies right above Lilith and lifts her off the ground. Angelica laughs as Lilith screams out, "Please God! Someone help me!"

Angelica laughs at Lilith as she continues to cry uncontrollably. She says, "It's funny how many fools find their faith at the end of their lives."

As Angelica flies back to the cemetery and over the circulating mist, Lilith screams, "But you promised to make us powerful! I wanted to be your student!"

Angelica looks down at Lilith, smiles, and says, "My dear. You're just another useful little bitch. You don't fit the bill to be one of my students. I'm bored with you."

Angelica opens up her hand and drops Lilith into the mist. Lilith lets out one final horrific death scream as she reaches the ground and then silence. Angelica and Pet both glide down to the ground as the mist grows bigger and gains centrifugal momentum before flying toward the skeletal figure. The figure absorbs the misty energy and begins to gain back his flesh and his youth. Pet turns his head in disbelief. Angelica pets the top of Pet's head and says, "It's okay, my dear. Now our family is reunited. Now, do me a favor?" Angelica points down toward the sight of three decayed human bodies and continues, "Take those pathetic bodies over to the crypt and shut the door." Pet performs his commands as the ghoulish figure walks over to Angelica.

The man grabs a hold of Angelica and gives her a kiss as he says, "Hello again." Angelica smiles from ear to ear as she says, "Welcome back, Alek!"

....

CHAPTER 16

NEWS RADIO AND OUR TOP STORY

Liam wakes up to the sound of Lady barking in the backyard as a nearby neighbor walks their dog down the street. Liam rolls over and looks at his alarm clock on his nightstand. It reads 9:03 a.m. He sits at the foot of the bed and smells bacon being cooked.

Boo walks into Liam's room while brushing her teeth. "Good morning, big brother. Sleep well?"

Liam smiles as he stands up. "Yeah. After the practice and finally finishing the game last night, I slept like a baby." He begins to walk toward his bedroom window and notices that his legs are really stiff and sore.

As he wobbles to the window Boo asks, "You feeling okay? You look like you're stiff as a board."

"I'm fine. I guess I'm paying the price after that final dash from third base and sliding into home last night."

Boo responds, "Yeah. Good game last night. I overheard Coach Phil say that he's going to recommend you for the All-Star Team this year."

Liam looks back at Boo and says, "Really? That's awesome! He gets to pick two players. If I'm one, I wonder who will be the other?"

Boo walks back into the bathroom to finish brushing her teeth. She then walks back into Liam's room and responds,

"Your guess is as good as mine. From an outsider's perspective, I think it's a toss-up between Tommy and Ryan. Both guys are on top of their game."

Liam replies, "I think you're right. Time will tell."

Liam looks out the window and sees his father, Will, get Lady from the backyard and bring her back into the house. Liam turns toward Boo and asks, "Did Dad talk to you about today?"

Boo answers, "He did. He said to let you rest and then we will go back to Grandmom's today to finish the job."

Liam says, "Sounds good. At least this is the last day. Were you able to take a better look at the journal last night?"

Boo says, "Only a little bit. By the time we came home and got settled for the night, I only read a few pages before I fell asleep. I guess I was more tired from doing the work at Grandmom's than I thought."

The household enjoys their breakfast together and slowly make their way down to Bethany's house to finish the work. As they crawl with heavy traffic on Interstate 294 South toward the southwest suburbs, Liam asks, "What do you think is causing all this traffic, Dad?"

Will answers, "I'm not sure, Son. If I had to guess, probably another accident further down the road. Let me see if I can get an update on the radio." Will switches radio channels from his classic rock station to the AM news station.

After a few commercials, an announcer from the station says, "Good morning, Chicago. And thank you for tuning in to news radio. Welcome to a start of another beautiful summer day. Currently, the temperature is 73 degrees going to a high of 87 degrees. The sun will continue all day. Winds out of the southwest at 10 miles per hour. Highways are moving fairly well except from the Tri-State Interstate 294. There's a crash in the southbound lanes involving a few vehicles and a semi-truck at the Interstate 88 junction. Police and fire crews are on the scene blocking the two right lanes."

Liam rolls his eyes and looks at Boo. "If there's anything worse than spending an entire day out of our summer cleaning up a hot garage, it's sitting in traffic on the way to cleaning out said garage."

Boo laughs. Will looks in his rear-view mirror and asks, "What's so funny back there?"

Liam quickly adds, "Nothing, Dad. Just keeping ourselves entertained."

The announcer on news radio continues saying, "The time is now 10:00 a.m. BONG! And at the top of the hour, we give our top stories of the day. Police are searching and requesting information regarding the disappearance of three teenage girls from the city's northwest side. Police say the girls were last seen by their parents shortly after 8:00 p.m. Police are requesting anyone with information to contact them immediately. In another unrelated story, police in the northwest suburbs are still continuing their search for an escaped patient from Northwest Cook County Hospital, which left two security guards dead. Area detectives state that the search and investigations are ongoing and will update the media when they have further details."

Liam and Boo look at each other. Liam points to his phone and gives Boo a signal to talk to him via text message. Liam texts: "After we get home, we have to get the crew together and try to find out what's going on around our neighborhood. Unrelated they say. I think not."

Boo looks at her phone and replies: "Agreed. Later tonight, you and I can spend time looking through that journal too. Something's going on, and police are coming up short. This is hitting too close to home."

✦ ✦ ✦

While Liam, Boo, and Will finally arrive at Bethany's home in Darien, Detective Cunningham is standing outside the Cook County Records Office near Roosevelt Road and Damen Avenue in the city. He wipes the sweat off of his forehead and neck as he checks his watch. It's 11:15 a.m. Detective Cunningham begins to wonder if Dr. Ross will arrive. He looks back at his notes. His follow up phone call with Dr. Ross confirms meeting her outside the building by 11:00 a.m. He begins to wonder if he should head back to his office and work on one of his other investigations.

He turns around and sees a beautiful young woman with long blonde hair and glasses walk down the sidewalk toward him. She smiles as she greets him. "You look like a detective if I had to guess. Detective Cunningham I'm assuming?"

Detective Cunningham extends his hand and greets Dr. Ross with a smile. "Your assumption is correct. I'll assume you're Dr. Ross?"

Dr. Ross smiles and says, "Yes, that's right. Nice to meet you. Sorry, I'm running a little late. Traffic was—"

Detective Cunningham interjects, "Of course. The traffic in this city is brutal. I have to plan my day around trying to get from one side of this city to another. That in and of itself is a full-time job." Detective Cunningham gestures his hand toward the building and asks, "Shall we?"

Dr. Ross answers, "Yes. Hopefully it will be a bit cooler in there."

Steve laughs. "Well, my office finally has the air conditioning up and running again. Thank God. But this building has some of the best temperature-control systems in the city." Steve and Dr. Ross walk up the long concrete steps toward the entrance. As Steve holds the door open for Dr. Ross, she is greeted with the wonderful rush of cold air from the inside.

Dr. Ross sighs and says, "Thank you. That definitely feels better."

They walk through security and show their credentials. As they complete their security check point they walk through the hallway toward a bank of elevators. Dr. Ross says, "I'm following your lead. I've never been to this building before."

Steve replies, "Yeah, no problem. We just have to take the elevator down to sub-level 2 and check in with their records clerk."

Dr. Ross asks, "Why does this building have the best temperature control, Detective?"

Steve answers with a smile, "I'm sorry. Please call me Steve. All of the formalities get old for me after a while. To answer your question, they need that to keep all of their records from aging and deteriorating over time. The only place that probably has a similar system will be—"

Dr. Ross interjects, "Let me guess. The Cook County Medical Examiner's Office."

As they arrive to the elevator bank, Steve presses the down arrow button. "That's right. You're familiar, aren't you? That's how Dr. Rodney knew you. Pleasant experience?"

Dr. Ross clears her throat and says, "Charming."

The elevator ring chimes, the double doors open, as a female voice says, "Going down."

Steve gestures for Dr. Ross to go first. Dr. Ross walks into the elevator and asks, "B2 you said?"

Steve answers, "Yes, that's correct. We just have to check in with Clarence. He's in charge of the Cook County Record Archive."

As they descend and reach their level, the elevator doors open and the same female voice says, "Basement Level 2."

Steve exits first and says, "Please allow me to lead the way."

Steve and Dr. Ross walk down a long hallway. The glossy light gray tile reflects the bright white florescent lights. They walk down the long corridor toward a sign reading: RECORDS ARCHIVE. Steve opens the light-brown stained door that has a small wire-mesh window along the top center. They enter a small sitting area and see an older man with short silver hair wearing a sweater and reading an old book. The older gentleman takes off his reading glasses, which are attached together by a wire. He slowly rests his reading glasses on his chest and stands up with a large smile that brightens his calm demeanor. He leans over the counter and extends his hand to Detective Cunningham.

Steve says, "Good morning, Clarence! Good to see you again, my old friend."

Clarence responds, "Steve! How the hell are ya? It's been too long. Haven't seen you since you were working that cold case about those victims along the Chicago River back in the day. How did that turn out by the way?"

Steve shakes his head. "Same as it began. Cold."

Clarence replies, "That's a real shame." Clarence's eyes open wide as he looks at Dr. Ross and asks, "Who is this beautiful young woman, Steve?"

Dr. Ross extends her hand. "Dr. Ross. I work for Northwest Cook County Hospital. I'm helping Steve with one of his current cases."

Clarence looks down at Dr. Ross's hand and says, "I notice no wedding ring. I'm guessing you're not married."

Dr. Ross blushes. "That's correct."

Clarence replies, "I see. Are you seeing anyone currently?"

Steve rolls his eyes as he looks at Dr. Ross. "Enough, Clarence!"

Clarence laughs. "Hey, you have to give me some points for at least trying."

Steve responds, "You'll have to excuse my old friend. He's an old smooth-talker." Steve looks down at Clarence's hand and continues, "I see you're still wearing your wedding ring, Clarence. How's the missus doing?"

Clarence answers, "She doing well and driving me nuts as per usual. Why do you think I haven't retired yet? At least down here I can mostly read in peace. Now, how can I help you, old friend?"

Steve answers, "We are looking for any old records that may be stored in the archive regarding the old Northwest Sanitarium."

Clarence rubs his chin. "There might be. Probably a few things anyway. Let me check the computer." Clarence does a quick online search of the archive and says, "Got it. You're in luck. We still have a few records, at least all that we were able to save."

Dr. Ross asks, "Save?"

Clarence gestures and waves his hands as he says, "I'll explain on the way. Follow me."

Steve and Dr. Ross follow Clarence through his office and into the records archive. They walk past several long and narrow corridors with row upon row of high shelves filled with file boxes. The archive is a large open floor plan with several round white pillars carrying the weight of the rest of the building. As they walk further into the older sections of the archive, both Steve and Dr. Ross smell a slight hint of mildew. Clarence turns back toward Steve and Dr. Ross and says, "Don't mind the smell. The county does what they can, but eventually the old records begin to the deteriorate."

Dr. Ross asks, "So, Clarence. How long have you worked for the county?"

Steve laughs as he interjects, "Believe it or not, I think he's been around longer than me."

Clarence answers, "That's for sure. In total, I've been working for the county for almost forty years."

Dr. Ross exclaims, "Wow! Forty years. That's impressive. Has all that time been here?"

Clarence answers, "Hardly. I've been working for the record's office for about twenty years. The last five years have been with the archive office. Believe it or not, I started working with the county as a young orderly at the sanitarium in question."

Dr. Ross responds, "You used to work at the old hospital? How was that?"

Clarence turns down an aisle, walks down a few feet, and begins looking through the box labels on the shelf. He responds, "It wasn't easy work. And unfortunately, most days were depressing and emotionally draining."

Dr. Ross sympathetically replies, "I'm sorry to hear that, Clarence. Must have been quite an experience for a young person to witness."

Clarence faintly smiles as "It's okay. In hindsight, I'm happy to witness an evolution in the way we treat the mentally ill." Clarence pulls out two file boxes. He hands one to Steve and one to Dr. Ross.

Steve looks at Clarence and asks, "That's it?"

Clarence answers, "That's it. That's all the records we still have. At least these are the records that survived anyway." Clarence points back to the main hallway and says, "On the way in, we passed by a couple of tables and chairs. Please feel free to take your time and go through the records. If you want to check out any records or make any photo copies, please come see me up front and I'll help you with that."

Steve smiles and says, "Thanks, Clarence. I think we will be able to gather what we need during our visit here. Thanks for your help."

Clarence says, "Anytime, Detective. You know that."

They all walk through the main hallway back toward a set of tables and chairs. As Clarence continues to walk, he stops, looks back at Steve and Dr. Ross, and says, "If you need anything else, you know where I'll be."

Dr. Ross opens her file box and removes the first document. The document is stained light brown with age and has a slight odor attached to it. She looks up as Clarence walks away and says, "Clarence. You mentioned that these were the only document to survive. What did you mean by that?"

Clarence smiles slightly. "I forget how old I am sometimes. Most of the original documents at the old Northwest Sanitarium were cooked after that horrible fire in the 80s. The fire department had a hard time with that fire. A lot of residents of the sanitarium including a few nurses died in the blaze. I'm sure Steve remembers the fire. Don't you, Steve?"

Steve nods his head. "Sure do. I grew up not far from there. I was in high school at the time. I could see the smoke from my house."

Clarence asks Steve, "Did authorities ever figure out what started that fire?"

Steve shakes his head. "Not that I'm aware of. If memory serves me correctly, they left the arson investigation unsolved after they discovered the origin but couldn't figure out the cause."

Clarence shakes his head. "It was such a shame. Horrible time. I had my suspicions, but anyway I'm heading back to my desk and finish a chapter in my book."

Clarence walks out of sight as Steve and Dr. Ross search through the records. They continue to search through the records for the next hour before they reach the unfortunate conclusion that none of the records show any correlation with Dr. Ross's patient. Dr. Ross and Steve begin to walk out of the office when Steve stops in front of Clarence's desk.

Clarence asks, "Find anything useful?"

Dr. Ross answers, "Unfortunately, no. But thank you, Clarence, for your time and help."

Clarence responds with a smile. "That's what I'm here for."

Dr. Ross looks at her watch and up at Steve and asks, "I really have to try to get back to my office before the end of the day. Is there anything else, Detective?"

Steve says, "No thank you, Dr. Ross. Thanks for your time. I'm gonna spend a little more time catching up with my old friend here."

Dr. Ross exits the office and walks down the hall. When she vanishes out of sight, Clarence says, "She's an interesting one, isn't she?"

Steve answers, "Sure is." Steve takes out his notepad, flips to a clean page, and asks, "Now Clarence, what else can you tell me about that fire?"

....

CHAPTER 17

WELCOME TO MY SHOP

While Liam and Boo are beginning their second day at Bethany's house, Ellie is on her way to pick up Simon in her dad's Ford Mustang. It's another beautiful day in Doylestown, Pennsylvania. The late morning sun continues to rise over the clear blue sky. Her jet-black hair whips through the refreshing summer breeze. Ellie has her sunglasses on and a smile on her face as she plays her favorite playlist from her phone.

She pulls up to Simon's house and honks the horn a couple of times. Simon looks through his storm door, waves, and blows Ellie a kiss. Simon grabs his skateboard and closes his front door. He tosses his skateboard behind Ellie and leans over for a kiss. Ellie smiles and asks, "Tell me again, Simon. Why do I date you?"

Simon answers, "I don't know why either. But I'm sure happy that you do."

Ellie smiles and gives Simon a kiss. Simon climbs into the front seat and Ellie asks, "So where is this legacy shop again?"

"It's over in Peddler's Village."

Ellie puts the Mustang in reverse and pulls out of Simon's driveway. As she puts the car in drive she says, "I've been to that shopping center more times than I can count, but I've never seen that shop. But I'll take you word for it."

Simon says, "I didn't know you to dislike any mall."

Ellie laughs. "Keep talking smart-ass and maybe I'll be busy for date night this week."

They cruise through the side streets until they merge onto York Road. It's a short trip down the road and they arrive to their destination, Peddler's Village. They find parking close to the main artery of the unique outdoor shopping outlet. They hold hands as they walk down the main walkway covered in red cobblestone. They take in the beautiful scenery—the bright and colorful planted flowers, the ducks swimming in the small pond, the small and quaint colonial shops, and the several American flags hanging on each of the lanterns along the walkway. Simon points to a restaurant and says, "Unless you change your mind and free up your schedule, I'm planning to take you there for dinner."

Ellie gives Simon a hug and a kiss and says, "I guess I can recheck my schedule."

Simon responds, "Oh! Did I mention? I'm also paying for it. I get paid the same day as date night."

"Okay, it's a date. You seem to be happy at your summer job."

"Hey, it's a record store and an arcade. I was spending most of my waking life at that place. Figure I could at least make it profitable."

They continue to walk down the windy walkway until Simon points out the shop and says, "Here it is. Family Legacy Shop."

Ellie looks at the entrance, shakes her head, and says, "No wonder I never saw it. The entrance is below street level and under an old men's clothing shop. How did you know about this place?"

Simon smiles and answers, "Look who you're asking."

They walk down the stairs and open the door. A small bell rings from the top part of the door frame. The shop is as seasoned as an original colonial property. They hear their footsteps echo off the lightly stained and weathered hardwood floors. A Tiffany-style window illuminates the small shop from the other side of the below-grade entrance. The ceilings are low with heavy timber wooden beams, which are surrounded by sections with chipped white paint. Family and noble crest pictures are scattered across the walls and floor while soft piano music echoes off the wood paneled walls.

An older gentleman steps out from the back office and walks toward the back of the main counter. He continues to clean his glasses but pauses briefly to brush back his ponytailed hair. He sees Ellie and Simon, smiles, and says, "I usually don't see a lot of young people in my shop. How can I help you today?"

Ellie asks, "What kind of people do you usually see in your shop?"

The man answers, "Usually a wife looking to get something clever for her spouse around the holidays. Come to think of it, I usually get a few young people in here around Father's Day."

Simon asks, "We were wondering if you can help us with a family legacy?"

The man nods his head. "Sure. No problem. Could you spell the name for me?"

Simon looks at Ellie and says, "Yeah, I can't help you with that. That's your department."

Ellie spells the name for the gentleman while he writes it down on a small scrap sheet of paper. He says, "That's quite a name! Definitely Polish in origin. Is that your last name?"

Ellie shakes her head and answers, "No, sir. That's my great-grandmother's maiden name."

The man says, "I see. And what are your names? I'm Sean."

Ellie and Simon exchange names and introductions. Simon looks at Ellie and says, "You should show him the family crest picture you got from Liam and Boo."

Ellie replies, "Oh, yeah! Thanks for reminding me." Ellie pulls out her phone, finds the picture, and hands the phone over to Sean.

Sean examines the crest and says, "This is very interesting. This is from the same family name?"

Ellie answers, "Yes, sir. That's correct."

Sean continues to examine the crest and says, "These symbols around the family crest are very interesting." Sean shakes his head as he continues, "My eyes are not what they used to be." He grabs a large magnifying glass from below the counter.

Ellie interjects and says, "Sir? Please, allow me. You can make the image bigger if you'd like. Here, I'll show you."

Sean smiles and says, "Would you look at that! That's amazing."

Ellie looks at Simon with a smile, and Simon rolls his eyes.

Sean takes a few more moments to examine the symbols and says, "I'll need a little bit of time to do a thorough examination into the family history. But I can tell you that this family crest is certainly something special."

Simon asks, "Really? How so?"

Sean answers, "These symbols mean that the family was a part of a noble class of warriors for the Holy Church, and if my theory is correct, it also means they were protectors against the forces of darkness."

Simon says, "Wicked!"

CHAPTER 18

....

THE JOURNAL

The following day, Liam walks into Boo's room. They are both relaxing today after a couple days of mandatory labor at Bethany's house. The temperature has finally dropped after several days of oppressive heat. Annie decides to give the air conditioning unit and her utility bill a break for the day. Most of the windows are open throughout the house. A cool breeze blows into Boo's room and brushes across the curtains.

Liam sees Boo looking over the journal at her desk and asks, "What have you gathered so far, Boo?"

Boo looks up at Liam and says, "It's very interesting stuff. Why don't you grab your desk chair from your bedroom, pull up next to me, and I'll show you."

As Liam pulls up his chair, Boo begins saying, "Like I said before. The first part of the journal was written in Polish. So, no help there. But the author begins each passage with a date entry." Boo continues, "The first entry is in 1894. But that's the part that was written in Polish. I'll begin here.

April 15, 1895: Per my teacher's instructions, I will begin to write in English as to help retain its comprehension. No word has been received from the church as to Angelica's whereabouts. The days are long without Father here to guide me. I thank God for the continuous guidance from Father Pawal who has been a father figure to me in the wake of his tragic passing.

July 2, 1895: Father Pawal continues to work with me and enhance my warrior skills. Each day we work on weapons training, strategies and tactics, hand-to-hand combat, and other skills such as studying local and neighboring maps. I go to bed every night exhausted. This has been an incredible challenge for me. For so long I've wanted to be a warrior like my father. Now, I yearn for the boyish days of my childhood. I long for the memories of innocence and the false dreams of a kind, gentle, and safe world.

October 30, 1895: I take a break from my training with Father Pawal after he receives a message via carrier from the church. Father Pawal informs me that the Bishops of the Silver Cross, Ireland Division, believe that Angelica traveled abroad with cargo shortly after our horrific encounter in 1894. The cargo is believed to be Alek's remains. The church has concluded that Angelica slipped past the surveillance parties as they waited for her in England. The church has also concluded that Angelica has been in America for quite some time.

December 1, 1895: I'm disappointed but also relieved. Father Pawal insists that we cannot travel to America until spring. He implores the church that traveling across the North Atlantic during the winter months is equally miserable as it is treacherous. During this time, Father Pawal continues to help me learn the English language and to perfect my warrior skills. I don't look forward to the long journey across the ocean, but I yearn to see America. I hear so many wonderful things.

May 30, 1896: We finally receive some more information from the church regarding Angelica and her movements. Partially genius on Father Pawal's part. For he didn't want to set a course to America until he knew where to look when he arrives. Due to the massive immigration to America, the church found it extremely difficult to locate the whereabouts of one woman and her cargo. They now believe that Angelica and her cargo arrived at Ellis Island, New York, in 1894. She used an alias name and used one of her mind control abilities to forego her quarantine period, which supposedly lasts several weeks. They found old documents from a mass transit railroad company that relayed information of a woman under the same alias name. The woman left New York City bound for Chicago. The church is sending a carriage straight away to begin our quest overseas.

June 10, 1896: I begin to travel across the North Atlantic with Father Pawal. I never in my life would believe that a body of water can be so massive and vast. As each day arrives with the rising sun along the oceanic horizon, and I grow more anxious and nervous about the dangers which lie ahead. I'm forever grateful for Father Pawal. Without him, this journey would have been more foreign and frightening. However, I should not fear. For I am armed with weapons and training from the church. More importantly, my faith will never be conquered by any advisory.

June 20, 1896: We arrive into the mouth of New York City just over a week since we began our long voyage across the Atlantic. We debark our ship at Ellis Island. As we debark, I thank God for safe travels along the lonely seas and high tides. I see the vast and beautiful Statue of Liberty. I read in a newspaper available on the ship that the statue was finished just a decade ago. A bishop from the order meets both Father Pawal and myself at the unloading dock. He instructs both of us to follow him and to not talk to anyone. He will do the talking for us. As we meet with members of the Port Authority, the bishop hands the gentlemen documents. I can only assume they pertain to us. One of the gentlemen hands back the documents and says, "Of course, Bishop. Anything for the church, sir. You and your party are free to go. God bless."

The bishop takes us to an awaiting carriage. He informs us that the carriage will take us to a train that is bound for Chicago later today. As we roll through the streets of New York, I am simply overwhelmed by the size and scale of the buildings encircling this incredible city. As I look out the carriage window, I'm also amazed by the amount of people that walk up and down every single street. In my life, I've never seen so many people. They said grand things about America. And they were right!

June 21, 1896: We boarded the train yesterday in the evening. The bishop accompanied me and Father Pawal to an entire rail transit car that was reserved for us. Inside, a few beds with fresh sheets were laid along the side of the car's wide and narrow windows. Father Pawal suggested to rest as much as possible on this first night after such a long journey.

This morning, I woke up to food waiting for me and Father Pawal and the bishop having a meeting over a long table looking over several maps and documents. As I step over, Father Pawal gathers my attention. He points to a document that he describes as a witch calendar.

The bishop states, "Angelica will probably attempt to resurrect Alek again in the fall of this current year. This is due to certain planets beings aligned with the crescent fall moon. She will also probably attempt to reassemble a coven in Chicago similar to her actions leading up to the encounter in 1894. If she hasn't already done so." The bishop suggests that Angelica has more than likely taken up residency along the South Shore neighborhood of Chicago. He explains that many young immigrants have settled in that area over the last couple of years. This is due to the massive expansion of that area during the construction of the World's Fair in 1893. The plan is to have all of us, including myself, pose as regular priests of the church. This will help us remain neutral and much more approachable to the local community. We will plan to use the newly constructed Saint Clara's Church as our home base, which is located in the heart of the Woodlawn neighborhood.

July 1, 1896: We have been moving slowly throughout the neighborhood over the last week. Attending masses and being involved with the local community. The community has successfully accepted us as their own after seeing us in and around the parish. The majority of the local community is that of Eastern European descent. Mainly German and Polish. The bishop and Father Pawal are both fluent in both native languages. This especially helps aid our cause. We have been keeping our eyes peeled for anyone who fits Angelica's description. So far our efforts have unfortunately concluded to no avail.

July 7, 1896: We received an interesting lead from a young lady talking to Father Pawal. Father Pawal showed the woman a picture of Angelica and stated that the parish has been looking for this woman in order to relay information about her family back in Europe. The woman states that a young lady fitting Angelica's description has been periodically stopping by her husband's general goods shop near the corner of Marquette and Jeffrey. She also states that she's sick of her husband constantly talking about such a beautiful woman coming into his shop. Especially a woman that's a young mother of a little baby girl. Father Pawal follows up asking when this young lady usually stops by the shop. The woman follows up with Father Pawal a few days later following the Saturday Vigil Mass. She states that the young lady seems to come by the shop every other Friday in the evening to gather supplies. Her husband believes it's probably the day the woman's husband receives his pay.

July 10, 1896: We work together to come up with a plan. After some long discussions, we believe that the best course of action is to dress as plain gentlemen. Concealing any armor and weapons over some light long evening jackets. We plan to stage on different corners outside the general goods shop and wait for the woman fitting Angelica's description to arrive. I am doubtful this will be Angelica. I just can't believe that such an evil creature like herself is even capable of bearing children.

July 11, 1896: To our amazement and good fortune, the woman fitting the description is Angelica! She arrived to the shop in the evening carrying a young baby over her shoulder. We watch her gather and pay for her goods and walk down Jeffrey Avenue. We cautiously trail her for several blocks until she enters the courtyard of the three-story building. I watch from the sidewalk as she ascends up the stairs and is welcomed by a man I can assume to be her husband. God knows if this man truly knows the woman he has been tricked to love.

July 12, 1896: We devise a plan to capture Angelica. Despite my objections, Father Pawal and the bishop want to capture and use her daughter as leverage to know the location of Alek's remains. Father Pawal and the bishop plan to infiltrate the house while the family is having dinner. The hope is to seize Angelica with the use of the silver chain mail net. Both Father Pawal and the bishop agree that the husband will put up a fight. The goal is only to subdue him and not cause him too much harm. The plan is set in motion for tonight. Years of training have been preparing me for this moment. I will pray at the altar of Saint Clara's that our mission will be successful.

July 15, 1896: I write this entry several days after the attempted capture of Angelica. One can say that our mission was successful. Another can say that our original plan lacked the capacity for collateral damage. Which unfortunately was the case. During our attempted infiltration into Angelica's home, we failed to remember Angelica's heightened sense of smell. Angelica smelled the holy oils that were carried by all three of us. She was able to attack the bishop before he was in position. Unfortunately, the bishop didn't survive the attack. Father Pawal was able to catch Angelica by surprise during her confrontation with the bishop. It was left to me to handle the defending husband. Angelica's husband attempted to defend his family, but he died in the struggle after falling on my war pick after it fell out of my hand. Angelica was seized and taken by both Father Pawal and myself back to Saint Clara's. It took both of us to carry Angelica out to an awaiting carriage and hold her down until we reached the church. She kept screaming out in pain and agony for her late husband and her young daughter. Father Pawal arranged for the Chicago Police to secure Angelica's home and establish custody over the young child. Chicago Police arrived and found the body of Angelica's husband and a ransacked apartment. Unfortunately, they arrived too late to secure the child. The child was nowhere to be found. Father Pawal insisted I go back to Angelica's home and follow up with police. The police confirmed earlier reports. The child must have been taken by someone. Probably a member of Angelica's new coven. Possibly someone in the same building. Father Pawal also insisted I look for Angelica's spell book inside her home. After turning over every corner of the apartment, I was unsuccessful in obtaining it. I returned to Saint Clara's and found four orderlies assigned to a sanitarium on the northwest side of the city standing alongside Father Pawal and Angelica. Angelica laughed through her pain as the silver chain mail net continued to drain her of her powers. She insisted that the church will never find her daughter, the spell book, or Alek's remains. She'd rather stay locked up forever before she ever gave up her treasures. Father Pawal granted her this wish. He told Angelica that she will spend the rest of her natural life locked away from the world until she gave up the location. We accompanied her to the Northwest Sanitarium with the intention to have Angelica remain there for the rest of her days."

Liam and Boo look at each other in amazement. Liam says, "Who is this Angelica? Is there anything else in the journal?"

Boo answers, "Yes. There's more passages. More about the author settling in Chicago. Finally finding his place in the world, meeting a young lady whom he marries, and purchasing a home near Archer and California Avenue."

Liam walks around the room. While he paces and thinks he asks, "What does all of this mean? You said that the first part of the journal is written in Polish?"

Boo answers, "Yup. That's correct. I could try to use the translate feature on the computer, but that might take a long time."

Liam replies, "Yeah that might be a pain to try to decode every single word on the computer. Hey, our church has both Polish- and English-speaking Masses. Maybe someone from the church can help us with the translation."

Boo smiles as she says, "Only one way to find out, big brother."

CHAPTER 19

REMEMBER, YOU HAVE SATURDAY VIGIL MASS TONIGHT

Liam stops pacing back and forth and looks at Boo. He starts to feel queasy and somewhat out of breath. He runs back to his room and grabs his inhaler. Boo follows Liam back to his room. Boo puts her hand on Liam's shoulder and asks, "What's the matter, big brother? What are you thinking?"

Liam catches his breath and says, "I'm starting to think all of this isn't a coincidence."

Boo nods her head. "I'm getting that feeling too. Especially with the cryptic messages I've been receiving from Misty. I haven't spoken to Misty since our last night at the Elk's Estate. Why has she waited until now to start talking to me? I mean, why would a giant flying monster be right outside our window? After everything we've been through. Why us?"

Liam replies, "I'm getting that same feeling again. The same feeling that I got back in Iron River and again at the Elk's Estate. And I had the same feeling the first time I saw that monster fly over my baseball game. That feeling like something bad is happening or is going to happen and we are right in the middle of it. I think it's time we get the crew together and update them on everything that's going on."

Boo replies, "I think you're right, but we can't gather the troops tonight."

Liam asks, "Why not?"

137

"Because you and I are altar servers for the Saturday Vigil Mass tonight."

Liam looks at the clock on the night stand. He replies, "You're right."

Just then, Annie shouts from the base of the stairs leading up the bedrooms. She says, "Hey, Liam! Boo! Come to the stairs for a minute!"

Liam and Boo walk out of the hallway and look down toward Annie. Liam says, "Yeah, Mom. What's up?"

Annie answers, "Hey! Remember you both are serving at the Vigil Mass tonight."

Boo interjects, "Yeah, Mom, we know. In fact, we were just talking about it."

Annie replies, "You two have been hanging out in your rooms all day. What have you been up to?"

Liam answers, "Not much, Mom. Just chilling and reading comics. Taking a break from the heat and running around today."

Boo says, "Yeah, and I've been working on this art project in my room and listening to music. It's been nice to chill at home today."

Annie says, "I understand. Sounds good. Hey, listen…I'm thinking of making my famous chicken fingers and fries after you finish up at church tonight. What do you think?"

Boo says, "Sounds good, Mom."

Liam replies, "Sounds good, but you know what would sound better?"

Annie asks, "What's that?"

Liam answers, "If you were also making your homemade coleslaw to go with it."

"Of course. Homemade coleslaw as well. In fact, I'll start getting that ready now before I drop you off at church. Can you two be ready to head out in about thirty minutes?"

Boo answers, "Sure thing, Mom. We'll be ready."

Within the hour, Annie, Liam, and Boo all leave the house and drive down the road toward church. The local neighborhood church is only a couple of blocks to the east of the crew's favorite BBQ restaurant where they enjoy hanging out after a round of baseball at Dunham Park. It's a small but quaint neighborhood church.

The exterior is made of white stone with a dark brown shingled roof. The exterior walls are lined with several stained-glass windows that reflect brilliant colors from the setting western sun into the church's aisles. Along the southern part of the church is an attached convention hall where the community typically holds their charity pancake breakfast and holiday celebrations. Next to the hall is a small elementary school where both Liam and Boo attend religious education classes on Monday evenings during the regular school year and another separate building that serves as a dormitory for the parish priests and nuns. All of which is connected by a large parking lot in the center. Annie drops Liam and Boo off in the parking lot.

As Liam and Boo exit the vehicle, Annie says, "Okay. I'll see you at 5:30."

Liam turns toward Annie and asks, "Aren't you staying for Mass, Mom?"

Annie shakes her head and says, "Nope. Got to finish a few things at home and then start making dinner. I don't have Dad's help tonight since he's at work. See you in an hour."

As Annie drives away, Liam and Boo walk into the church. Boo notices Liam in deep thought and asks, "Anything else on your mind, big brother?" Liam turns to look at Boo and answers, "Oh, I'm good. Just curious why Mom hasn't been staying back for church recently. She made it a habit for a while. Especially after what happened at the Elk's Estate." Boo answers, "I don't know. Maybe she feels that her time is better served doing other things. It sounds like something that maybe you should ask her."

As Liam and Boo walk down the main aisle toward the altar of the church, they see Father Luke walking down the aisle with another priest wearing a gray cassock with a silver cross stitched along the center of the chest. Liam and Boo pause to say hi to Father Luke. Father Luke pauses with the other priest and says, "Ah. Liam and Boo. My favorite sibling duo. I saw that both of you were serving this evening. Tell me, how is your summer going? Staying out of trouble, I hope."

Boo shifts her eyes toward Liam and begins to laugh as Liam responds, "So far so good, Father. Baseball is going well. I might get picked to be on the All-Star team again this year."

Father Luke replies, "Well, that's wonderful, Liam! Good to hear." Father Luke looks toward the man standing to his side and says, "Oh, please allow me to introduce you to Bishop Michael. He's visiting us from overseas."

Boo says, "Overseas? That's interesting. Where are you from, Bishop?"

Bishop Michael answers, "My functions with the church are mainly out of Poland."

Liam notices Bishop's Michael's accent and asks, "That's an interesting accent, Bishop. Is Polish your first language?"

Bishop Michael smiles as he answers, "Yes, that's correct. But I'm happy to report that I'm fluent in English, German, and Italian."

Liam replies, "Wow! That's really cool."

A shimmering light from the setting sun glows through the stained-glass windows and dances along Liam's silver cross. Bishop Michael looks down and notices the light reflecting off Liam's cross and says, "That's a lovely silver cross, young man."

Liam replies, "Thank you, Bishop. It's my shield."

Bishop Michael is intrigued by Liam's response and says, "Indeed, my son." Bishop Michael points to his silver cross on his gray cassock and says, "I, too, have a silver cross that acts as my shield."

Boo interjects, "Will you be joining us for Mass this evening, Bishop?"

Bishop Michael answers, "Yes, indeed. In fact, I was invited to be a guest speaker for today's homily by Father Luke." Bishop Michael looks down at his watch as other members of the parish begin to enter through the main entrance. Bishop Michael continues, "Well, Mass will be starting soon. I shouldn't keep you. It's been lovely to meet you both. See you at Mass."

Liam and Boo both smile and say goodbye as they walk toward the dressing room.

Bishop Michael pauses and turns back to Liam and Boo walking away. Father Luke asks, "Anything wrong, Bishop?"

Bishop Michael answers, "Not at all, Father. I'm curious about how that young man described his silver cross. They seem to be two very special souls."

Father Luke nods and says, "Indeed they are, Bishop. Those two have a very interesting back story. Come. The sisters are always good about making coffee for me in the sacristy. Let's have a quick cup of coffee before Mass and I'll tell you about it."

Father Luke and Bishop Michael walk into the sacristy. Two tall and narrow stained-glass windows illuminate and bounce bright colors off the white painted walls. There they find two matching vestments and stoles hanging on a hanger along the wall with a wooden bench underneath. The pleasant aroma of sweet-smelling coffee lingers in the air as a coffee pot on a nearby counter finishes brewing. Before Bishop Michael gets ready for Mass, he sits down at a chair with arm rests facing another chair and a small table. Bishop Michael says, "Smells delicious. Thank you, Father."

Father Luke opens a cupboard and pulls out two large cups. As Father Luke gathers the sugar from the counter he says, "Not a problem, Bishop. I always like to have a large cup of French vanilla coffee before the evening Mass. I always feel like I'm dragging toward the evening hours. Helps me get through Mass. I could only imagine how you're able to function. Working in the shadows in the middle of the night."

Bishop Michael smiles as he answers, "I, too, enjoy my coffee. I usually make some in the morning and in the evening. I got used to working into the twilight of the evening and in the middle of the night when I was a soldier in the special forces."

Father Luke replies, "I'm sure. How do you like your coffee, Bishop? I like mine with a lot of cream and sugar."

Bishop Michael answers, "Just black will be fine, Father."

Father Luke pours a tall cup of black coffee for Bishop Michael. After he hands Bishop Michael his coffee, Father Luke walks over to a small refrigerator on the counter and pulls out a tall container of half-and-half creamer.

Bishop Michael takes a few sips of his coffee and says, "Thank you, Father. The coffee is excellent."

Father Luke replies, "You're welcome. One of our parishioners owns a small coffee shop off Gunnison. He donated a few pounds to the church after I kept coming into his shop."

Bishop Michael interjects, "So, Father, you were going to tell me more about the two young people who will be the altar servers this evening. You mentioned they had an interesting backstory."

Father Luke stirs his coffee, takes a sip, and sits down across from Bishop Michael. He begins saying, "Yes. Those two have quite a unique backstory. You might find it intriguing considering the special nature of your order. So...a couple of years ago, those two were vacationing with their family in the Upper Peninsula of Michigan. In a small town called Iron River. The family used to have a summer vacation home there until it happened."

Bishop Michael asks, "What happened, Father?"

Father Luke continues, "At first it was a hard pill to swallow, but they had an encounter with a werewolf."

Bishop Michael raises his eyebrows in disbelief and says, "A lycanthrope!"

Father Luke continues, "If that's what you call it when a man turns into a wolf under the moonlight and hunts and kills the innocent."

Bishop Michael interjects, "I believe I heard of this incident. It led to many casualties, correct?"

Father Luke continues, "Yes. Several people died. The two young people, Liam and Boo, were right in the middle of it. They were lucky to survive."

Bishop Michael takes another sip of his coffee and exclaims, "Jesus! That's incredible! I can't believe it."

Father Luke takes another long sip from his coffee and continues, "But wait...there's more, Bishop."

Bishop Michael asks, "More? What else happened?"

Father Luke responds, "Last summer, the family was on the East Coast visiting the father's side in Philadelphia. They were helping the family with the restoration of this massive estate in Elkin's Park, Pennsylvania. Well, they had a run-in with some type of dark entity and several bad spirits."

Bishop Michael asks, "A poltergeist?"

"Something like that. It also led to several casualties, including a young local boy from Elkin's Park. There was this engulfing fire, and Liam and Boo were both lucky to escape the blaze. Did you and your order hear about this?"

Bishop Michael nods his head. "Yes. There were mentions of this incident at one of our conferences at the Vatican. To my recollection, a few members of the clergy died in this incident."

Father Luke answers, "Yes, that's correct. A priest and one of our sisters. Very sad. But they helped save both Liam and Boo."

Bishop Michael exclaims, "That's unbelievable! To think that both of these incidents happened to these two young people and they both survived to tell the tale."

"Yes indeed, Bishop. After everything that happened in Iron River, the family naturally gravitated toward therapy to help their children cope with the trauma. It helped, and the family was able to heal gradually. But after the events at the Elk's Estate, especially after such a battle in spiritual warfare, the family gravitated toward the church for help as well. We did what we could. Helped them in any way we could. And in the end, I think we were able to help. Their faith is still intact."

Bishop Michael looks at his watch. "It's about that time that we get ready for Mass, Father. Thank you for the coffee and sharing their story with me."

Bishop Michael and Father Luke leave the sacristy to find Liam and Boo dressed in their white altar server albs. Liam is carrying the cross while Boo carries a large brass candle. Liam says, "We are all ready, Father…Bishop."

Bishop Michael looks down and smiles at both Liam and Boo. "Thank you. Both of you seem to be ready for anything,"

The Mass continues without incident. Bishop Michael gives an intriguing homily. He talks about the battle between good and evil and that forces of darkness are alive and well in our modern-day society. The Mass ends as Annie makes her way back to the church to pick up Liam and Boo. As Liam and Boo put the cross and candle away and secure their albs on the proper hangers, Boo says to Liam, "You know, I really like that Bishop Michael. There's something about him. I just feel very safe around him."

Liam responds, "You know something? You're right. I feel the same way."

Boo looks over to her left to see a cloudy apparition begin to form next to her. It's Misty! Boo says, "Misty! Where have you been?"

Misty smiles and gives Boo a hug. Boo shivers as a chill goes down her spine. Misty says, "Sorry. I know my hugs are not all warm and fuzzy."

Boo turns to Liam and says, "Hey, Liam! Misty is here!"

Liam says, "Cool! Why is she visiting us now?"

Boo turns to Misty and asks, "What's the occasion, Misty?"

Misty smiles as she answers, "I've come to give you some advice. You should mention to Bishop Michael the journal you found in your grandmother's attic. He's here to help."

Boo tells Liam Misty's message. Liam asks, "Why is Bishop Michael here? To help with what?"

Misty tells Boo, "I wish I knew more. That's all the instructions I was given. Be sure to mention it to Bishop Michael on your way out of the church."

At that moment, Misty fades into a brilliant blue light and vanishes from the living world. Liam asks, "What's up, Boo?"

Boo answers, "Misty's gone. That was a quick visit. I guess that's all she needed to say."

On the way out of the church, Liam and Boo see Bishop Michael talking to a few parishioners. As Liam and Boo approach Bishop Michael, he says, "Thank you both for your help this evening. It was a lovely service thanks to you both."

Liam says, "Thank you, Bishop. Happy to help."

Boo turns to Liam, smiles, and then turns back to Bishop Michael saying, "Thank you, Bishop. Listen, I was wondering if you'll be able to help us with something."

Bishop Michael replies, "What can I help you with?"

Boo answers, "We found this old journal in our grandmother's attic. Its possibly from an old relative of ours. It's an interesting read from back in the 90s. Sorry back in the 1890s. The first narration in the journal is written in Polish. Is it possible that we bring it to you and you can help with the translation?"

Bishop Michael smiles and says, "Of course. Feel free to come by the rectory and ask for me. I'll be happy to help you."

Liam says, "Thank you for your help, Bishop."

Bishop Michael replies, "Of course. It's my job."

Liam and Boo both say their goodbyes and head toward the parking lot where Annie is waiting patiently for them to arrive.

Bishop Michael watches Liam and Boo as they approach Annie. Liam and Boo both wave at Annie as she rolls down the window saying, "Hey, you two! You hungry?"

Boo says, "Sure am."

Liam says, "Absolutely. Starving actually."

As Liam and Boo both enter Annie's van she says, "Good, because dinner is all done and ready. Let's head home and eat. Maybe after dinner we can play a board game. How does that sound?"

Boo says, "Sounds great. Can we play Clue?"

Liam says, "No. We played that last time. How 'bout Monopoly?"

Annie, Liam, and Boo drive down the street toward home, and a *swoosh* of air flows through the evening sky as Pet swiftly lands on a tall tree. Two red eyes glow and watch Annie's van drive down the road. As Annie turns onto Gunnison, Pet extends its massive wings and takes flight to follow the van.

While this is happening, Bishop Michael is back in the sacristy with Father Luke. As Bishop Michael puts his vestment and stole back on their hook, his silver cross begins to glow. Bishop Michael grabs hold of the silver cross. Father Luke notices the glowing cross and asks, "What is it, Bishop?"

Bishop Michael dashes out of the sacristy, down the hallway toward an exit, and out to the parking lot. He sees Pet glide its massive wings as it heads to the west and quickly vanishes out of sight.

CHAPTER 20

....

A MEETING ON THE FRONT LAWN

Bishop Michael dashes back into the parish and quickly makes his way toward his quarters. On his way, he sees Father Luke. Father Luke notices an overwhelming look of concern over Bishop Michael's face. Father Luke asks again, "What's the matter, Bishop? Is something wrong?"

Bishop Michael asks, "Father! I just saw the flying beast! Do Liam and Boo's parents own a van?"

Father Luke thinks quickly as he responds, "Yes. I believe so. I've seen them go into a dark-colored van when they exit church after mass."

Bishop Michael exclaims, "That's the one! Quickly, Father, I'm going back to my room to gather my tools. Can you search the church registry and tell me the family's address?"

"Yes, of course. I'll meet you back at your room."

"Thank you, Father."

The two men quickly make their way toward their objectives.

Bishop Michael opens the room to his quarters. There, he opens a door leading to a small bedroom closet. Inside he quickly finds his chain-mail vest hanging from a heavy metal hanger, his silver sword secured in its scabbard, his brown leather satchel with a silver cross stitched along the opening flap, and his gray hooded overcoat. In a flash, Bishop Michael dons all of his protective gear, throws on his overcoat and picks up his weapons. As he finishes getting ready, there are a few loud knocks on his door. Bishop Michael opens the door to find Father Luke holding a small piece of paper. Father Luke hands Bishop Michael the piece of paper. "Here, Bishop! The address you requested."

Bishop Michael takes the piece of paper from Father Luke's hand and says, "Thank you, Father. Is their house far from here?"

"Not at all, Bishop. It's less than a mile from here. Just take Gunnison Avenue down to the street on the piece of paper and head north. You should find it easily." Father Luke continues to chase Bishop Michael out to the parking lot where the bishop has his car parked. Father Luke asks, "Is there anything else I can help you with, Bishop?"

As Bishop Michael opens the trunk and throws his weapons inside, he turns toward Father Luke and says, "I wish you could, but I fear that this task is only meant for my order. Have your phone by your side. I may call upon you."

Father Luke nods at Bishop Michael as he fires up his car and dashes out of the parking lot toward the main road.

Bishop Michael drives as quickly and safely as he can heading west down Gunnison Avenue. He hits the accelerator as he begins to cross Austin Avenue just as the light turns yellow. As he continues to drive, he observes the road and looks up to the dusk-filled sky looking for the flying beast. The sky is colorful as the sun continues to set, turning the sky from a vibrant pink to dark orange. The shadows begin to increase, and so does Bishop Michael's level of concern. He passes several blocks and then sees the sign for Liam and Boo's block. He turns to head north. As he approaches the house, he sees two glowing red eyes pierce through the ever-growing shadows from a tall oak tree branch. He stops the car in front of Liam and Boo's house. He looks at the home and sees movement in what appears to be the family's dining room. Bishop Michael observes the family as they sit down to enjoy their dinner. While Liam and Boo find their seats, Annie walks toward the window and closes the blinds, not noticing Bishop Michael's car idling with him inside.

Bishop Michael exits his car and observes Pet as he flashes his radiant red eyes and disgustingly long teeth. He quickly scans the block to gain better situational awareness. He sees one car going down a side street and a neighbor walking a dog in the opposite direction. Other than that, the street is calm and lacks much activity. At least for the moment. Bishop Michael pulls back his gray hooded overcoat, dons his scabbard holding his silver sword, and throws his leather satchel over his shoulder. At that moment, his whole silver cross begins to glow incredibly bright. Bishop Michael grabs hold of his silver cross and observe its remarkably vibrant glow. He has never seen his cross react this vividly before. He looks up at Pet. Pet looks down the block toward the southeast corner. Two figures turn the corner and begin to walk down the block toward Bishop Michael. As the two figures approach, Bishop Michael notices that it's a man and a woman. As they walk ever closer, he fully realizes his predicament. It's Alek and Angelica walking hand-in-hand toward him!

Angelica smiles and waves to Bishop Michael. Bishop Michael says to himself, "Oh, my God! She's done it! Her teacher is back, and he looks as like a young man!"

Alek and Angelica walk past a large cement flower pot of a neighbor's home near the public sidewalk. Alek pauses and observes the dozens of bright and beautiful flowers as they gently move to the soft breeze coming out of the west. Angelica asks, "What is it, my love? Is something wrong?"

Alek smiles at Angelica, and says in his harsh dark voice, "These flowers are the problem. They're far too peaceful." Alek spits inside the flower pot. Instantly, all the flowers begin to wither and die as if they were sprayed with a strong weed killer. Angelica laughs as Alek continues in his native tongue, "Much better." Alek and Angelica continue to walk gingerly toward Bishop Michael.

Bishop Michael begins to breathe heavily. He can feel his hands start to shake, and his heart starts to pound, seemingly out of his chest. He looks back toward Liam and Boo's house. Bishop Michael thinks quickly and grabs a few items from the trunk of his vehicle. He opens another bag and pulls out a large container of salt. He opens the package and begins to quickly sprinkle a small line of salt along the front part of house and sidewalk. He sprinkles a line of salt and then grabs a few vials of oil from his leather satchel and pours them on the ground. He quickly finishes his task and says a protection prayer from memory: "Oh, mighty and most gracious Lord. Make this line of salt and holy oils be the shield to protect your servants from the powers of darkness. In this Lord's name we pray for your protection and grace. Amen!"

Alek and Angelica walk within the property line of Liam and Boo's home, and they pause as Bishop Michael pulls back his gray robe and reveals his brown leather scabbard. He unlocks the thin leather strap securing his silver sword in his scabbard and places his adrenaline-filled hands on his sword handle. He steadies his breathing and tries to control his ever-increasing heart rate. He backs up behind the line of salt and holy oils. Bishop Michael stares at Angelica and Alek as they halt their progression and Angelica sniffs the air in front of her. Alek smiles at Bishop Michael, looks at Angelica, and asks, "What do you smell?"

Angelica says, "Figured as much when I saw the priest walking around so quickly. He put some of his church's magic around the property."

Bishop Michael exclaims, "Alek and Angelica! By the name of God and the Order of the Silver Cross, I command you to leave this area at once and leave this innocent family alone!"

Alek looks confused. He doesn't understand the words Bishop Michael stated. Alek looks at Angelica and asks in his native language, "What did this priest say to me?"

Bishop Michael realizes then that Alek only knows his native language of Polish. So, he repeats his commands in Polish before Angelica is able to answer. Impressed with Bishop Michael's dialect, Alek looks to Angelica and says, "This baby priest speaks to me as though he knows me. Is this the same priest as before?"

Angelica answers, "Yes, my dear. Similar to the priests who took me away all those years ago. But I imagine that this one is another American."

Bishop Michael responds in his native language, "I am not, Angelica. I am from the same place you call home."

Angelica attempts to interject, but Alek raises his hand to command the floor. Angelica bows to her love and teacher as Alek smiles and says, "You seem like a nice little soldier for the church, Priest. I don't intend to do any business with you. I have unfinished business with that so-called innocent family inside that house behind you." Alek looks toward Pet who awaits the order to attack from his masters.

Bishop Michael responds, "I know your beast is in the tree across the street. It doesn't matter. I'm ready to engage all of you if need be."

Alek's eyes flash from dark green to bright glowing red as he looks the bishop up and down. Alek smiles and says, "Your body says otherwise, baby priest. If that mortal heart of yours beats any faster, you'll be venturing into the void between life and death." Alek looks around, smiles, and continues in his deep thunderous voice, "Three against one aren't good odds, baby priest. I'll tell you what. If you leave now, I'll spare your life. Like I said, I'm not here for you."

Angelica attempts to attack as she lounges forward and says, "I can take care of this priest all by myself. Not the first time." Angelica attempts to cross the line of salt and oil, and her feet begin to burn! Alek laughs as Angelica screams in pain, backs away from the line, and tends to her wounds. Alek looks up at Pet and then looks at Bishop Michael as he says, "Well played, baby priest. Well played."

Bishop Michael responds, "Be careful where you step, Alek. Before you is holy ground. Secured by the power of God!"

Alek looks down at Angelica and asks, "You, okay?"

Angelica answers, "I'll be fine, my love."

Alek looks back up at Pet and gives a command in a deep, low voice. Pet nods its head and begins to fly off into the eastern evening sky. Alek says, "You know something? I've been in America a long time, but unfortunately, I haven't done any sightseeing. Looks like tonight is a fine night to explore. God only knows what trouble we could get into." Alek looks at Angelica as she begins to laugh and hug Alek across his waist. Alek looks back toward Bishop Michael and continues, "I guess you have a choice to make, baby priest. Stay here and defend this family or follow us?"

Bishop Michael responds, "Us mortals always have to make a choice, Wizard. It's called free will. Something you gave up a long time ago. I will always defend the light. Down to my last breath."

Alek and Bishop Michael pause and turn toward a house across the street as a man comes outside to walk his dog. The man gives each of them a suspicious look and continues to walk past the group. Alek nods his head as he says, "Good to know, baby priest. Have a good evening. See you soon." Alek and Angelica both turn, lock hands, and walk in the opposite direction.

Bishop Michael breathes a huge sigh of relief. He lifts his hands from his sword handle and observes how much they continue to uncontrollably shake. He looks around and thinks for a moment before he grabs his phone out of his pocket. He calls Father Luke.

Father Luke quickly answers, "Yes, Bishop! What do you need, sir?"

Bishop Michael responds, "I can use your help, Father. Please come meet me at the family's household. I think it's time for us to have a conversation."

CHAPTER 21

....

GOOD EVENING, MA'AM. MAY I COME IN?

Bishop Michael opens the trunk to his car and secures his weapons, tools, and silver chain-mail vest and patiently waits for Father Luke to arrive. Within minutes, Father Luke pulls up behind Bishop Michael's car. The bishop extends his hand to offer Father Luke a hand shake. He says, "Thank you, Father. I appreciate you coming over so quickly."

"No problem. Your hands seem shaky, and you sounded nervous on the phone, Bishop. What's going on?"

Bishop Michael answers, "She's done it, Father! She resurrected the wizard! Her evil teacher."

Father Luke blesses himself with the holy cross and says, "Dear God! How do you know?"

Bishop Michael answers, "I just had a little meeting with them right here where you are standing. And both Angelica and Alek both wanted...." Bishop Michael pauses as he points toward Liam and Boo's home. He continues, "The family inside this home."

Father Luke exclaims, "What! Why?"

"I don't know. But I have a feeling their past encounters with the forces of evil were not due to blind coincidence."

Father Luke shakes his head. "How can I help, Bishop?"

"You're very close with this family, especially after they sought the church's counsel. I need you to handle the introductions and then I'll proceed from there."

Father Luke says, "Of course, Bishop. Anything I can do to help this poor family. They've been through enough already."

Bishop Michael and Father Luke begin to walk toward the front door as the bishop continues, "I fear they are currently facing something far worse than anything they have encountered before."

Father Luke rings the doorbell. The bell chimes through the house and echoes along the hallways. The family is finishing their delicious home-cooked meal and break away from their fun conversation at the dining room table. Liam and Boo look at Annie who says, "I wonder who that could be?" Annie stands up and walks over to the front door. She peels back her handmade white curtain from the front door window.

Liam stands up from the table and asks, "Who is it, Mom?"

Annie shakes her head. "It's Father Luke and another man who looks like a priest." Annie begins to worry about her husband, Will, who is currently on duty with the fire department. She reluctantly opens the door saying, "Good evening, Father. Please, tell me you're not here to deliver bad news. Is it Will?"

Father Luke looks puzzled for a moment and asks, "Is Will on shift this evening?"

Annie says, "Yes, he is. He must be busy. I haven't heard much from him all day."

Father Luke continues, "I'm so sorry to give you a scare, Annie. We are definitely not here in regards to Will. I'm sure he's doing just fine. We are here on another important matter, I'm afraid. May we come inside?"

Annie says, "Of course, Father." Annie looks at Bishop Michael and asks, "And who is this, Father?"

Father Luke begins to talk, but Bishop Michael quickly interjects, "Sorry for not introducing myself, ma'am. I'm Bishop Michael. I'm currently a guest at your parish on church business. I've had the luxury of meeting your children during Mass this evening."

Father Luke and Bishop Michael walk into the house. Liam and Boo both smile. Boo says, "Bishop Michael. Nice to see you again."

Father Luke says, "Evening, Liam and Boo. I hope you're doing well." Father Luke looks back to Annie who's closing the front door and says, "So sorry to be disturbing your dinner, Annie."

Annie says, "Oh, not to worry, Father. It's fine. We were just finishing up. Are you hungry? I always make extra."

Father Luke says, "No, thank you, Annie. I appreciate the offer."

Annie looks to Bishop Michael and says, "Can I get you anything, Bishop. Water…coffee?"

Bishop Michael smiles. "Coffee would be lovely. Thank you, ma'am."

"Please, call me Annie. Ma'am is my mother. Please have a seat, and I'll back in a minute."

Father Luke and Bishop Michael sit down at the dining room table, and Lady runs down the stairs and walks over to Bishop Michael. The bishop smiles as he greets the friendly family dog.

Liam shakes his head and says, "Some watch dog. Good job watching the house, Lady."

Father Luke says, "I was wondering where Lady was. Anytime I've come over to the house, Lady is right at the front door barking her little head off at me until your mother opens the door."

Liam says, "Yeah, something weird happened during dinner. One minute, she is next to me trying to get some table food. The next minute, she puts her tail between her legs and runs upstairs."

Father Luke turns and looks at Bishop Michael as he says, "You don't say."

Boo says to Bishop Michael, "Yeah, it was weird. After she ran up the stairs I felt like something was off but then it went away quickly. Lady likes you. She's wagging her tail and smiling."

Bishop Michael says, "She's a lovely dog."

Boo responds, "I think she feels safe around you. You have that energy about you."

Annie comes back with a cup of coffee for Bishop Michael and says, "Would you like any cream, Bishop? Sugar? I forgot to ask what you like in your coffee."

Bishop Michael answers, "Thank you, Annie. It's fine the way it is. Thank you for your hospitality."

Annie laughs briefly. "Of course. It's not every day a bishop stops by your house with your parish's priest."

Bishop Michael says, "I'm sure this is awkward for you. You are probably wondering why we are here."

Annie says, "It happens to be the elephant in the room, Bishop. So, if you would, please."

Bishop Michael responds, "Annie, are you familiar with what has been happening around the area?"

Annie sarcastically answers, "If you mean the flying-whatever-thing over Liam's baseball game, the crazy stuff being reported on the news, and the neighbor's dog disappearing. Yeah, I'm quite aware. Way too close to home, Bishop."

Father Luke interjects, "Annie, Bishop Michael is from a special order of priests in the church. Because of his specialty, I took the liberty of enlightening him on your family's history."

Bishop Michael says in a serious tone, "Liam, Boo…Annie. I regret to inform you that your family is in grave danger by a powerful evil."

Annie asks, "What the hell are you talking about? What powerful evil?"

Father Luke interjects, "Annie. Bishop Michael had to intervene and place a blessing of holy orders around your house to protect you from this…evil."

The bishop nods his head. "Like you said, Annie. Too close to home."

Annie fearfully asks, "What! Why?"

Father Luke answers, "Annie. That's why we are here. We don't know the answers right now, but we are trying to figure it out. Bishop Michael was sent by the church to vanquish this evil."

Bishop Michael says, "This is true. I'm from a special order. The Bishops of the Silver Cross. We are an order of priests that are trained to be the shield and last line of defense between the good and the evil forces of this world." Bishop Michael looks around the table over to Boo and continues, "Boo mentioned to me an old family journal she recently discovered. May I see it, please?"

Annie looks at Liam and Boo who now look like two kids getting caught by their mother for doing something they shouldn't have. Annie crosses her arms and gives both Liam and Boo a piercing look. "A Journal? What journal?"

Liam gives Boo a nod as she walks out of the dining room to retrieve the journal. Liam looks away from Annie. Annie continues to look at Liam and says, "Liam!"

Liam answers, "Yeah, Mom."

Annie responds, "What journal?"

Boo rushes back to the dining room with the journal in hand. She holds it up and says, "This journal, Mom." Boo hands it to Bishop Michael.

Bishop Michael says, "Thank you, Boo."

Boo answers, "No problem." Boo looks over to Annie and continues, "We found this journal at Grandmom's when we were clearing out her attic."

Annie, in a serious tone, says, "Thanks for telling me."

Bishop Michael examines the journal. Annie walks over to Liam and Boo's side and says, "Now. No more secrets. No more lies. I want the truth. And this goes for both you. Is there anything else you are hiding from me and your father? Let's air out the laundry right here and right now."

Liam and Boo look at each other.

Annie interjects, "What else are you hiding?"

Liam asks, "Do you promise not to get mad?"

Annie answers, "I'm already mad. Too late for that. But I promise not to get furious if you're honest with me. Right here and right now."

Liam gives Boo another nod as Boo ducks her head and runs up the stairs toward her room. Boo comes downstairs and places the items found in the attic onto the dining room table.

Bishop Michael looks up from the journal and examines the items. He says, "Good God!"

Annie interjects, "Boo! Liam! You found these things in Grandmom's attic! Why didn't you tell us? Especially your father!"

Liam says, "I'm sorry, Mom. It's my fault. I wanted to find out more on my own."

Boo says, "Because we know that you and Dad would have flipped out."

Annie interjects, "I have every *right* to flip out! Especially after everything this family has been through! Wait until your father hears about this. I'm not going to call him at work, but he's gonna find out as soon as he walks in that door!"

Father Luke, feeling uncomfortable, says, "I'm sorry to bring all of this to light, Annie. Truly. The last thing I want to do is upset the household."

Annie clears a small tear from her eye. "It's okay, Father. I had a feeling that these two were up to something. I'm upset and disappointed in both of you. You should have told us."

Liam says, "I'm sorry, Mom."

Boo adds, "Yeah, me too, Mom. Sorry."

Bishop Michael looks up from the journal and says, "Annie, if I may interject."

Annie responds, "Please."

The bishop says, "I mean this in all sincerity. We are so incredibly fortunate that Liam and Boo discovered these items. These items, and especially the journal, are the missing pieces to this puzzle." Bishop Michael stands up and looks down the hallway toward the office. He asks, "Annie. I have to contact the church and make them aware of the situation. May I use your office?"

Annie says, "Sure, Bishop. Whatever you need."

Bishop Michael walks into the office and calls his headquarters. He informs the order of Alek's resurrection, the family connection between the family and Angelica, the journal, the weapons, and the gear discovered. He asks for additional resources to assemble and immediately travel to Chicago. His command informs him that additional resources will take several days if not a week to coordinate, dispatch, and assemble. All bishops who work in the field are all currently on other assignments. Bishop Michael feels his stomach turn as his order informs him that he will unfortunately be on his own until then.

Bishop Michael walks back into the dining room and rejoins the group as Father Luke attempts to provide some words of comfort. Annie sees Bishop Michael walk back into the room. She stands up and asks, "Bishop, what can we do? And why is my family back in danger's crosshairs?"

Bishop Michael sits down and explains what he found in the journal, the ancestral connection that links their family back to Angelica and Alek, and the weapons that were discovered. He opens the journal and says, "Liam and Boo. You mentioned that you read the section of the journal written in English and you wanted my help in translating the section written in Polish."

Boo says, "Yes, Bishop. Liam and I read the rest of the journal together. What can you tell us about the opening section?"

Bishop Michael reads and summarizes this section to the group. He informs them that the opening section of the journal describes Jacek's first encounter with Angelica, the lives that were lost, and how the survivors attempted to recover Alek's buried remains days after the attack, only to discover that his remains were removed.

Liam asks, "Does the journal describe how to stop Alek and Angelica once and for all?"

Bishop Michael shakes his head. "Unfortunately, no. Maybe they weren't sure at the time. How do you kill something that extinguished its mortal life so many years ago? But my training and studies suggest that the key to stopping Alek and Angelica lies within their spell book."

Liam asks, "What do you mean, Bishop?"

Bishop Michael answers, "Covens, witchcraft, warlocks, and evil wizards are real, young man. Magic—good and evil magic—are all real things. As real as the faith you have in that cross you wear around your neck."

Liam looks down at his silver cross and holds it in the palm of his hand.

Bishop Michael continues, "You say that your silver cross has been your shield. It's protected you from the forces of evil before."

Liam nods his head.

"Bishops from my order are trained to vanquish these types of evil forces from our world. The history of battling covens and witchcraft lies mainly in retrieving their spell books and destroying them. Most real witches and wizards create an unholy bond between their souls and their spell book. The spell book is the key to their powers."

Boo interjects, "That's right! In the journal, Jacek tried to retrieve the spell book after Angelica was captured but he couldn't. Someone took it before he could get to it."

Bishop Michael says, "And that's another factor to consider."

Liam asks, "What's that, Bishop?"

Bishop Michael answers, "Who has been helping Angelica? Someone had to help her. Otherwise, she would still be locked up in that institution."

Father Luke says, "I pray for all of you."

Annie asks, "Bishop, what can you do to protect my family?"

Bishop Michael nods his head, drinks the rest of his coffee, and says, "Talk to your husband, Annie. Inform him of everything. Don't hold back any details. I'm sure he'll understand. I can't promise you I can stop it. I'm on my own. Angelica…maybe, but Alek is much more powerful. He is her teacher, after all. But I can promise you that I would rather die before I let anything happen to your family." He pauses for a moment as he looks at Liam and Boo.

Annie asks, "What is it, Bishop?"

"My order is supposed to be the last line of defense. But maybe that doesn't have to be the case."

Annie asks, "What do you mean?"

"The last line of defense is self-defense, Annie. If something happens to me, my soul cannot rest knowing that Liam and Boo stand defenseless. They have proved their bravery and defeated monsters before. I can train them."

Annie shakes her head. "No! That's completely out of the question! Bishop, they're just kids, after all. Plus, my husband and I are supposed to protect them. These types of things are supposed to be handled by grown-ups."

Father Luke interjects, "Annie. I know this is a lot to take in, but listen to reason. For the last couple of years, you've been asking why. Why have these horrible things been happening to your family? This is the answer."

Annie asks, "What's the answer, Father?"

Bishop Michael says, "That your husband's family's bloodline is linked with the descendants of monster slayers. Soldiers, like me, who battle the forces of darkness in order to protect the good and innocent. What's been happening to your family is fate. Nothing happens by coincidence. Annie, whatever you do you can't stop this evil from harming your family. Angelica, her monster, and especially Alek will cut through you like the evening air. This is Liam and Boo's bloodline. And at the end of this. Angelica wants both Liam and Boo."

Scared and upset, Annie stammers, "Fo-fo-for what reason?"

Bishop Michael answers, "Simple answer. Perhaps it's vengeance. For the family's involvement in her capture, her imprisonment, the loss of her husband and child. All of it. At the end of this road, I fear that it will be Liam and Boo standing together and fighting for their very lives. I don't have much time. Please, Annie. Let me show them how to protect themselves. It could mean all the difference."

Bishop Michael stands up and gathers the journals and items. He motions for Father Luke to do the same. Bishop Michael says, "I think it's time we leave for the evening. You have much to discuss."

Annie says, "You're just gonna leave us after you just spent all this time telling us how much we're in danger?"

Bishop Michael answers, "Don't worry. I'll be moving around the property for a little while. I'm going to add several other layers of protection. It's going to be a long night, but I'll take watch."

....

CHAPTER 22

LOCK THE DOORS AND CLOSE THE SHUTTERS

Bishop Michael and Father Luke walk outside and talk for a few more moments before Father Luke leaves in his car. Bishop Michael gathers a few items from the trunk of his car and begins to work around the property. Annie waits by the front door and observes Bishop Michael as he turns on a small hand light; dusk has now turn into the early evening.

Liam and Boo approach Annie who is visibly upset. She begins to cry. Liam says, "It's okay, Mom."

Annie grabs a tissue from a box in the living room and replies, "No! It's not okay. Why can't the monsters in this world leave my family alone!" Annie looks at both Liam and Boo as she continues, "And you two. I'm very disappointed in both of you. After all we've been through. You decide to keep things from me and your father. What did you think? That we wouldn't believe you?"

Boo replies, "It's not that, Mom. We didn't know what to think. We were just trying to figure it out on our own."

Annie says, "Oh, yeah. Just like you tried to figure out Iron River, Michigan, and Elkins Park, Pennsylvania, on your own. Do you know the definition of insanity?"

Liam and Boo are quiet as Annie waits for some type of response. Annie continues, "I try not to talk about stressful stuff at home when your father is at work, but this can't wait. I'm going into the office and calling your father. He needs to know what is going on." Annie walks away from Liam and Boo, grabs her phone from the living room end table, and closes the door as she enters the office.

Boo looks at Liam and asks, "Do you want to have some soda and chips? I'm craving some salt and sugar right now."

Liam nods his head. "That sounds like a great idea. Let's do it. I'll grab the sodas from the basement fridge, and you grab the chips from the cabinet."

Liam and Boo reconvene at the dining room table. Liam takes a big gulp of his cold soda and says, "Good idea, Boo. I needed this too."

Boo smiles. "Thanks. I get a craving for chips and soda when I'm stressed out."

"I know what you mean."

"So, Jacek has to be, what? Our great-great grandfather?"

Liam quickly does a calculation in his head and answers, "That makes sense. I heard Dad mention our family history before.. So yeah, that would be our great-great-grandfather, Jacek."

Boo washes down some chips with a large gulp of her soda and says, "Yup. A family of monster slayers. Who knew? You nervous? What do you think of all of this?"

Liam answers, "I'm beyond nervous. We've been through so much already. I feel uncomfortably numb. Like I don't feel anything. That's weird, right?"

"It makes sense. I guess it's your way to take it all in."

"How do you feel, Boo?"

Boo gives her brother a hug, holds him tight, and says, "I'm scared, Liam. That's how I'm feeling."

"It's okay, Boo. I'm your big brother. I will always be there to protect you. You can count on it."

"Yeah, well, I'm your little sister and I'll always be there to make sure you'll be okay."

There's a slight knock at the front door. It's Bishop Michael. Liam walks over and opens the door. Bishop Michael steps into the foyer and says, "Thank you, Liam. Sorry to be a bother, but may I see your mother?"

Liam says, "It might take a minute. I think she's still talking to my dad on the phone."

At that moment, Annie walks out of the office saying, "Nope. I just finished talking to Will."

Bishop Michael asks, "How did your conversation go with your husband, Annie?"

"As good as can be expected, I guess. He's just as shocked as I am, but he understands what you are trying to do. He said to do whatever is necessary to protect the family. Even if that means showing Liam and Boo how to defend themselves."

Bishop Michael looks at Liam and Boo and says, "Very well." Bishop Michael looks back toward Annie and continues, "We can begin training as early as tomorrow if I may. But for now, your home is as safe as it can be. I put markings from burned lent palms around all of your outside threshold doorways and windows, salt and holy oil lines around the entire perimeter of the property, and several blessed statues of Saint Joseph at different parts of the property. I only need to place a few more layers of protection over your upper floor bedroom windows. By any chance do you have a ladder that can reach?"

Annie answers, "Yeah, sure. No problem. Liam, why don't you help Bishop Michael. There's a large ladder in the garage."

Bishop Michael replies, "That's quite all right. I appreciate the offer to help. But it's best for Liam and Boo to remain inside tonight. If you would just open the garage for me, I'll take care of the rest."

Annie opens the garage from the opener in the kitchen. Annie watches the bishop quickly complete his work. As he moves around the backyard, he continuously scans the twilight sky. As the bishop works toward completing his work, Annie pours the rest of the coffee into his cup and walks toward the side entrance door. Bishop Michael greets her at the door and says, "Thank you, Annie. My work is done here. Your ladder is put back, and I closed the garage. The property is as safe as it can be." Annie hands Bishop Michael the cup of coffee as he steps inside the house. "Thank you. I could use a refill."

Annie replies, "Thank you for everything. What do we do next? What's the plan?"

Bishop Michael answers, "No other plans for tonight. At least for you and your family. I, on the other hand, will be on watch tonight."

Annie says, "Would you like to sit down with the family for a little while longer, Bishop? I would like to learn more about your order and your previous encounters."

Bishop Michael smiles. "Sure. Of course."

"Well, Liam and Boo are in the dining room finishing their munchies. Let's sit with them."

Bishop Michael and Annie sit down with Liam and Boo. Bishop Michael says to Boo, "Father Luke mentioned that you have abilities, Boo. Do you mind describing them to me?"

Boo talks about her first encounter with her abilities with Misty at the Elk's Estate and everything leading up to now.

Liam says, "Yeah, if it wasn't for Boo's abilities and some help from above, we wouldn't have made it out of the Elk's Estate."

Bishop Michael asks, "Is that right, Boo?"

Boo answers, "Yes, that's correct. But I had help along the way."

Bishop Michael replies, "It's simply amazing. All of you have shown some incredible bravery in the face of pure evil."

Annie asks, "And what about you, Bishop? I'm sure you have a very interesting story. The order, your accent, and the work you do of course. And your English is amazing. Also, you seem young to be a bishop for the church. Most bishops are...you know."

Bishop Michael answers, "Old with gray hair and a raspy voice."

Liam, Boo, and Annie laugh.

Bishop Michael continues, "Thank you. My mother was an American. She met my father during a college exchange program in Poland. They fell in love, got married, and decided to stay in Poland. I'm named after my grandfather on my mother's side. I wasn't always a priest. In my youth, I was a soldier and a medic. Special Forces."

Annie asks, "How does one go from soldier to a priest?"

Bishop Michael responds, "I was wounded in combat. My unit was attacked."

Annie replies, "Oh God! I'm so sorry."

Bishop Michael says, "It's okay. I was wounded but not completely broken. Had to spend a long time recovering but I pulled through. Unfortunately, the wounds meant early retirement from military service. I loved being a soldier and was lost for a little while when I came home. I went to my local church and prayed to God. I asked him to send me in the right direction. I sat there for a short while until the parish priest came into the church and saw me sitting in a pew. He approached me and asked if I needed help with anything. A special blessing or confession. I guess he could tell I was dealing with a lot of unanswered questions at the time. I politely said I'm okay and he let me know that he would be in his office if I needed anything and he would be happy to help. I looked up at the altar and said, 'Thank you.' I stood up, walked over to the priest's office, and asked what I needed to do to become a priest. Before long, I was in the seminary studying to become a priest. Ready for my new service. After taking my vows, the church recruited me for the order based on my service background."

Boo says, "Wow! That's pretty cool."

Liam says, "Have you had any run-ins with other…you know?"

Bishop Michael smiles. "Monsters?"

Liam and Boo laugh.

Annie asks, "But have you? I'm curious."

The bishop nods his head. "Yes. I've had a few encounters with monsters in other parts of the world."

Liam asks, "What was the first monster you had to face?"

"My first encounter was a nest of vampires in the French countryside."

Annie exclaims, "What! Vampires are real too?"

Bishop Michael nods his head as he says, "Most monster stories are layered in legends, myth, and truth. Most monsters, even the ones in popular culture, are in fact real. As you, unfortunately, are well aware."

Liam asks, "Were you scared when you had to face the monsters for the first time?"

"Of course I was scared."

Boo exclaims, "Even a trained solder like you gets scared?"

"Of course I get scared. At the end of the day, I'm a human being. But just because I'm scared doesn't…how do I want to say it?"

Liam interjects, "That some things are more important than being afraid."

Bishop Michael smiles. "Well said, young man."

Bishop Michael looks at the clock in the living room. "It's getting late. Thank you for your hospitality, but I should be leaving."

Annie says, "I was hoping you were going to stick around for a bit. This whole thing just makes me scared."

Bishop Michael stands up. "Of course. I understand. But not to worry. I'll be close by. Remember when I said I have watch tonight? Try to get some rest. Father Luke has your contact information on file at the parish office. I'll contact you tomorrow."

Boo asks, "Any advice before we begin training with you tomorrow?"

Bishop Michael answers, "Yes. Bring water and wear comfortable clothes. You'll thank me later."

CHAPTER 23

. . . .

SHOW ME YOUR CITY

Alek and Angelica walk hand-in-hand back toward Gunnison Ave. A young man with music blaring through his car flies down the street and zooms past Alek and Angelica. Alek looks at Angelica and asks, "These machines are everywhere! And the mortals move so much faster now. Are they some type of modern-day steam engines?"

Angelica answers, "Yes, my love. Think of them as a modern-day metal horse and carriage."

Alek replies, "It's fascinating." Alek looks up to the sky as an airplane descends toward the west. "These mortals have been busy while I slept. They can even fly now."

They look around and assess the area before ducking down an alley at the end of the street. They walk over to a group of garbage cans where they placed two large tree branches before their encounter with Bishop Michael. Angelica replies, "Yes…they have, my love. But you showed me how to fly generations before these pathetic mortals even took their first steps off the ground. Do you remember our first flight together?"

Alek smiles coldly. "Why don't you show me your city?"

Alek and Angelica look around the alley. No movement, just a dog barking further down the street. Alek and Angelica mount their branches and leap into the evening air. They quickly gain speed as Angelica leads the way. She steadies to a comfortable altitude, and Alek glides close to her. Angelica turns toward Alek as he asks, "Where are we going first?"

167

Angelica answers, "Downtown Chicago."

They glide and ride the power of the western blowing wind as Angelica and Alek reach the Dan Ryan Expressway. Angelica turns and follows the expressway toward downtown. Alek looks down and sees the endless line of headlights and break lights. They fly southeast toward the city, and the skyline of downtown Chicago quickly comes into view. Angelica looks at Alek and says, "Welcome to Chicago, my love."

Alek asks, "This mortal city is massive. Is this the biggest modern-day city in the new world?"

Angelica answers, "No, my love. That's New York City. We traveled through there when you were resting."

They soar over Downtown Chicago's tallest skyscrapers. Alek asks, "Amazing! Are these all modern-day castles?"

Angelica answers, "Not to my understanding. These are simply meeting places where mortals come and go and perform their various professions."

Angelica and Alek watch as the city's skyline zips past them as they glide over the shallow coastal waters of Lake Michigan. Angelica turns toward the south and uses the shoreline and Lake Shore Drive as her guide. Angelica says, "I'll take you to where I lived when I first arrived to this city."

"Does it have a different village name than Chicago?"

"You can think of it like that. This city is a group of dozens of villages. They are only divided by different neighborhood names. I lived in one called the Woodlawn/South Shore neighborhood."

They quickly head south and within minutes arrive at the Museum of Science and Industry. Angelica and Alek encircle and hover over the green domed roof of the vast white building. They both glide down and land on top of the roof. Angelica looks around in bewilderment. Alek studies her and asks, "You seem lost. What's the matter?"

Angelica answers, "It looks so different now. I wanted to wait to come back here with you."

"What's so different about it?"

"There were so many buildings here when I arrived that are gone!" Angelica looks down and points to the green roof as she continues, "This is one of the only buildings that I recognize. This neighborhood was the beacon for a great world's fair that took place just a couple of years before my arrival. Think of it, Alek. The whole world was on display right here. You know how much I wanted to see the world. That's what drew me to this area. And you know I always gravitated to live around the shorelines. I would take my daugh—" Angelica pauses as Alek approaches her.

Alek asks, "You had a child? A family?"

Angelica answers, "Yes. Met a very nice man after I moved here. He was also from our homeland. I had to wait so long for the right conditions to bring you back. I just longed for a sense of... family. We had one child together. We would take her for walks along the shore. She would play in the sands of Jackson Park Harbor."

Alek approaches Angelica and places a hand on her shoulder. "And then the priests took them away from you."

Angelica says, "Yes." Angelica turns toward Alek. She notices his skin as it begins to turn a pale green. She places a hand on his face and says, "Your skin, my love. It's changing color and it's already cracking and dry."

Alek examines his hand and replies, "Yes, it is. Looks like I'll need more life energy soon."

Angelica grabs her branch and says, "Follow me."

Alek and Angelica both take flight and glide over the lakefront parks, which are slightly illuminated by tall lanterns along the winding running trails. The fly over South Shore Drive and descend over the Jackson Park Harbor. As they descend, Angelica scans the area and looks for anyone in the immediate area. No one at the harbor. Just a few runners and bikers moving in opposite directions further up and down the trail. Angelica takes in the sound of the shallow waves as they ripple over the lakefront sand and the larger waves as they crash along the breakers farther out along the deeper ends of the harbor. Angelica says, "You don't know how much you miss something until it's gone, do you?"

Alek nods as he places his branch into the water and says, "You and I both know the feeling of loss. Comes with the length of our timeline." Alek slowly stirs his branch in the water.

Angelica asks, "Creating mist and shadows, my love?"

Alek smiles slightly. "If I need more energy, it's better that others don't see us." Alek looks at Angelica and continues, "Looks like you can use more energy too."

Angelica examines her hands and notices that they are also starting to look pale and gray. Angelica says, "I believe you are right, my love."

From the small whirlpool from Alek's spinning branch, a thick mist begins to form in the center of the centrifugal force. The thick soupy mist begins to the spread quickly and hangs low over the shallow beach waters and the busy pathway of the nearby expressway. Alek asks, "Now that we have the fog of war, where shall we hunt?"

Angelica answers, "I saw a spot not far from here. Just a few miles to the north. Decent number of young people, full of life and energy. And a lot of corners and shadows."

Alek smiles as he and Angelica soar into the murky air. Angelica turns her branch to the north and says, "Follow me. This way."

They glide on the crest of the fog that continues to expand over the lakefront and the inner parts of downtown. The fly over the Shedd Aquarium. There they see several people moving along the trail doing various types of exercises. Alek and Angelica quietly land and place their branches on the gray stone barrier wall, which separates the running path along the far end of the Shedd Aquarium from the saturated and foamy rocks of the breaker wall below. Alek and Angelica watch as the mist blankets the skyline of Chicago. In the distance, they hear the sound of cars tapping their breaks and the echo of several car horns as traffic slows down to a crawl along Lake Shore Drive. Angelica says, "This city looks so different for even me to understand. When I arrived, this city was still rebuilding after a great fire swept through most of it."

A young couple exercising along the trail quickly jogs past Alek and Angelica. Alek looks at the young couple and gives Angelica a head motion to follow them. As they move to catch up to the young couple, Alek says, "Look at those two happy, healthy, and young mortals. They are beautiful, aren't they? The young lady reminds me of you when we first met." Alek smiles as he reaches into his long jacket and pulls out his long walking cane. He rubs the cane, and as it begins to glow, he aims and fires a violet-colored ball of energy toward the young couple. The ball of energy engulfs the young couple who freeze in their present stance and immediately turn into stone! Alek smiles as he walks up to admire his handy work. He says, "Don't they look marvelous? Forever preserved in their youth. Most mortals aren't so lucky."

Angelica and Alek turn toward the northern end of the trail as they hear a group of runners head in their direction. Alek looks at Angelica and says, "Time to go. Let me lead the way. I want to do some exploring." They mount their branches and glide up into the mist-filled night air. Angelica looks back and laughs as the group of runners stop and look at the two stone figures.

Alek leads the way as the Downtown Chicago skyline sails past him on his left side. The dense fog has now engulfed the majority of the inner city. They fly past several high-rise buildings, running trails, baseball diamonds, and tennis courts until Alek sees a small fire burning near a tent next to a Lake Shore Drive overpass. Alek points while descending behind two men sitting by a fire. They glide down gracefully without detection due to the fog. Alek looks around and notices several people pushing around shopping carts, going through garbage cans, and sitting near small fires. Alek looks puzzled. "Modern-day camp settlement?"

Angelica shakes her head. "No, my dear. I've seen this type of thing even before I was locked away from the world. These people are very similar to poor peasants and drifters we saw along busy trails and villages back in our world."

Alek nods his head and smiles at Angelica. "That's my kind of people. The outcasts and drifters. You know what I like most about this class of people?"

Angelica asks, "What's that, my love?"

Alek answers, "I will assume the same rules apply that applied even in our time." Alek gives Angelica an evil grin as he continues, "It's getting a little cold. Why don't we warm up by their fire."

Angelica casually walks over to the two men trying to keep warm as a cool wind picks up. Alek walks closely behind. Angelica says, "Good evening, gentlemen. My partner and I are a little chilled. Do you mind if we stay warm next to your fire?"

The two men are startled at first and suspicious of the two strangers. The suspicions are lifted as they see Angelica's beautiful smile. Most of the decaying changes to her skin are hidden by the gloom of the evening and the slight glow of the fire. The two men give each other a look, and one of them says, "Go ahead. Help yourself."

Angelica says, "Thank you. You are too kind."

One of the men asks, "So, where are you from?"

Angelica looks at Alek who smiles as she replies, "I'm from the South Shore neighborhood. I'm just showing my friend the better parts of this city."

The other man asks, "And what about your friend? Where is he from?"

Angelica looks at Alek who doesn't understand what the man is asking. She responds, "Oh, please excuse my companion. He's from a foreign land and doesn't know the language."

One of them continues to look at Alek. "So, what's wrong with your friend? He looks ill."

Alek blows on the fire. The fire almost goes out. Angelica says, "Oh, dear. The fire is almost out. Do you have any more kindling nearby?"

One of the men says, "Yeah. Help yourself, they're right next to your sick friend."

Angelica looks to Alek and says, "My love. Why don't you make this fire a little bigger."

Alek nods his head, smiles, and grabs a few small sticks lying behind him. He places the kindling into the smoldering fire. It creates a decent amount of smoke. As it does, the men cough as the smoke puffs and drifts toward them. Alek grabs his walking stick and creates an encircled smoke around the two men. The men cough and shout as they try to escape. But it's too late. The coughing and cries for help last for only a few more seconds and then silence. The illuminating energy from their bodies lifts and floats in midair toward Alek and Angelica. Alek and Angelica both enjoy and savor the moment and feeling of mortal energy as their decaying bodies begin to heal and repair. By now, other people take notice of what's happening. They start to shout and scream as the encircling smoke clears and lifts, revealing the decayed remains of the two men. A few moments later, a police car on patrol around the lakefront pulls up to a nearby stop sign. The officer takes notice of the activity and activates the flashing and glowing blue lights on top of his squad car. Angelica takes notice of the flashing blue lights and says to Alek, "My love. I think it's time we leave."

Alek says, "Hmm. This always feel so good. Like taking a bath in the warm spring waters back home." He takes notice of the flashing blue lights and asks, "Modern-day knights?"

Angelica walks over to the branches and says, "Yes, my love. And they can be a pain. Let's make haste."

Alek and Angelica quickly mount their branches and launch into the night sky. The officer pulls up to the site. He quickly exits his vehicle, looks up, and asks, "What the hell was that? What did I just see?"

Several other people shout and point at the officer to take notice of the site. The officer directs his attention to the site, grabs a flashlight from his belt, and turns it on. A beam of light cuts through the mixture of fog and smoke and reveals the remains of the two men! The officer says to himself, What the hell? He presses the push-to-talk button radio button on his shoulder and says, "Beat 8877 to Dispatch."

Dispatch replies, "This is dispatch. Go ahead 8877."

The officer replies, "Dispatch, send my supervisor and area detectives to my current location. I don't know what to say.... I think I have victims of a double homicide. Send the appropriate response. Do it now!"

....

CHAPTER 24

TRAINING BEGINS

Liam wakes up to the sound of Annie making breakfast in the kitchen while listening to the radio. The smell of country sausage, eggs, and biscuits fill the air. Liam walks across the hallway and notices his parents' bedroom door closed. The whole family knows that if the door is closed, that means Will had a long night at work and is trying to get some rest.

Liam comes down the stairs and greets Boo who's in the process of making her plate. Annie hears Liam entering the kitchen and says, "Hey, honey! How did you sleep?"

Liam answers, "Not bad. Honestly, I felt better with Bishop Michael 'on watch' as he calls it. How 'bout yourself?"

Annie answers, "Not great. I went to bed late. My head was spinning. Couldn't shut it down for a long time."

Boo asks, "Did anyone see Bishop Michael last night?"

Annie answers, "I didn't see him in the backyard when I let Lady out for the night. But his car was out front. He must have left sometime overnight. I asked your father if he noticed the car outside when he came home from shift."

Liam asks, "Did Dad see him."

Annie shakes her head. "No. Your father had a busy night. Plus, even if he wasn't busy, he couldn't sleep. He was too worried about us. Why don't you make a plate for yourself, honey."

As Liam starts to make a plate, the announcer on the radio on the windowsill says, "Thank you for tuning in to news radio. At the tone it's 9:00 a.m. *BONG!* Good morning, Chicago. And welcome to another day. Today it will be cloudy with a slight fog that's been burning off since the evening hours along the city's lakefront. The fog that blanketed the majority of our listening area caused major backups on all expressways until the early hours this morning. Besides the weather, our top stories are two bizarre cases that happened miles apart from each other along the city's lakefront. Police discovered a pair of stone statues near the running trail along the Shedd Aquarium. Police say the statues fit the descriptions of two missing person reports filed by family members early this morning. How the statues, who police say weigh several hundred pounds, arrived along the city's lakefront remains a mystery. One of our reporters is on the scene of a separate incident a few miles north of downtown involving two victims. Here's Gene on the scene with the latest."

Gene interjects, "Thank you, team. This is Gene on the scene with the latest. Police have the scene secured with police tape. Witnesses state, 'The two bodies looked like they were in the late stages of decomposition.' However, witnesses also state, 'The two men in question were seen just moments earlier talking to a couple of people before they disappeared into the sky.' Area detectives are currently on the scene, and the victims have been transported to the medical examiner's office. And in other news...."

Annie steps away from completing her meal prep and walks over to the radio. She says, "That's enough news for one day."

Liam says, "It's only nine in the morning."

Annie flips a switch to turn off the AM radio as the news radio report fades out.

At the scene where the two men became victims, area detectives continue to question witnesses and search the area. A car pulls up behind the news radio van. Gene from news radio hands the mic back to his team. He says, "Thanks, everyone. It looks like a wrap around here. Let's head back to the station. We have a catered breakfast arriving soon."

As the news radio team finishes packing up at the scene, Detective Cunningham exits his car and walks over to the detectives searching the scene. Steve recognizes one of the detectives who he has helped him in the past. Steve walks up to him and says, "Hey, Rory. How are things going?"

Rory looks away from his notes, smiles, and extends his hand. As they shake hands, Rory says, "Hey! Good to see you, Steve. Things aren't too great right now. I was supposed to get off this morning when I got called into this mess."

Steve nods his head. "I know what you mean. Had many late nights that blended into early mornings."

Rory asks, "So, what brings you over to the lakefront on this fine cloudy summer morning?"

Steve answers, "Well, I heard an early AM radio report while I was on my way into my office. From what I heard, this sounds like similar cases that are currently on my desk."

Rory replies, "Is that so? Interesting. Well, come with me and I'll show you what I got, and then if the shoe fits, maybe we can help each other with the case." Rory pulls up the yellow police tape that surrounds the site. He says, "Here, step into my office."

Steve smiles. "Thanks. I appreciate it."

Rory adds, "So, basically the two bodies that were here are being brought over to the medical examiner's office as we speak."

Steve says, "Dr. Rodney will probably receive them unless, of course, he clocked out and finally went home."

Rory interjects, "You know that man doesn't go home. He probably just sleeps in that office of his next to all the body coolers. So, anyway, the witnesses said that the two guys in question were talking to a young woman and some other guy. Next thing they know smoke swirls around, the two guys turn into something straight out of a horror movie, and the girl and guy they were talking to just fly into the air."

Steve asks, "Did they give a description of the woman?"

Rory searches his notes briefly and says, "Let me see. Yeah. One of them mentioned that she looked pretty young but her complexion was off. Figure she was on something. Pretty with long black hair."

Steve nods his head. "Yup. This is all starting to sound pretty familiar to my case." Steve looks beyond the group of onlookers and sees a man wearing a hood over his head. Steve points at the hooded man and asks, "Hey, Rory."

Rory turns toward Steve's pointed finger and asks, "What's up?"

Steve answers, "Did anyone question that guy over there?"

"Which one?"

"The younger man in the hood. That guy."

Rory replies, "I don't think so. Probably not. Probably another drifter like the rest of them."

Steve shakes his head. "Don't be so sure."

"Why's that, Steve?"

"Because he doesn't look like a drifter. His clothes are clean, and he's clean cut. Like military clean cut."

Rory says, "You're a better detective than me. If you want to question him, go for it. I'm still trying to search for anything that can put a name to the face on these guys."

Steve says, "You know what? I will. Thanks, Rory. If you need anything call me." Steve walks over toward Bishop Michael. Bishop Michael takes notice of Steve walking toward him. The bishop turns about face and heads back to his car. He quickly unlocks the vehicle, gets inside, turns the ignition, and puts the car in drive. Steve sees Bishop Michael attempt to leave the scene quickly. He begins to quickly jog over to the bishop before he leaves. Steve exclaims, "Hey you! Sir! Stop for a second! I want to ask you a few....!" Before Steve is able to reach the bishop's car, Bishop Michael drives away quickly and immediately enters the Lake Shore Drive feeder ramp to head north.

Steve slows down and says, "Damn it. I didn't even get the plate number." He paces back and forth for a minute as he tries to figure out his next step. He grabs his cell phone out of his pocket and attempts to call Dr. Ross. After a few rings, his call goes to voicemail.

Bishop Michael checks his rear-view mirror several times before he is satisfied that he's not being followed. As he starts to head west toward Jefferson Park, he calls Annie. Annie answers, "Hello, Bishop. Thank you for everything last night. My husband is on board with anything that will help protect the family. He said he'll be willing to accompany Liam and Boo to wherever you need them."

Bishop Michael responds, "Thank you, Annie. I'm glad the family is on board. No need to worry about driving Liam and Boo anywhere. I'll be in contact with Father Luke. He and I will pick up Liam, Boo, and your husband. If you feel safer with us, you can come with us as well."

Annie answers, "Thank you but I feel safe at home."

Bishop Michael replies, "That's fine, Annie. Father Luke and I will be at your house within the hour."

Within the hour, Will wakes up from his much-needed rest. He slowly makes his way downstairs and into the kitchen to make his coffee. Will sees Annie as she climbs up from the basement stairs. Annie gives Will a long hug. He notices that Annie needs to hold on to him for a few extra moments. He gives Annie a kiss on the cheek and says, "It's okay, honey. Everything is gonna be okay."

Annie continues to hold onto Will for another few seconds before she releases and says, "Thank you. I know. I just needed that."

Will asks, "Where's Liam and Boo?"

"They're both downstairs playing a video game. I guess it's their way to escape reality for a little while."

Will nods. "I understand. Believe me."

"Bishop Michael said that both he and Father Luke will be here soon. I suggest getting in the shower, and I'll get your coffee ready."

"That's fine. But first I need to do something."

"What's that, honey?"

Will pulls out his phone from his pocket. "Call my mom. See what she knows, if anything, about the stuff Liam and Boo found in the attic."

Will calls. After a few rings, Bethany answers the phone sounding tired. Will says, "Good morning, Mom. How you feeling?"

Bethany answers, "I feel lousy. I think I overworked myself today while I was cleaning up in this heat.."

Will replies, "Sorry to hear that, Mom. Do you need anything from myself or Annie?"

Bethany adds, "Don't worry about me. I'll be fine. Plus, you live far. If anything, I'll reach out to one of your cousins or my sister. They live a lot closer."

Will replies, "Sounds good, Mom. Listen. Totally off topic, but Liam and Boo found an old wooden chest when they were cleaning up your attic. Do you know anything about it?"

Bethany thinks for a minute and says, "A wooden chest... I believe it belonged to my mother. She received a lot of family heirlooms after her parents passed away. And your grandfather was just like your father. That man couldn't throw anything away. When your grandparents passed away, a lot of stuff from their garage ended up in our garage. Hence, all of the stuff we had to sort out and throw away. The dumpster company should be picking up that dumpster today in fact."

Will asks, "Did you ever open it?"

Bethany answers, "I only saw it once when your father was putting stuff from your grandparents' garage into his truck. I saw it had a lock on it. I joked with your father that maybe part of my inheritance will be in it. Your father found a couple large coffee cans with some keys in them. Not sure if he ever opened it. Did Liam or Boo open it? Is everything okay?"

Will answers, "Yes, Mom. Everything is fine. Liam and Boo mentioned it to me, and I was just curious. But feel better soon."

Bethany adds, "Goodbye, honey. Love you."

By the time Will gets showered, dressed, and sips on his coffee, the front doorbell chimes. Will walks to the front door and sees Father Luke and another man who he assumes is Bishop Michael. Will opens the door. Father Luke shakes Will's hand and says, "Hello, Will."

"Father."

Father Luke continues, "I'm sure this is a lot to take in."

Will replies, "It is, but I had a feeling something was eventually going to happen."

Father Luke asks, "Is that right?"

"Yes. When I saw that flying creature over Liam's baseball game I thought, *This is it. It's starting again*. It was quiet for too long." Will looks at Bishop Michael.

Bishop Michael extends his hand and says, "Will. Nice to meet you, sir. I wish we could have met under less stressful circumstances."

Will replies, "Thank you for keeping my family safe while they slept, Bishop."

Bishop Michael replies, "Of course. It was my pleasure to help your family. Speaking of which, are you, Liam, and Boo ready to leave?"

Will says, "Of course. Just give us a minute, and we'll be outside."

Liam, Boo, and Will get inside Father Luke's vehicle and within a few minutes they arrive at their church. Bishop Michael and Father Luke escort the family through the auditorium area of the church's campus and down to the cool basement. Father Luke opens a door and turns on the lights. The large basement is surrounded by old wood paneling on the walls and light brown ceramic tiles on the floors. As they walk through the wide open space, they see a long plastic table set up with two crossbows and two targets approximately fifteen yards down range in front of a padded section of the wall. Liam notices another plastic table with the war pick and a body opponent dummy approximately ten yards away. In the center of the room is a large padded blue floor mat and another punching dummy used in mixed-martial-arts gyms. In the far corner of the space, Boo notices a treadmill, a weight lifting bench, and other fitness equipment.

Bishop Michael says, "Welcome to my training room. Will, if you need anything like coffee or water, Father Luke is going to set up a table of refreshments in the auditorium upstairs. And Liam and Boo, if you need to take a break at any time to catch your breath or get some hydration, please feel free."

Liam says, "Wow! This is pretty impressive."

Will says, "I'll say. Looks like you set up a nice personal training room for yourself." Will looks at Father Luke and asks, "Are you using any of this equipment, Father?"

Father Luke laughs. "Not at all. I'm happy with my walks around the parish. This was all set up by Bishop Michael's order. They sent over the equipment right before his arrival."

Will whispers to himself, "This is awesome. If I knew that part of my weekly donation was going to this stuff, I probably would have thrown in a couple extra bucks."

Boo asks, "So this is how bishops from your order train?"

Bishop Michael answers, "Yes. We go through extensive physical training and attend many classes on how to vanquish various types of monsters from this world. The physical training isn't anything new for the majority of men in my order. Most of them, like myself, attended basic training, other military/paramilitary boot camps, and special forces training. The order requires us to be the sharpest weapon in the church's arsenal. If a member such as myself is sent on assignment for a prolonged period of time, the order sets up training equipment for us."

Liam says, "Well. How would you like to start, Bishop?"

Bishop Michael takes off his hooded overcoat. Under his hooded overcoat, he wears a comfortable sweatshirt and sweatpants. "Very good question. How can one go through this type of training so quickly? I figured we will start with some long-range training and work our way down to self-defense." Bishop Michael walks over to Liam and Boo and continues, "Because what is the last line of defense?"

Boo answers, "It's self-defense."

Bishop Michael smiles and says, "That's correct, Boo. Self-defense. Let's begin."

....

CHAPTER 25

LAST LINE OF DEFENSE IS SELF-DEFENSE

Will shakes his head and asks, "Bishop Michael? Is all of this necessary?"

Bishop Michael walks over to one of the tables as he replies, "Is all of this necessary, you ask?" He picks up Jacek's journal and says, "This journal belonged to your bloodline. The author describes in detail Angelica's brutality. How much trouble she went through to bring Alek, her teacher, with her." Bishop Michael pauses in mid-thought and asks Will, "Do you have your phone?"

Will reaches into his pocket. "Yes. What about it?"

Bishop Michael answers, "Look up the local news. The top story. Several bodies were discovered this morning. Each of them was an innocent human being. Alek and Angelica took their lives to harness their life energy. A young couple was turned into stone! They were simply taken just for wicked fun and to send a message." The bishop places his hands on Liam's and Boo's shoulders and continues, "This is all completely necessary. We don't have much time. We must begin."

Will, Liam, Boo, and Bishop Michael walk over to a table where two unused bows and several practice arrows currently rest. Bishop Michael picks up the bow and hands it to Boo. He says, "This is your ancestor's original bow. It's only fitting that you have it and learn how to use it. I replaced the cord with a new one. I fired a few practice shots earlier. Seems to be working quite well."

Bishop Michael picks up a practice arrow with a rounded metal end and continues, "These are practice arrows. The arrows I have for you have solid silver tips. That's, of course, when you are ready to receive them."

Boo smiles as she places the practice bow in the correct position, lines up down range with her target, gets into a proper firing stance, and releases. She almost misses the target but still makes contact. Bishop Michael exclaims, "Wow! Not bad, Boo. Have you fired a bow and arrow before?"

Boo nods her head. "Yes, sir. I trained with Liam on a few scouting trips."

Bishop Michael looks at Will and asks, "Is that right?"

Will answers, "Yeah, she's actually a scary good shot. Almost as good as her mother."

Bishop Michael asks, "And how is your shot, Will?"

Will replies, "Let's just focus on the kids."

Bishop Michael hands Liam a slightly bigger bow. He says, "Now, I gave Boo the smaller bow. You're a little older and bigger. I picked up this bow from a local sporting goods store. I tweaked a few things to make it better."

Liam smiles and says, "Thank you, Bishop." Liam attempts a few practice shots down range. Most of his shots are able to hit the target. One almost hits the center mass!

Bishop Michael says, "Look at both of you. You're naturals! Continue with some practice shots. I will help you adjust to make you better shots. At the end of the session, we will add a few more variables."

Liam asks, "What kind of variables?"

Bishop Michael smiles. "I want you to start at the back of the room. Run up to the table. Do a few push-ups, and then quickly aim and fire."

Boo says, "What! Why?"

Liam says, "I think I know." Bishop Michael gestures for Liam to answer. Liam says, "To make the body feel like it's under stress."

Bishop Michael smiles and says, "That's correct, Liam. Well said. It's easy to stand here in a controlled environment and simply point, aim, and fire at a non-moving, non-threatening target.

It's another thing to think and perform while you are under stress. In the special forces, we would try to add stressful variables to training in order to simulate real-life scenarios. Let's continue."

After some extensive practice and adding more stress to the training, Bishop Michael decides to have Liam and Boo rest for a short while. Next, he moves Liam and Boo over to another table with the war pick. Boo picks up the weapon. They all agree that it's too heavy for Boo to use practically. Bishop Michael says, "I think it's best that we pair Liam with the war pick, and I'll have you, Boo, continue to practice with your bow and arrow."

Liam attempts to throw the war pick similar to axe throwing. He does surprisingly well hitting the target down range. Bishop Michael studies Liam and says, "Excellent work, Liam. Well done. Have you done something like this before?"

Liam answers, "Yes. I went with my baseball team to axe throwing and pizza after the All-Star Game last year."

Bishop Michael breaks away from being serious for a moment, laughs, and says, "Axe throwing and pizza. What an interesting combination."

Will walks past and says, "It's probably safer than axe throwing, pizza, and beer with the guys from work."

Bishop Michael continues to laugh and says, "Agreed. Okay, Liam let's move closer to the target."

When Liam and Bishop Michael move closer to the target—a mixed-martial-arts plastic dummy—Bishop Michael says, "Hopefully you don't have to get too close. But be fair warned. Angelica and Alek are both dangerous from both near and far."

Liam asks, "How so, Bishop?"

"She can make almost anything around her a weapon. Stones, sticks, fire, etc. She can create fog to add to her aid. Create her own fog of war."

Liam cautiously asks, "What about this Alek? What should we be worried about with him?"

Bishop Michael nervously shakes his head. "The scary answer. I honestly don't know. The order is currently searching the old record archive. Hopefully they can find something. I know he's very old. His power goes back to the dark times in human history. If you have to strike in a close quarters combat, I want you to practice using your weapon and strike this dummy at certain key points. Let me show you. Let's begin."

After some time passes, Bishop Michael decides it's best to have Liam and Boo take another break. After Liam and Boo rest and replenish with some protein bars and water, they slowly make their way back over to Bishop Michael. Liam looks at Boo's tired eyes and asks, "You look as tired as I feel."

Boo says, "You're not kidding. Haven't worked this hard in any of my sports."

Liam says, "Me either."

Will and Bishop Michael break away from a friendly conversation as Liam and Boo approach them over a large blue padded mat. The bishop recognizes Liam's and Boo's fatigue and says, "Good, you're getting tired. This is where we train the hardest." Bishop Michael gestures to Liam and Boo to follow him to the center of the mat. As they approach he continues, "Now, Liam and Boo, have you ever taken a martial arts class?" They both reluctantly shake their heads. Bishop Michael adds, "That's okay. Are you familiar with mixed-martial-arts?"

Liam answers, "Yes. Dad likes watching the main events with his buddies. Doesn't let us watch it. But Dad used to workout at an M.M.A. gym when he was younger."

Bishop Michael turns to Will and asks, "Is that so?"

Will answers, "In my youth. That was before I had kids, a big mortgage, and had a lot more energy, money, and time on my hands."

Bishop Michael smiles and asks, "What disciplines do you mean when you say M.M.A.?"

Will answers, "Mostly boxing, Brazilian Jiu-Jitsu, and Muay Thai."

"Exactly! Boxing. Striking with the upper body. A combination of strikes such as"—Bishop Michael demonstrates as he continues—"jab, hook, cross, and upper cut. Muay Thai is a striking with the lower body through a series of different types of kicks. And finally wrestling or Brazilian Jiu-Jitsu. When you are fighting your opponent at the closes range possible."

Bishop Michael looks down at Boo and says, "Now, Boo. You are the smallest. With being small, you have less range for strike using your lower body and upper body. In a stand-up fight, a larger opponent is more likely to win. But if you take them to the ground and use some basic wrestling or Jiu-Jitsu moves, you'll have a fighting chance. Because you'd be on the ground, the size of your opponent doesn't matter. On the ground, it's skill and determination that will separate the winner from the loser. Lucky for us, Father Luke was a former inner-city youth boxing champion. You will go over boxing with him. I'll teach you the rest. Let's begin."

After some more time goes by, Bishop Michael knows it's time to finish for the day. He looks at Liam and Boo and says, "Okay. That concludes our training for today." Liam and Boo look at each other with great relief pouring over their faces as much as the sweat hits the blue mat below them. He continues, "Good training today. You're breathing heavy and your body is tired. You'll need to recover and rest before another training session tomorrow." Bishop Michael takes a knee next to Liam and Boo who are cooling off with some water and wiping their sweaty faces with a dry towel from Father Luke. "Our final lesson for today. And please remember this if nothing else. This especially goes for when you get knocked down and you're not sure if you can go forth. As long as you still have air in your lungs, you can stand, fight, and defend your ground."

Bishop Michael stands and Will extends his hand. "Thank you for everything today. I'll make sure that they have everything they need to recover and rest at home."

Father Luke gets the car ready while Bishop Michael gathers a few items and meets one last time with Liam, Boo, and Will. The bishop hands Liam the war pick and Jacek's silver chain-mail vest. He hands Boo the bow and silver-tipped arrows. Finally, he hands Will the family journal. He says, "I put a few sticky notes inside the journal. The notes are a summary of the text translated to English. Please take the time to read and discover your family's legacy."

Will nods. "Of course, Bishop. Thank you again."

Bishop Michael replies, "Of course. Father Luke and I will make sure you get home. Stay there tonight."

Will asks, "What will you being doing tonight, Bishop?"

Bishop Michael answers, "Doing what I can and what I do best. Going on the hunt and working in the gray."

CHAPTER 26

....

THE HUNT

Bishop Michael makes sure that Liam, Boo, and Will arrive home safe for the evening. When he arrives back to his quarters, he pulls out his laptop and an old-fashioned paper map. He pulls out his silver cross from under his shirt, opens his phone to the police scanner app, and gets to work. He begins his research by placing red pins on his map where any previous incidents occurred. He continues further research by looking up news articles on his laptop.

First, he searches for any updated information relating to the escaped mental patient from Northwest Cook County Hospital. Next, he looks into the incident at the airport, Pet's monstrous fly over Dunham Park, the three missing teenagers from the area, and the young lady who died in Robinson Woods. He digs into his bag and finds his red string. By using the red string to link all of the incidents line for line on the map, he notices something and says, "Good God! Liam and Boo's house is right in the middle of everything that has been happening. The airport and the young woman from Robinson Woods to the west. The disappearance of the three teenagers to the east. Pet's fly over to the south. And Angelica's escape from the hospital to the north/northwest. But where is Angelica and Alek now?"

The bishop continues to examine the map and comes up with only one logical conclusion. He thinks out loud, "She hasn't been anywhere near that hospital since she escaped. I found her in the Robinson Woods with her monster. I doubt she's been back since. When her monster left Liam and Boo's street, he flew off to the east.

I have to look further into the disappearance of these three girls. Three girls? That's it! Angelic used the three girls to resurrect Alek just as she attempted all those years ago! I found her hiding in the forest preserve before." Bishop Michael examines the map and says, "That's where I must look." He points to forest preserve next to the intersection of Foster and Cicero and continues, "My best guess is she's hiding somewhere in those woods. Time to go out on the hunt."

✦ ✦ ✦

Back at Liam and Boo's house, Annie calls Coach Phil. Coach Phil answers, "Hey, Annie. How can I help you?"

Annie replies, "Hey, Phil. How are things?"

"Doing good. Just on my way home from work, making a quick dinner, and then heading over to the park for practice tonight."

Annie replies, "Yeah. That's why I'm calling. Unfortunately, Liam won't be able to make practice tonight."

"Oh, that's too bad. I hope he's feeling okay. Especially with the All-Star Game coming up soon."

"I'm sure he'll be thrilled about that. Have you made the official announcement yet."

Phil shakes his head. "Nope. Not yet. I was planning to send out an email later this week to all of the families. But I already picked my two players."

Annie smiles as she responds with a slight white lie, "That's wonderful. Some good news, but I'll be sure to keep it to myself until you make it official. Tonight, unfortunately, Liam and Boo have to help their grandmother."

Phil exclaims, "Who? Bethany? I hope she's doing okay?"

Annie answers, "She's doing fine. But she needs extra help over the next few days. She's moving out some more of her husband's things."

Phil says, "I love seeing her at the games. She's Liam's biggest fan. She hasn't missed any of the All-Star Games. Even if it meant that she had to walk to the park from the burbs. And if you guys need anything, you know the team always has your back. Just ask."

Annie says, "Thanks, Phil. I hear Liam coming up the stairs from the basement so let me let you go. Take care."

✦ ✦ ✦

Angelica, Alek, and Pet are watching the sun set on another day from the cracked and mossy steps of the mausoleum. Pet chews on a few small forest animals as Angelica asks, "What are we going to do tonight, my love?"

Alek stands up and starts to walk around. He thinks for a moment and says, "That baby priest had a magic cross that helps him locate us."

Angelica responds, "Yes, he does. That order is able to use those crosses to sense our magic."

Alek looks at Pet who is just finishing his meal. Alek asks, "Where did Pet first find the children? Away from their home?"

Angelica briefly examines Pet's visions and answers, "Pet first found the children at a park near their home. They were playing an American sport called baseball."

Alek chuckles. "Human mortals are silly. They believe there's safety in numbers. Maybe they're playing this game at this park as you call it. They might be away from that fortress they live in."

Angelica asks, "What do you propose?"

Alek replies, "I suggest we divide and conquer. Just a little bit, at least. Let's have some fun with these children. Let's use the baby priest's magic against him. We'll lure him away from the area. Closer to the high castles and the large body of water. Let's take him for a ride just...you and me. And let Pet check the park for the children."

Angelica smiles as she approaches Alek and gives him a kiss. She says, "That's sounds wonderful, my love. I want that little girl. She has the same gifts I once possessed. If we can get her then—"

Alek interjects, "Let's not put the cart before the horse. Let's place the wheels in motion first."

Darkness falls across the city as the evening sky turns from dark purple to navy blue as thousands of street lights begin to illuminate the endless pathways across the city. Bishop Michael dons all of his gear and sets off to search the forest preserve to the east. As he approaches the forest in his car, his cross begins to shine and point to the east. Bishop Michael says, "Got you." He finds a place to park. He exits his car, opens his trunk, places his sword in his scabbard, and throws his satchel over his shoulder. Bishop Michael looks at his cross as it continues to glow brighter as he heads into the tree line. He says to himself, "It's time to end this."

Angelica smells Bishop Michael as he approaches. She turns to Pet and Alek "He's here! He's close! We must accelerate our plan."

Alek says, "Good. Let's take flight." He turns to Pet and says, "You stay here until we are out of sight. You know what to do after." Pet nods his ugly head.

Alek and Angelica mount their branches and ascend over the tree line. Bishop Michael looks up as his cross begins to illuminate. He catches sight of Alek and Angelica as they take flight into the evening air with their silhouettes in front a silvery moon above them. Bishop Michael says, "Damn it! They're on the move. But I found you. And I'm not gonna lose you this time." Bishop Michael runs back to his car, throws his sword and satchel on the passenger seat, and zips the car toward Alek and Angelica's direction of travel.

Alek looks back to see Bishop Michael attempting to follow in his car. Alek looks at Angelica and gives her a nod. Angelica smiles as she sends a message to Pet saying, "It's time, Pet. Go forth with your mission." Pet receives the message, bows his ugly head, and begins to flap and soar into the evening sky. Angelica speeds up to Alek's side and says, "Pet is on the way, my love."

Alek smiles. "Good. Let's take this baby priest for a ride around that lake." Alek and Angelica continue to glide east toward Lake Michigan. Alek continues to check and see if Bishop Michael is still in pursuit. Alek continues to look back and watch the bishop zip in and out of lanes and attempt to catch up, and he says, "Foolish priest. A mouse cannot compete with the flight of an owl."

Pet arrives at the park. He lands quietly on top one of the tall oak trees that surround the outer lining of the park. He takes notice of his surrounding environment. He sees people running along the park trail, a couple walking their dog, and a group of children playing baseball under the park lights. He nestles into the tree and examines the children as they continue to run, laugh, and play. Angelica and Alek continue to glide through the air as a cool lake breeze whips past them. Angelica's long beautiful black hair flows through the wind as they continue to travel ever closer to the lake.

She examines Pet's vision and says to Alek, "Pet's at the park, my love. The children are playing their game."

"Good. Let's pick up the pace and lose this fool."

"You take the lead, my love."

Alek and Angelica enter the Uptown neighborhood of Chicago. They pass Broadway Avenue and increase their speed. They dash past several high-rise buildings and quickly zoom over Marine Drive and Lake Shore Drive. Alek says, "Let's go out a bit over the water until the baby priest loses sight of us, then we flank from the south and head back west."

Angelica laughs. "You're a genius, my love! That sounds perfect."

Alek replies, "It's time we pay a visit to the children."

Bishop Michael stops the car. He is blocked by a traffic jam near Wilson Avenue and Broadway. He looks up and sees Alek and Angelica dash out of sight and out to the lake. He says to himself, "Damn! They're gone." He looks down at his cross. The cross's illuminating light begins to fade as Angelica and Alek continue their flight over the lake. He looks up at the evening sky and says, "Where the hell are they going?"

Alek and Angelica flank Bishop Michael and quickly head back to Dunham Park. As they get close to the neighborhood, Alek asks, "Are the children still at the park?"

Angelica quickly searches Pet's vision. "Yes, my love. They are still there. But I see a lot of cars arriving. Probably the parents coming to take the children home. I see one of those modern knights arriving to the park flashing their blue lights."

Alek replies, "Then let's move in quietly. Knights are trouble regardless of the times."

The couple quietly glide and land softly next to Pet. They land on a large adjacent tree branch, making sure not cause any extra noise or movement. Pet sees Alek and Angelica and points to the children as they are finishing up their baseball practice. Alek asks Angelica, "Are any of these children the ones we are looking for?"

Angelica examines the children as each one gets picked up by their guardians. She lifts her head, breathes in deeply through her nose, and says, "No, my love. None of them have the stench of Jacek's bloodline."

Alek shakes his head as most of the children leave the park.

The police squad car drives onto the trail, parks, and talks to Coach Phil for a moment. Inside the police cruiser, Officer Jeremy and Officer Paul briefly talk to Coach Phil.

Coach Phil smiles and shakes their hands. "Hey. Thanks for stopping by, guys."

Jeremy says, "No problem."

Paul replies, "Yeah, we just finished our dinner over at that barbecue joint down the street, so we were in the neighborhood anyway."

From behind Coach Phil, Tommy exclaims, "Hey, Coach!"

Coach Phil turns around to see Tommy and Ryan. Coach Phil asks, "Yeah, boys. What's up?"

Tommy asks, "You need help cleaning up before we leave? Ryan and I willing to help."

Coach Phil sees Tommy's and Ryan's parents waiting patiently in their cars and says, "Don't worry about it. I'll take care of it. Thanks for the offer though."

Tommy says, "Okay. Have a good night, Coach."

Tommy and Ryan pick up their packs and walk together to their awaiting rides.

Coach Phil asks, "Busy shift so far?"

Jeremy answers, "Nope. Not bad for a summer evening. But the night is young."

Paul interjects, "Yeah, we're on overtime. They want as many squad cars out as they can. There's been too much stuff going on."

Coach Phil replies, "I understand. The families appreciate you watching out for the kids so we can finish our practice. Means a lot."

Jeremy says, "No worries. All a part of the job."

Dispatch echoes through the radio saying, "Dispatch to Beat 1635, come in."

Paul picks up the mic, presses the push-to-talk button, and replies, "This is 1635 Bravo. Go ahead, Dispatch."

Dispatch replies, "1635, take in an accident at the corner of Lawrence Avenue and Central. Fire department is on scene."

Paul answers, "1635 Bravo en route, Dispatch."

Jeremy smiles and says, "Told you, the night is young."

Coach Phil says, "Indeed it is, gentlemen."

Paul says, "Have a good night. Be safe."

Coach Phil says, "You too. Thanks again."

Jeremy and Paul back out of the running trail and head toward Gunnison Avenue as they reactivate their flashing blue lights and sirens. The sirens fade out into the distance as the police cruiser continues to move east toward the call.

Angelica turns to Alek. She notices Alek's skin is beginning to turn a grayish green as it begins to look drier and more cracked. Angelica says, "My love. You're turning again."

Alek breaks away from his pondering thoughts and examines his hands. He replies, "I'm going through this mortal energy quicker than expected." Alek pauses mid-thought and looks down at Coach Phil who is cleaning up some equipment from baseball practice. He delivers a wicked smile as he continues, "Not to worry. This mortal is a friend of the children, yes?"

Angelica answers, "He must be." She exchanges a similar wicked smile and asks, "Thoughts?"

Alek answers, "Let's send a message. That nowhere and no one is safe. Especially the people they care about close to their hearts and home."

As Coach Phil completes his tasks in the quiet and now vacant park, most residents who usually use the park trail to exercise and walk their dogs have made their way home for the evening. The neighborhood is quietly restless and anxious to have a lot of unanswered questions be finally resolved. Most hope to have their summer evenings back to normal before the end of the season. As Coach Phil gathers the rest of the baseball equipment into his long red plastic wagon, he sees a couple walking down the trail toward him. He doesn't think anything about it and continues to walk his wagon toward his car. Coach Phil pauses along the trail as the couple stops and waits for Coach Phil to pass them on the trail. He starts to feel as though something is wrong. Alek and Angelica flash their red radiant eyes at Coach Phil. He gasps and tries to turn his wagon around to head in the opposite direction. His escape from Alek and Angelica is immediately halted by the sweeping wings of Pet as it breaks the nearby light post and lands right in front of Coach Phil. Pet flashes its glowing red eyes through the darkness, outlining its grossly sharp, bloody teeth. Coach Phil screams in terror and tries to turn around, only to discover he's surrounded by Alek, Angelica, and Pet. The coach's desperate cries for help are quickly silenced as an encircling mist surrounds him, and his life energy is sucked away from his body.

Alek and Angelica relish for a moment, enjoying the energy being poured over their bodies like a hot shower on a cold morning. As the energy absorbs into their bodies, Pet turns to the sound of an approaching dog being walked by their owner. The three quickly take flight and dash away from the park. The man holds back his dog and attempts to understand what he just witnessed. The mist quickly fades into the summer air, just as the man notices the decayed remains of Coach Phil.

Bishop Michael continues to head back west when he hears a request on his police scanner. Dispatch says, "Any available units in the northwest area district, respond to a report of another body being discovered at Dunham Park. Victim is an adult male."

Bishop Michael says, "Good God! They struck again!" He zips past the intersection of Lawrence Avenue and Central as he hears Officer Paul respond, "Dispatch. This is 1635 Bravo. We're finishing up at this traffic accident. You can put us on the ticket."

Dispatch replies, "Message received, 1635. Be advised supervisors and detectives are en route. Per command, the S.W.A.T. team from the airport will be en route to secure the skies surrounding the park via their helicopter."

Within minutes, dozens of emergency vehicles enter the area. Lights and sirens reflect and echo from every direction. Paul and Jeremy are the first to arrive. They are waved down by a gentleman with short spiky hair. Paul says, "This guy looks familiar. I think he's on the job."

Jeremy takes notice of the man in the park. The man pulls a police badge out of his pocket. Jeremy says, "Looks like you're right."

Paul and Jeremy drive their police cruiser back up the trail. Paul says, "Jesus Christ! I think it's Phil!"

Jeremy gasps. "Oh, God! We were just talking to him."

The man on the trail approaches the police cruiser with his dog and says, "Evening, gentlemen. The victim is right up the trail."

Paul and Jeremy exit the vehicle. Paul asks, "Thanks. Saw you flash your badge. Where are you assigned?"

The man answers, "Airport S.W.A.T. I'm Commander McKinley. This is my neighborhood. Had the evening off. Thought I could take old Rex here for a walk on the trail. And then all of this happened. Saw the whole thing. I still can't believe my eyes."

Within a few minutes of Paul and Jeremy arriving on scene, another unmarked police car arrives and parks along Narragansett Avenue. Detective Cunningham reaches for his mic and presses the push-to-talk button. "Dispatch. I'll be available on the scene of this potential homicide at Dunham Park. CPD has the ticket. I'm just here to assist."

Dispatch replies, "Message received, Detective."

Detective Cunningham exits his squad car, walks past dozens of onlookers, and walks up to the police barricade. He looks overhead and sees a police helicopter encircle the park continuously flashing and moving its spotlight up and down the trail and into the trees. Jeremy is along the yellow police tape securing the scene. He gives Detective Cunningham a sign to stop, but the detective flashes his detective badge at Jeremy. Jeremy's supervisor sees Detective Cunningham at the barricade. He exclaims, "Hey, Jeremy. Let the detective through, will ya!"

Jeremy answers, "You got it, Sarge." Jeremy lifts the yellow police tape.

Detective Cunningham says, "Thank you, young man."

Detective Cunningham approaches the now blanketed remains of Phil. He continues to talk to fellow investigators as Commander McKinley steps away from the social circle to take a call from one of his S.W.A.T. officers inside the helicopter. Commander McKinley continues to talk to Chris inside the helicopter and says, "Chris, I don't care if this isn't exactly in our wheelhouse! Whatever monsters are causing this death, chaos, and fear in our backyard, we are gonna hunt them down and take care of it ourselves. Phil was a neighbor of mine for Christ's sake!"

From the dark shadows of a nearby oak tree, Bishop Michael steps into the light and approaches Commander McKinley. Commander McKinley takes notice of the man in the gray overcoat with a silver cross around his neck. He says to Chris, "Hey, keep searching the area. If you find out anything else, call me back." Commander McKinley on guard asks, "Is there something I can help you with...Father?"

Bishop Michael nods his head and answers, "Thank you. My name is Bishop Michael. I'm currently staying at the local church down the street from here. If you can spare some time. I think we can help each other."

Robert, who lives closest to Dunham Park, sees several police and other emergency vehicles fly down his block. He hears the whipping helicopter blades echo down the block. He says to himself, "What the hell is going on?" He grabs his phone and calls Ryan.

Ryan answers, "Hey, loser. What are you up to?"

Robert replies, "Dude, no bullshit! Are you still over at Dunham Park finishing your practice?"

Ryan answers, "Not at all. I'm back home. I just opened up a family-size bag of rippled chips, cracked open a can of soda, and I was turning on the ball game. Why? What's up? Do you want to come over and hang out?"

Robert replies, "Dude, I don't think my mom is gonna let me out of the house right now. Haven't you've been hearing all the sirens in the area?"

Ryan says, "Yeah, but it's the city, bro. There's sirens going up and down the main streets all the time. Especially over the summer. Why?"

Robert exclaims, "Dude. I think something major just happened over at Dunham Park! My mom just walked down the block to see if she can find out what happened. Was Liam there?"

Ryan shakes his head as he answers, "Nope. He couldn't make practice."

Robert's mom walks back into the house looking distraught with her hand over her mouth. Robert pauses in mid-thought as he looks at his mother.

Ryan asks, "Dude, you still there? What's going on?"

Robert replies, "Hold on a sec. My mom just walked back inside." Robert looks back at his mother and asks, "What happened, Mom? Is everything okay?"

Robert's mom shakes her head. "No. Nothing is okay. Phil, the baseball coach, was…now you listen to me." Robert's mom pauses and walks closely to Robert as she continues, "You don't go outside unless you ask first. Especially after dark until further notice. Is that understood?" Robert nods his head and his mom continues, "Now, you can watch TV, play video games, or talk to your friends over the phone for the rest of the night. That's fine. I have to call your father. If you need anything, I'll be upstairs."

As Robert's mom grabs her phone out of her pocket, she promptly walks up the stairs and closes her bedroom door behind her.

Ryan asks, "Dude! Dude? You still there? Don't keep me hanging, bro?"

Robert finally replies, "Ryan. Something really bad must have happened to your baseball coach."

Ryan exclaims, "What! Something happened to Coach Phil! What happened?"

Robert answers, "I can only assume that it's bad enough to have a lot of cops, a helicopter, and yellow-and-red police tape going around the park. This is all getting too familiar right now."

Ryan says, "You got that right. I'll call Liam and you call Boo so we can all be on the call together. They have to find out what's going on."

Robert and Ryan catch Liam and Boo up on the events of the evening. Liam and Boo are huddled upstairs in Liam's bedroom. Ryan asks, "Hey, Liam, are your parents around?"

Liam says, "They are both down in the basement watching a movie together. They probably don't know anything yet. At least for now."

Boo says, "We have to figure out something. Before someone else gets hurt or worse."

Liam says, "We still don't know anything about Coach Phil yet."

Robert sees a news van roll down his block. He adds, "Well, we will probably know more when the evening news comes on. The news vans are here."

Ryan asks, "What can we do? Honestly, it's just us."

Liam and Boo fill in Ryan and Robert with everything they've been doing with Bishop Michael.

Robert says, "Wow! That's amazing. This sounds a lot like… like?"

Ryan interjects, "Sounds a lot like Iron River, Michigan, but this sounds worse. And what makes it worse is it's happening in our backyard. Honestly, Liam, what are we gonna do?"

Liam contemplates his answer for a moment. He then says, "Bishop Michael is planning some more training tomorrow morning. Maybe we can figure out a way to get together afterward. Give me tonight to figure something out, and I'll get back to you first thing tomorrow."

....

CHAPTER 27

THAT'S NOT A GARGOYLE ON THAT BUILDING!

Will and Annie go to bed without watching the news, unaware of the horrific incident that occurred down the street from their house. The following morning, Annie wakes up to her phone ringing. She turns over and looks at the caller ID. It's her cousin, Brock. She thinks, *I wonder why he's calling now?* Annie answers, "Hey, Brock. What's up? How are things at your suburban department?"

Brock answers, "Hey, Annie. Morning. That's one of the reasons I'm calling you."

"Why? What's going on?"

Brock replies, "Look, I'm just coming off shift, and the ambulance just went out to your mom's address."

Annie jumps out of bed and says, "What! What was the nature of the call?"

Brock answers, "The nature was a woman complaining of shortness of breath."

Annie says, "I'll call you right back! Let me try Mom."

Brock replies, "Sounds good. I'll try to get a hold of someone on the ambulance and see if they can tell me anything."

Annie attempts of call Tina. No answer.

Will rolls over in bed and asks, "What's the matter, honey?"

"It's Mom! I'm trying to figure it out. An ambulance is on the way to her house."

Will exclaims, "Oh, God!"

After a few missed attempts to reach Tina, Annie calls back Brock. Brock answers, "Hey, Annie. Tina saw that you were trying to call, but the medics were putting her on some oxygen. I talked to the medics myself. They know this call involves family and they said Tina gave them full permission to disclose everything. Tina got up this morning feeling dizzy and out of breath. She was home alone at the time since your dad left early for work. She called 911 right away. The medics said she's doing well. But they're taking her to Hinsbrook Hospital just as a precaution so they can run some tests."

Annie says, "Brock, thank you so much. I appreciate it. I'll make my way over to the hospital in a few minutes."

Annie wants to leave quickly but Will reminds her that Bishop Michael is planning to meet Liam and Boo this morning to continue their training. Annie says, "Okay. That's right. What are we gonna do?"

Annie thinks for a moment as she grabs her phone off the nightstand. She gasps as she reads several texts from other parents regarding Coach Phil.

Will asks, "What is it, honey?"

Annie looks at Will and says, "The parents from the baseball team have me on this group thread. It's Coach Phil! He's…he's dead!"

Will exclaims, "WHAT! What do you mean he's…dead? What happened?"

Annie reads are few more messages and then responds, "I think it's best if Liam and Boo are with Bishop Michael." Annie hands the phone over to Will so he can read the message feed.

After a brief moment, Will nods his head as he says, "You're right. It's not safe for them to leave the house without him. I'll get the van ready while you contact him."

Annie explains to Bishop Michael their predicament. The bishop agrees that it's best for Liam and Boo to stay with him. Bishop Michael says, "That's fine, Annie. I'll be there in a few minutes. While you're waiting, take the time to explain the situation with Liam and Boo. It's best for them to understand just in case something goes wrong with your mother."

Annie asks, "Bishop. Are you aware of what happened to Liam's baseball coach?"

Bishop Michael answers, "I am aware of what happened. I didn't know it was Liam's coach. Good God! I'll add some additional prayers this morning for everyone involved."

Annie replies, "Thank you, Bishop. I will certainly talk to Liam and Boo before you arrive. I'm so worried. Especially for Liam. How much can a young man take? We will be here waiting."

Within minutes, Bishop Michael arrives and Will and Annie leave for the hospital. Bishop Michael takes Liam and Boo back to the church where they spend the rest of the morning training with him and Father Luke. Bishop Michael offers his condolences to Liam for the loss of his baseball coach. He could tell that Liam looked distraught all morning. As the morning progresses toward midday, Bishop Michael gets a call from Commander McKinley. He walks over to his phone and answers, "Hello, Commander. Thank you for responding. How can I help you?"

Commander McKinley replies. "I've given this whole situation a lot of thought when I arrived to work this morning. Ever since I witnessed that monster fly over the northwest side of the city and after I saw what I saw last night, I'm convinced that maybe we need help from a higher power. I'm a Catholic soul, after all. So is the majority of my team. I talked it over with them, and they would like you to meet with us as soon as possible."

Bishop Michael looks at Liam and Boo as they both take a break from training and talk to Father Luke. Bishop Michael says, "Let me see what I can do. I'll get back to you shortly."

Commander McKinley says, "Sounds good, Bishop. I'll be awaiting your call."

Bishop Michael walks over to Liam and Boo and says, "I think this is a good place to end our training for today. Both of you are very quick learners. I've seen some significant improvement."

Liam says, "Thank you, Bishop."

The bishop replies, "It's been my pleasure. You're very welcome."

Boo asks, "Have you heard anything from our parents?"

"I haven't. Not yet at least. Have you heard anything?"

Liam and Boo check their phones. No messages yet.

Bishop Michael says, "Hmm. I hope everything is going okay. I know it takes time to receive results from all those medical tests.

I have to leave shortly. There's a team of men who are willing to help even the playing field against Alek and Angelica. But I feel that shortly after meeting this team and doing some preparation, it will be time for us to do our work. Which leads me to what will be best for both of you."

Liam looks at Boo. Boo winks back at Liam. Liam says, "Honestly, Bishop. I think it's best for us to stay at our friend Robert's house. He lives right down the street."

Boo adds, "Yeah. We know he's home and at least one of his parents are home. We can stay there until we hear otherwise. At least we'll be with friends and close to home."

Bishop Michael thinks it over for a minute, *That's probably not a bad idea. Alek and Angelica will most likely look for Liam and Boo at either their home or outside the church. And I know Father Luke has a laundry list of other church obligations that await his attention.* He says, "It's probably for the best. Let's plan on that then. Please, talk to your friend and allow me to talk to the parent over the phone before we arrive. And I'll also call your mother. Let her know about your whereabouts." Liam and Boo both agree.

After a quick discussion over the phone with Robert and his mother, Bishop Michael drives Liam and Boo over to their house. He checks his silver cross. No signs of activity. He thanks the family for their hospitality, but before he leaves, he bends down and looks at Liam and Boo. "I talked briefly with your mother. Your grandmother is doing fine for now. They are awaiting some more test results. They are fine with you staying with this family. Now, please. If you get a message from me, have this family take you back to your house. That's where you'll be safest. The backup plan, if Father Luke arrives to your friend's house, you are to go with Father Luke back to the church. I added some extra layers of protection there as well." Liam and Boo nod their heads. Bishop Michael looks at Liam's and Boo's backpacks and says, "Do you have most of your supplies?"

Boo says, "Yup. I got my bow and arrow. Packed it in my bigger camping backpack."

Liam nods his head as he says, "Yes, sir. Got my silver chain mail and the war pick. My bag weighs a ton."

Bishop Michael nods his head and says, "Now, one last thing."

Liam asks, "What's that, Bishop?"

Bishop Michael answers, "Keep your supplies in your bags. Don't show them off to your friends. They aren't toys."

Liam says, "Understood, sir."

As Bishop Michael drives away, Robert's mother welcomes them into the house and says, "Isn't that so nice that the parish priest is willing to help the family? Sorry to hear about your grandmother. I hope she's doing better. Why don't you make yourself comfortable down in the basement. I'll warm up some of my husband's homemade pizza. I know how much you like it. I'll let you know when it's ready."

Liam, Boo, and Robert make their way down to the basement. Robert goes over to the television remote and turns up the volume. Liam asks, "Did you text Ryan that we are over here yet?"

Robert says, "Yeah. He said he's finishing a snack and he'll be right over."

Boo asks, "Didn't he know your mom was warming up your dad's famous homemade pizza?"

Robert nods his head. "Yup. He knew but he said he wanted to have a pregame snack before the main event."

Liam and Boo laugh. Liam says, "Thanks for the laugh. I kind of needed that."

Robert says, "No problem." Robert smiles at Boo and asks, "Any news on your grandmother, Boo?"

Boo answers, "They're running some tests. Sounds like she's doing okay. She's a tough lady."

Robert responds, "Glad to hear. I'm glad that you're safe after what happened last night."

Boo blushes. "Thanks. I usually go to the practice so I can hang out with Maddie, but it was best for us to stay home."

Liam gives Robert the side-eye. "Yeah. I'm sure you were concerned about my safety too...right, buddy?"

Robert laughs it off as he responds, "Yeah. Sure. Of course. Brothers for life, you know."

Boo tries to change the subject. She looks at Liam and asks, "Hey! Did you ever hear back from Ellie and Simon? Maybe they found something."

Liam thinks for a moment. He answers, "You're right. I haven't heard from them."

There's a ring at the doorbell. Robert receives a chime on his phone. It's Ryan with a simple message saying, "Here."

Robert's mother answers the door and escorts Ryan down to the basement entrance. As he walks down the stairs she says, "Pizza will be ready in a few minutes. I only ask that you eat it up here. I'm tired of cleaning up leftover plates and soda cans."

Robert says, "Thanks, Mom. Will do."

As Robert's mother walks away from the basement entrance, Ryan says, "Okay. What did I miss?"

Robert responds, "Nothing yet. Liam is trying to get hold of his cousin back in Philly."

Liam hears Ellie's phone ring a few times before she answers, "Hey, Liam! How are things in Chicago? I'm here with Simon right now. I have you on speaker."

Simon interjects, "What's happening, monster slayer?"

Liam puts his phone on speaker and says, "It's going. That's for sure. Boo's here along with Robert and Ryan. They were with Boo and me when this all started back in Michigan."

Simon says, "Ah. The other fellow monster slayer associates. Nice to finally talk to you. We helped Liam and Boo vanquish some evil spirits here last summer."

Ryan and Robert laugh, and Ryan says, "Hey! Thanks for looking out for our friends. Sounds like that Philly crew really stepped up when the time arrived."

Ellie responds, "No worries. What's families for?"

Liam asks, "Hey! Were you and Simon able to find out anything else regarding our current predicament in Chicago?"

Simon says, "Yeah. The old dude that owned the legacy shop confirmed the details of that journal you found. Turns out, the family has a history and a long-standing alignment with the Catholic Church. They were working together for a long time while being defenders against the forces of darkness. As it shows on the family crest. Which is so incredibly awesome and wicked, by the way."

Liam responds, "Thanks. But we have another situation that's kicking up momentum really quick around here. This Angelica is starting to stack up victims all across the city."

Simon says, "Yeah. I've been following this story. The news articles are wild! I've been trying to figure out more about this Angelica. I can't find much about her online, but I have another avenue that you might want to try."

Boo asks, "What's that?"

Simon answers, "Here's what I'm thinking. After I came to a lot of dead ends in my research, I shifted my focus. I started to focus more on the rich history of Chicago to see if I can find some parallels between Angelica's story and the historical timeline with the city."

Ellie interjects, "Get to the point, Simon!"

Simon says, "Sorry. Anyway, the Chicago Public Library. Have you ever been to that really big library downtown? It's supposed to be one of the oldest libraries in the city."

Liam says. "I haven't been there. No."

The rest of Chicago crew shake their heads as Simon continues, "Okay, so there's this huge library that holds the largest archive and record preservation for the city. The site was chosen to hold all of the records due to its fire-resistant construction after the Great Chicago Fire of 1871. The records include building blueprints after Chicago had to rebuild itself and all of the old records of cemetery lots. According to my research, a lot of coffins and graves had to be moved during the reconstruction of the city. I know it's a shot in the dark, but maybe you can find out when, where, or if Angelica purchased a lot under the same alias she used when she crossed the great ocean blue."

Liam smiles at Boo and says, "Simon, you're a genius. Thank you."

Ellie interjects, "Don't help that massive ego of his. He already has the biggest head ever."

Boo laughs. "Thanks again. I'll call you later, Ellie."

Ellie responds, "Yes, please do."

Simon says, "Well, I'll leave you to it. The library is off State Street and Van Buren Avenue. You can't miss it. It's a massive building of red brick and a jade green roof. If I'm ever in town, I would love to check it out. Looks amazing. Be safe out there, monster slayers."

The phone call ends, and Liam looks at his watch. Robert's mother calls down from upstairs, "Okay! Come on up and make a plate! Pizza is ready. If you want any soda, just help yourselves to anything in the fridge in the basement."

Robert exclaims, "Thanks, Mom! We'll be up in a minute!" Robert lowers his voice to a whisper as the crew huddles together. "Okay, so what's the plan?"

All eyes focus on Liam. Liam looks at his watch and says, "Maybe we can head down there. As quickly as we can at least."

Ryan asks, "What? Downtown? Are you serious?"

Liam continues, "Look, it's simple. We take the bus over to the blue line train station and head straight downtown." Liam reaches into his pocket and pulls out some money. He continues, "I got this cash from my grandmom after we helped clean out her garage."

Boo interjects, "Yeah. I got my cash on me too."

Liam continues, "We take a quick cab as soon as we reach downtown over to the library. We do our research and be home before sunset."

Robert says, "Yeah, that sounds easy in theory, but you're forgetting one thing."

Liam asks, "What's that?"

Robert answers, "What do we do about the parental unit upstairs?"

Ryan says, "A little lie never hurt anybody."

Robert says, "Now that statement alone is a total lie. What are you thinking?"

Ryan continues, "I'll try to pull a fast one. Tell them we are planning to meet up with Tommy and Maddie back at my house. Say that we are gonna stay at my house and play a few video games. Keep the bullshit story short and sweet. No details. It might work."

Boo adds, "I don't think so."

Liam interjects, "Actually, we pulled a few quick ones off Robert's mom before."

Boo adds, "What? What are you talking about?"

Ryan and Robert smile at Liam.

Liam says, "We pulled stuff like this so Robert, Ryan, and I could head down to the city to check out a couple of ball games last summer."

Robert smiles, "Yeah. We figured out how to navigate the different train lines. Hey! Do you think Tommy, Timmy and Maddie will be on board?"

Liam texts Tommy. As Liam awaits a response, Robert's mother yells down to the basement, "Hey, all! The pizza is getting cold. Come on up!"

Robert shouts back, "Sorry, Mom! Be up in a minute!"

Liam receives a message from Tommy saying, "Timmy is out but Maddie and I are game. Whatever you want."

While Liam, Boo, and Ryan are finishing their pizza, Robert attempts to convince his mom. Robert always knew how to perfectly set up his mom. Ryan went right to work in the kitchen by cleaning all the dishes and loading the dishwasher. As the rest of crew finishes their meal, Robert takes each of their plates, wipes down the table, and puts all of the soda bottles into the recycling can. Robert notices the recycling starting to fill up. Robert winks at Liam and says in a low voice, "Dude, grab the trash bag and follow my lead."

Liam picks up the trash bag and begins to follow Robert toward the side entrance door. The rest of the crew follows suit. Robert's mother says, "Well, thank you all for helping me clean up this kitchen. That's so nice of you."

Ryan says, "Hey, it's the least we can do after a wonderful meal."

Boo adds, "Thank you so much."

Robert's mother asks, "Now, what are you kids thinking of doing this afternoon?"

Robert answers, "Actually, we were thinking of meeting up with Tommy and Maddie, after we throw out the trash, over at Ryan's house. He just got a couple of new video games. Figure we can check them out."

Robert's mother says, "Well, I guess that's okay. It's right down the street. Oh, go ahead. Have fun and please just stay on the block and be home before dinner. Deal?"

Robert smiles. "Deal. Thanks, Mom."

Robert's mom adds, "And Liam and Boo, if you hear from your folks that they are on their way home, please come back and I'll be happy to drop you off."

Boo smiles and says, "Of course. Thank you."

Liam, Boo, Robert, and Ryan start walking down the block toward Ryan's house. Robert looks back as he gives one more wave to his mother before she steps back inside the house. Robert says, "I think we're in the clear."

Liam nods his head as he notices Tommy and Maddie walking down the street toward them. As they approach each other, Tommy asks, "So, what's the plan?"

Liam asks, "Did you eat lunch?"

Tommy and Maddie nod their heads, and Tommy says, "Yes. Maddie and I both some had some fruit, chips, and sandwiches."

Liam replies, "Perfect. Then let's keep moving. We don't have much time."

Tommy asks, "Where we going?"

Ryan answers, "To the blue line. We are going downtown."

Tommy stops in his tracks and holds back his sister. He exclaims, "Wait! What do you mean we're going downtown? And the blue line train station is like six blocks from here."

Robert says, "Look, Liam has a plan. Maybe we can find out more about the mystery guest who's been tearing up this city."

Liam stops the group and looks at Tommy. He says, "Sorry I didn't tell you all the details in the text. I get it if you don't want to go. But we might have a chance to find out where these monsters might be hiding. And I have a feeling if we find them, we'll probably find the three high school girls who went missing too. We might have to search through a lot of old records in a short amount of time, so we need all hands on deck. We can use your help."

Tommy looks at Maddie and asks, "Are you up for some walking?"

Maddie says, "Yes. Anything to get away from home for a little bit. I've been cooped up the last couple of days."

Tommy nods and says, "Okay. We're in. But we have to get back as soon as we can. My folks think we are at Ryan's house too."

Liam says, "Of course. Promise."

The group makes their way to the blue line train station and into downtown. When they arrive downtown they find a taxi van big enough to fit everyone. Liam tells the driver where he would like to get dropped off. As they arrive, they quickly marvel at the structure that seems to be frozen in a time when literary assembly halls were turned into cathedral works of art. They walk through the main doors and see the reflection of each of their steps off the high gloss marble tile floor. Liam approaches the main counter and asks where to find the old record archive. A woman working at the counter cautiously asks the group why they want to see the archive. Ryan, who always been the fast smooth-talker in the group, quickly interjects, "We're all in the Scouts, ma'am. And we are working on a merit badge for research and discovery. We figured this is the place to go."

The woman smiles as she stands up from her desk and insists the crew follow her toward the back of the library. They walk past stunning works of stone and canvas art, dozens of occupied desks, several rows of computers, and almost a countless number of books awaiting their next readers. They walk through a glass door with black writing along the side reading: ARCHIVE SECTION.

Inside the Archive Section, they see old maps of the city limits in the early part of the nineteenth and twentieth centuries, a painting of Chicago burning during the Great Fire, and old posters advertising the Chicago World Fair. The woman directs them to a computer station in the center of the room. She says, "From here, you can look up almost anything that is within the archive. You can look up old buildings, street maps, deceased residents from the city, and areas that were later annexed as additional sections of the city. If you need anything, please let me know. Good luck with your project."

Robert jumps onto the computer. He looks at Liam and asks, "What should we look up first?"

Liam tells Robert to look up the alias name of Angelica. Liam adds, "Figure that has to be the starting point. If we can't find it here, we won't be able to find it."

Robert searches the name and says, "Son of a bitch! I've got something!"

Boo interjects, "Really? Where should we look?"

Robert answers, "This name appears on a few documents relating to the purchase of some property in the Cook County Forest Preserve and the construction of a mausoleum inside the Saint Lucas Cemetery. Check cabinet B12 and a file numbered 167452 and cabinet C17 and a file number 193830."

Tommy and Maddie look for the file in cabinet B12, while Ryan and Boo look for the file in cabinet C17. They bring the files over to a nearby unoccupied table. Tommy searches the file until he sees the name. He says, "Here it is! So, this lady purchased some land near the Saint Lucas Cemetery. But wait. That doesn't make any sense. That would make this lady…?"

Liam smiles as he interjects, "Yeah. We know, Tommy. She's like super old. That's our mystery lady. An old witch that has family ties to Boo and me."

Tommy adds, "Okay. So, this is what you guys do when I'm not around. Got it."

Boo searches the other file until she finds the record of the mausoleum construction. Boo says, "Yup. This is her alias name. Looks like she used an alias name for our other mystery guest, Alek. It says someone else is buried there. But she probably used a phony name to hide Alek from the order."

Tommy asks, "Wait...what? Who's Alek? And who's the order?"

Liam smiles as Boo answers, "Alek is an evil wizard who was resurrected by his ancient witch girlfriend. The order is a group of secret elite priests of the church who fight against the forces of evil."

Liam adds, "And that thing that flew over our baseball game is like their own personal big ugly monster."

Maddie hugs Tommy as Tommy says, "Jesus! Anything else?"

Liam looks up at the old maps of the city. He pulls out his phone and searches the location of Saint Lucas Cemetery.

Boo asks, "What are you doing, big brother?"

Liam answers, "Looking up something. Robert, you said the Saint Lucas Cemetery, correct?"

Robert looks at the computer to verify and says, "Yup, that's correct. Why? What's up?"

Liam answers, "I'm reading a quick article. That cemetery was closed and later abandoned after all living relatives of anyone buried there finally died off. It's now minimally maintained by the Cook County Forest Preserve." He approaches the map on the wall and finds the intersection of Foster and Cicero. He points to it and says, "That's where it is! Right in that forest preserve close to home. That's gotta be it." The crew gathers around Liam and looks at the map.

Boo asks, "So what's the next move?"

Liam answers, "It's time to head back. We got what we needed."

As the group exits the library, the woman who walked them to the archive stands up and asks, "Did you find what you were looking for?"

Ryan answers with a smile, "Yes, ma'am. We sure did. Thank you."

They exit the library, and Liam tries to locate—and hopefully wave down—another taxi van so they can make the journey back home. The crew takes the moment to look at the majestic beauty of their marvelous city. They admire the tall buildings, the classic architecture, and the jade green gargoyles on top of the library roof. Ryan says, "This place is pretty amazing."

Robert says, "Yeah, you can say that again. How often do you see buildings with concrete gargoyles hanging over the towers and roofs?"

Liam flags down a taxi van as it drifts away from the lane and slows down next to Liam. Tommy looks up and says, "That's funny."

Ryan asks, "What's that?"

Tommy answers, "Well, these other gargoyles on the roof are that cool green color. But this one over here is gray."

Robert adds, "Must have been added on later or something."

Boo looks up and asks, "What are you guys talking about?" As she looks up at the gray gargoyle, its eyes flash radiantly bright red.

Ryan exclaims, "Holy shit! That's no gargoyle on that building!"

Boo shouts to Liam. Liam looks up and shouts at everyone to get inside the taxi van. The crew flies inside the taxi as Pet begins to take flight and swoop down toward them. The taxi driver asks, "Everyone on board?"

Liam exclaims, "Yeah! Just go! Train station and step on it!"

CHAPTER 28

....

THE CHASE

The taxi speeds away toward the train station as Pet dives down and scrapes the top of the taxi van's hood. Pet expands his mighty wings and ascends to the top of nearby skyscrapers. The taxi driver exclaims, "Jesus Christ! What the hell was that?"

Liam replies, "I don't think Jesus has anything to do with that thing. Just keep driving, please!"

Ryan looks out the back window and says, "Anyone see him? I don't see him." All eyes are glued across nearby windows.

Tommy looks with his sister and says, "You see anything, Maddie?"

Maddie shakes her head.

Tommy says, "Nope. We don't see anything."

Liam looks at Boo and asks, "See anything, Boo?"

Boo looks at Robert, and they both shake their heads. Boo says, "No. Maybe he lost us in the sea of taxis on the road. But I feel like it's not gone."

Liam says, "I'll take your word for it. That thing knew exactly where we were and probably followed us all the way from the neighborhood." Liam looks up toward the taxi driver as he wipes the sweat off his wet and wrinkly brow. Liam asks, "How much further till we get there?"

The taxi driver nervously replies, "Jus-just a co-couple of blocks until we get there. I've been living and driving in this city for a long time. Thought I saw everything until just a few minutes ago."

Ryan jokingly says, "Yeah, well, that's Chicago and the Liam and Boo Crew for you."

A slight chuckle from everyone inside helps dissipate the tension between the crew and their driver. They continue to look out their windows as the taxi driver approaches the destination and pulls over along the curb. The taxi driver says, "Okay, kids. We made it. Now get home safe, okay?"

The crew exits the taxi. They look up toward the sky and scan the surrounding area. Liam is the last to exit the cab. Liam asks, "How much do I owe you, sir?"

The driver looks at his meter and says, "Let's make it twenty bucks and call it even."

Liam reaches into his pocket for a twenty-dollar bill. Robert looks up at a towering skyscraper across the street. He sees something moving along the gray stone luxury penthouse suites. He takes a more concentrated look as Pet flashes his radiant red eyes and opens its massive wings. Robert exclaims as he points upward, "Guys!"

Boo asks, "What do you see?"

Robert replies, "We didn't lose shit!"

Ryan says, "Oh, shit!"

Tommy grabs Maddie's hand.

Boo exclaims, "Liam!"

Liam hands the driver a twenty-dollar bill and quickly exits the van. They witness Pet dive from the top of the building down toward them. Liam looks at everyone who seems to be frozen in fright and exclaims, "Everyone! Into the train station! Now!"

Ryan replies, "I agree. Time to go!"

Pet screams a loud howl as it sees the crew scatter into the train station. He continues his quick descent and lands on top of the taxi's roof before the driver is able to pull away. Tempered broken glass showers and sprays in all directions as the roof caves into the taxi's interior. The loud thump and crashing bang startles all nearby bystanders, and the flow of traffic slows down to a screeching halt. The sight of Pet as he screams and displays his impressively sharp teeth sends everyone away in a frenzy. The taxi driver crawls out and away from the van as some decent bystanders help the man to his feet. A nearby woman wearing medical scrubs grabs a plastic bag of tissues from her purse and applies direct pressure to the man's head as a steady stream of dark red blood oozes from his forehead. Other bystanders attempt to back away to a safe distance as they pull out their phones and try to record the flying beast. A few other bystanders run in terror and scream, "Call 911! Call 911!"

Pet stomps off the roof and jumps away from the taxi. The remaining bystanders and onlookers who want to record the monster run away in horror as Pet briskly stomps toward the entrance of the train station. The automatic doors slide away from Pet when he crosses the threshold of the train station. He continues his frantic search for the crew as frightened travelers desperately dash away in opposite directions. Beyond the screaming and shouting, a recorded message echoes through the long corridor saying, "Welcome to Chicago. Please watch your step and have a safe day. If you see something, say something to our courteous staff members and security teams."

✦ ✦ ✦

While Pet makes a loud entrance through a train station, Bishop Michael is meeting with Commander McKinley at his headquarters along the airport. Bishop Michael concludes his briefing on the order, Angelica, Alek, and their wide array of monsters, powers, and magic. Commander McKinley shakes his head. "This has to be the wildest story I've even heard in my whole life. But I've seen what I've seen. I hate to admit it, but I can't help but believe you. My team was one of the first ones on the scene when that flying beast tore through and killed a maintenance worker and a security guard right here at the airport. I've never seen penetrating wounds like that. And you're talking to an experienced veteran on the force. The question I have to you is how can we stop it?"

Bishop Michael answers, "With your help, we can even the playing field. When they take flight, we'll take flight and bring the fight to them. I can track them with my silver cross."

Commander McKinley nods his head. "Well, that's sounds just fine for you. But what about myself and my men? We don't have fancy holy weapons. Just the standard weapons to take down almost anything. Except, of course, monsters in your line of work."

Bishop Michael answers, "Holy water won't work well with your brass shells and standard tips, Commander. I can, however, spray your rounds with holy oils. It won't affect their functions."

Commander McKinley rotates in his chair as he contemplates this plan. He stops in mid-motion and nods his head. "Okay, Bishop. We'll do it your way." Commander McKinley looks at Chris and says, "On my orders, empty all magazines and hand each round to the bishop." Chris nods his head and heads toward the armory.

Chris walks back into Commander McKinley's office with the magazines. Commander McKinley says, "Chris, the bishop here is a man of service who served down range in several drop zones. I'm sure he'll be an excellent addition to our team and the hunt for these monsters." Commander McKinley adds, "Chris is our sharp shooter."

Bishop Michael asks, "Is that right?"

Commander McKinley answers, "He's the best shot we have on the team. He's like a skilled craftsman with his weapon. Still makes his own rounds in the armory."

Bishop Michael says, "That's excellent. In fact, I have an idea for you, Chris."

Chris asks, "What's that, Bishop?"

Bishop Michael goes into his satchel and pulls out a small bag containing pebble-sized nuggets of silver. He says, "Please allow me to accompany you to your armory. If we can, I'll give you a weapon's upgrade to your ammunition."

Chris looks at Commander McKinley who nods his head. Chris says, "That's sounds fine, Bishop. Follow me."

Pet leaves a trail of destruction in his path. Anything in his way is ripped off the hinges and foundations. The crew flies down the stairs to the mezzanine level. They run through the white-tiled halls and the dirty concrete floors of the long passage as they hear the sound of an approaching train. They follow the blue line down to the platform sub-level. Maddie slips and falls as a frantic middle-aged man pushes her out of the way. Maddie screams and begins to cry, "Tommy! Please, help me."

Tommy hears the shallow cry of his sister and turns abruptly. He runs back and kneels down next to his sister. Liam is the last one from the crew to make it down the steps to the platform. He sees

Tommy block his sister from the panicked travelers as they run past. Liam stops in front of Tommy as he gets shoved by another terrified bystander. He asks, "What's the matter, Tommy?"

Tommy picks up Maddie and says, "It's her knee. She hurt it bad when that asshole pushed her down."

Liam commands, "Okay. Let's scoop her up and get on this train!" Liam looks up the stairs back toward the mezzanine level and sees Pet flash his ghastly red eyes at him. Pet howls down the narrow stairway corridor as he locks eyes on his target. Liam looks at the crew inside the train. Boo sticks her head out and waves for them to get on the train. Boo hears a bell tone and an overhead voice saying, "Caution. The doors are about to close."

Boo shouts, "Liam! Come on! The train is leaving!"

Liam grabs Tommy by the shoulder and runs alongside him and Maddie as Pet quickly advances from behind. Pet knocks everything out of his way. Metal trash cans and anchored benches get ripped out of their foundations and thrown out toward the tracks. Large glass poster signs shatter and break like small cheap toys. Liam, Tommy, and Maddie step across the threshold just as the doors close behind them. Pet scratches and claws at the metal and reinforced glass. The crew and other bystanders scream in horror as Pet desperately attempts to gain access. The train begins to pull away from the platform. Pet attempts to follow and locks eyes with the crew. He stops at the end of the platform as the train disappears into a dark tunnel underground.

Terrified passengers shake and try to calm down after their dangerous encounter with Pet. Several people each ask: "What was that thing?" "Is it still following us?" "Did anybody dial 911?"

Tommy finds an open seat and places Maddie down. Liam goes over to better assess the wound. Tommy, with tears in his eyes, looks up at Liam and says, "We'll have to get Maddie to a hospital, Liam. She hit that concrete floor really hard with her right knee."

Liam assesses the knee. The right knee continues to swell as it changes color from bright red to dark purple. Liam says, "I don't think it's broken. Maybe a decent sprain."

Tommy shakes his head. "I knew this was a bad idea. I should have stayed home. My parents are gonna freak out."

Liam replies, "Don't worry. It will be fine. Just put it on me. I'll take the heat. Most importantly, we are all here and doing okay." Liam, out of breath, pulls out his inhaler and takes his medicine.

Ryan peeks over at Tommy and Liam and asks, "How's she doing?"

Maddie continues to cry and shake, between the pain and panic.

Liam says, "We'll be okay."

Ryan asks, "Do you think we lost it?"

Liam looks out the window at the pitch blackness as several small lights dash alongside the tunnel. He says, "I can't tell. Can't see anything out there."

They begin to hear screams erupting from the farthest trailing train car. The double sliding doors at the end of the crew's car slams open as several people run away in horror. Liam looks at Boo and nods his head. Boo opens her backpack as Liam opens his backpack. Boo throws a leather quiver holding a dozen silver-tipped arrows over her shoulder and grabs her nearly reconstructed bow. Liam dons the silver chain mail and grabs his family's war pick.

Ryan asks, "Wait! You guys have been carrying that stuff around all day?"

Boo looks at Robert and Ryan and says, "Stay here."

Liam looks at Tommy and Maddie says, "Yeah, stay here. Let me and Boo handle this."

Liam and Boo push past the panicked passengers as they rush past Liam and Boo and run way from danger. They enter the last car and see what is causing all of the commotion. Pet is running and gliding as he attempts to follow the train moving along the tracks. They see his glowing eyes flash and grow bigger as Pet moves within striking distance of the train. The recorded voice overhead says, "The next stop will be Division Street. Followed by Damen and Western Avenues." Pet leaps to close the gap between himself and moving train. Pet is able to grab hold of a u-shaped metal handle on the outside rear door. He uses all of his strength to tear the door clear off its hinges! Liam and Boo scream as Pet's strength and force causes the train car to shake.

Boo says, "What are you thinking? This train is gonna slow down any second for the next stop."

Liam sees the flashes of energy spark and arch from the electrified third rail running parallel to the train. He says to Boo, "If we can get him to land on that third rail, he'll be toasted like a critter in an old cartoon."

Boo grabs an arrow out of her quiver and lines it up along her draw string. She asks, "How do you know about a third rail? What are you, a train conductor on the side?"

Liam shakes his head and firmly grips his weapon. "No. I heard Dad talking about it. He has to go to incidents on the subway every once in a while."

Boo approaches the ripped-apart rear hatch and says, "Time to test out this bow for real. Just hold on to me."

Liam nods his head, grabs a hold of her backpack, and steps behind a row of seats. Boo draws back her bow and attempts to line up her target. She focuses on her breathing just as Bishop Michael instructed. She releases the bow. The arrow flies through the dark tunnel toward its target. Pet ducks down just as the arrow sails past him. Boo says, "Damn it!"

Liam starts to feel the train begin to slow down. He says, "Just try again. We're out of time!"

Boo grabs another arrow and draws the string on her bow. She takes a wider stance as she begins to feel the momentum of the train try to pull her backward. Pet closes the gap as the train begins to pull into the station. Pet growls at Boo. Boo releases the arrow at the fast-approaching target. It punctures Pet and tears through its gray hairy flesh in between its webbed wings and its shoulder. Pet screams out in horror as the pain of the silver arrow rips through his body. Pet stumbles and trips over its own momentum and feet. It tumbles onto the third rail and screams in shear agony as hundreds of electrified volts travel through its monstrous body. The lights on train begin to flicker as the train reaches the platform. The train doors open and terrified passengers run away in horror. The power from the third rail launches Pet away and he bounces off the tunnel wall. It quivers as the remaining joules of energy continue zapping through its roasted body. Liam says, "Good job, Sis."

The lights stop flickering with the sound of running power being restored through the third rail. The train pulls away from the station. Pet is left to die alone in the slightly illuminated gaping tunnel.

The conductor, unaware of what's been happening in the back of the train, continues along the track as Liam and Boo rejoin their crew. Boo asks, "Where the hell are we?"

Robert looks at the map along the wall. Before he answers, a recorded voice says, "The next stop will be Logan Square. Followed by Belmont, Montrose, and Jefferson Park." As the train continues along the path and makes a few stops, the tracks ascend from the subway tunnel to street level and run along the expressway. The recorded voice comes overhead and says, "Next stop will be Jefferson Park. Followed by Harlem and Cumberland. Last stop will be the airport."

Robert says, "Thank God! We're almost home."

Liam interjects, "We have to get off at the Harlem Avenue stop."

Robert asks, "What are you talking about?"

Liam answers, "We have to get Maddie to a hospital. The closest hospital from the neighborhood is walking distance from that station. If need be, I'll help Tommy carry her."

The crew continues to ride past the Jefferson Park station as the overhead voice says, "The next stop will be Harlem Avenue." As the train arrives on the outdoor above-grade platform, the crew exits the train. Tommy scoops up Maddie in his arms, and Maddie continues to cry from the ongoing pain.

Liam walks alongside Tommy and says, "It's okay. The hospital is right down the street."

As the train prepares to leave the station, the overhead chime echoes along the outside corridor and the overhead voice says, "Caution. The doors are about to close."

The crew walks down the platform toward the Harlem Avenue ramp, and they suddenly hear a crashing swoop go through the air. The sound sends a chill down everyone's spine. Ryan asks, "Liam... Boo did you hear that?"

Robert says, "We all heard it, fat boy."

Ryan replies, "Shut up! I thought Boo killed that damn thing."

The crew look around to see if they can find Pet. Not a sign. Boo says, "I thought I killed it too."

Liam interjects, "That thing took a silver arrow and rode the lightning with hundreds of volts. Should be enough to finish it off."

Maddie starts to cry more and hug her brother tighter. She quivers, "Is the bad thing back? Please, no. Make it stop, Tommy."

Tommy says, "It's okay, Maddie. I'm here. I won't let any—" Tommy pauses.

Pet dives right in front of him and crashes into the concrete. The bursting shock causes the concrete platform to shake and crack. Pet flaps open his wings, which knocks Tommy and Maddie down onto the concrete platform. Pet sees Maddie lying on the floor crying and shaking. She screams out in terror as Pet grabs her with his large claw-filled hand. Tommy sees Pet grab his sister while Liam and Boo attempt to attack Pet with their weapons. Tommy steps in front of Liam and Boo and tries to pull Maddie free. Pet lunges several claws from his other foot toward Tommy and pierces through his skin right into his abdomen. Tommy screams out in pain as blood flows freely from the open wound. Maddie screams for her brother. Pet grabs hold of Maddie tightly and soars into the open air. Within moments, Pet is out of sight.

Tommy grabs his abdomen and looks down his shirt. He cries out in pain and sheer terror as his whole T-shirt quickly gets saturated with his own blood. Liam bends down and starts to shake. His heart rate skyrockets, and his adrenaline rushes through his body. Liam quickly presses his hands along Tommy's abdomen and applies direct pressure to the wound. Ryan and Robert are frozen in stunned fear and disbelief. Unable to accept that their friend is seriously injured. Liam looks at Boo and shakes his head. He says, "Boo! Call 911! Get an ambulance here now!" As Boo calls 911, Liam tells Tommy, "It's okay, buddy. It's okay. Help is on the way. Stay with me, Tommy."

As the crew desperately waits for help to arrive, Commander McKinley and Bishop Michael finish prepping and loading rounds into long magazines. Chris bursts into the commander's room and says, "Commander! Sir, I think we have something. They're sending a massive response along the blue line. And it just came over the scanner that there's someone seriously injured at the Harlem Avenue station. Reports of a flying monster in the area."

Commander McKinley looks at Bishop Michael who nods his head. Commander McKinley says, "Chris, have the team ready to leave. Run and have the pilot prep the chopper. It's time we bring this fight to them."

Bishop Michael adds, "It ends now."

CHAPTER 29

....

HOW IS YOUR TEA?

The ambulance flies south down Harlem Avenue toward the scene. The paramedic in the passenger seat checks the notes on his computer screen and says, "I'll grab the pediatric bag. Sounds like it's a kid."

The paramedic driving says, "Jesus! I hate calls involving kids. It's just not the natural order of things."

As they arrive on the scene, they see several police cruisers parked alongside the entrance of the Harlem Avenue Train Station. One of the police officers waves down the ambulance. The officer's arms and hands are covered in blood. Liam tries to help lift his friend inside the ambulance, but the officers instruct him to stand back. One of the officers say, "It's okay, kid. The ambulance is here. They'll put him on the stretcher".

The medics grab the medical bags and ask the officer to give them room. One of the medics grabs his trauma scissors and cuts away the blood-soaked T shirt. He applies a field trauma dressing as his partner gets the oxygen kit ready for use. The medic gets the oxygen ready and asks his partner, "How's he doing?"

His partner says, "Not good! This damn wound won't stop bleeding. Looks like he's gasping for air. Let's get him loaded up and ready for transport."

As they load Tommy in the stretcher, Liam tries to stay by his friend's side. Liam exclaims, "It's gonna be okay, Tommy. Just stay with us!"

Tommy says in a low voice, "Maddie. Bring her home…I'm scared."

The ambulance stays on scene for just a few moments. The driver comes out the side of the ambulance and ask the officers, "Can anyone hop on board and give us a hand just in case?"

The officer who's covered in Tommy's blood doesn't hesitate. He exclaims, "I've got it. I used to be a medic in the army." The officer jumps on board and the ambulance pulls away.

The crew stand by the officers along the sidewalk. In shock and disbelief, they don't know what to do. Boo tries to rally herself but is overtaken by her emotions. One of the remaining officers come up to Liam and says, "Come on, kids. I'll drive you over to the hospital. From there, we'll find out more about your friend and get in contact with your folks."

The police officer driving the crew activates the cruiser's lights and sirens and pulls away from the scene. The cruiser moves quickly toward the hospital. The officer gives dispatch an update on the situation. Dispatch says, "Message received. Command wants you to remain at the hospital until another beat car arrives. They'll handle the protective custody assignment for the minors. Be advised the ambulance from the scene just updated EMS dispatch. They arc initiating CPR."

The officer says under his breath, "Shit. Damn it." He presses the push-to-talk button and says, "Message received, Dispatch. I'm pulling up to the hospital now."

The police cruiser pulls up alongside the ER entrance. The crew witnesses as Tommy gets rolled into the ER. Doctors and nurses meet them at the entrance to assist with CPR measures. Onlookers put their hands to their mouths as Tommy rolls past them. The officer brings the kids over to the waiting area. There he sees officers Jeremy and Paul. Jeremy says to the fellow officer, "Hey. Are these the kids we have to look after?"

The officer says, "Yes." He points to Liam and continues, "I'm taking this kid over to a washroom so he can clean himself. Maybe they can give him a hospital shirt or gown to wear."

Paul says, "Jesus. Is he hurt?"

The officer replies, "No. It's his friend."

As the officer walks away with Liam, Paul instructs Jeremy to stay with Ryan, Robert, and Boo. Paul says, "Just stay here. I'll try to find out more about their friend."

As the remaining members of the crew wait in the sitting area, Boo sees Misty glide through the room. Her bright blue figure looks at Boo, smiles, and waves. Boo asks Jeremy, "Excuse me, Officer. May I use the washroom?"

Jeremy says, "Yeah. Go ahead. But come right back. I need to get your parents' information so I can start making some phone calls."

Boo motions to Misty to follow her. They make their way into the washroom and Boo locks the door. Boo asks, "Misty? Why are you here? And we could have used your help several times, but you were nowhere to…wait…you're not here for me or Liam, are you?"

Misty offers a kind but sad smile as she ducks her face and says, "I'm afraid not. I was sent here for your friend, Tommy."

Boo gasps as she puts her hands to her mouth and asks, "Tommy's not gonna make it?"

Misty answers, "I'm afraid not. I'm here so he doesn't have to be afraid and he won't be alone. I'll make sure he goes to where he supposed to go. Sometimes kids, take me for example, cannot fathom crossing over, and their spirits remain here…trapped. They're scared because they have no one to guide them. This is one of the tasks I do now. He's going to the best of places. From what I heard, he was a great young man. And he gave his life trying to protect his sister. Think of me as a guide bringing him to his new home."

Boo asks, "Is there anything else you can tell me?"

Misty answers, "Yes! Thank you for reminding me. I was told that if you want to help end this whole ordeal, you need to leave now. Sounds like you and Liam know where to go. You and Liam need to decide if your friends come with you. That's up to you."

Misty gives Boo a cool hug. A cold chill goes down Boo's spine. Boo shakes it off as Misty laughs and says, "Sorry. I never mean to do that. It's good seeing you, Boo. I have to go now. Goodbye." Misty fades away in a blue mist as Boo heads back to the sitting area. In the hallway she sees Liam walking with the officer.

The officer says, "I'm glad the hospital had an extra shirt in their supply closet." The officer looks at Boo and says, "Now, I have to go and check on your friend. Both of you head back to the sitting area and wait there with the other officer. You understand?" Liam and Boo nod their heads. The officer marches down another hallway away from the sitting area.

Boo pulls Liam aside and tells him about her encounter with Misty and the unfortunate reason why she is here. Boo starts to get choked up as she sees her brother break down in tears. She holds him tight. Liam cries, "It's all my fault. If we didn't go downtown, he and Maddie would be—"

Boo interjects, "You're not the one who caused this. It was Alek, Angelica, and their...monster."

Liam tries to walk away as he shakes his head. Boo catches him before he walks back into the sitting area. She grabs him and says, "Now, listen. If you don't want the loss of Tommy to be for nothing, we have to leave now. I know that's the opposite of what you want to hear. Tommy was my friend too. But we have to help finish this before more friends meet the same fate, and we don't know what's happening with Maddie...We have to get her home."

Liam nods his head. He pulls the silver cross out from under his shirt. The light from the overhead florescent bulbs reflects off its shiny surface. Liam, with tears in his eyes, says, "You're right. That was what Tommy wanted. His last breath on this earth was about bringing his sister home. That's what we are gonna do."

Boo looks behind Liam toward Robert and Ryan who are being questioned by Officer Jeremy. Boo asks, "What about Robert and Ryan? Do they come with us this time?"

Liam looks at his friends who look like they're trying to talk their way out of trouble and says, "No...I can't drag another friend into this. Especially now. This is our fight. Now, let's find another way to exit this place. It ends now."

Back at Northwest Cook County Hospital, Dr. Ross is finishing up for the day. She quickly finishes a few notes on a patient file on her computer when she gets a knock along the door jam. It's Detective Cunningham. Steve says, "Hey. Afternoon, Dr. Ross. Do you mind if I come in?"

Dr. Ross, surprised to see Detective Cunningham, delivers a smile. "Not at all. Anything to help local law enforcement. Please come in."

Steve closes the door behind him and takes a seat next to Dr. Ross's office desk. He looks around and says, "This is a nice office. I always like when people add plants and color to the room. Always feels more welcoming."

Dr. Ross replies, "Yes. I've been a huge fan of botany. Always marveled at the beauty and brilliance of plants. Now, I'm sure you're here for a reason."

Steve grabs his notepad from his sport coat pocket and says, "Sorry. Yes, you are correct. The reason why I came back this afternoon is in regard to a follow-up interview I had with my old friend from the Cook County Records Office."

Dr. Ross smiles as she stands up, walks around the desk, and steps over to her beverage counter. She asks, "I'm in the mood for tea. Would you like some? It's just a simple black tea."

Steve nods. "Yes. That's sounds nice."

Dr. Ross begins to warm up her electric counter tea pot and asks, "How do you like it?"

Steve answers, "I'll have honey and sugar, if I may."

Dr. Ross replies, "Of course."

Steve looks at his notes. He shakes his head and says, "Well, after talking to my old friend, I'm afraid I have some answers and yet again more questions."

Dr. Ross replies, "Sounds like a riddle. How's that, Detective?"

Steve looks closely at his notes. "Well, the whole thing still doesn't make any sense. I started to describe your patient from my notes. He said your patient was in fact a patient of the old hospital back when he was just a young man. He said when he met her she looked middle aged already. That would mean that she's over a hundred years old."

The tea kettle begins to whistle. As Dr. Ross adds the tea to each cup she says, "That sounds crazy, doesn't it."

Steve replies, "And he also said that he remembers her especially after a huge fire engulfed most of the old hospital back in the 80s. So many people were killed, and the county lost records on the majority of their patients. He remembers her because the authorities at the hospital believed that she was to blame for the blaze. They put her on isolation for a considerable amount of time, especially after they had to rebuild a good portion of the hospital."

Dr. Ross hands Steve his tea cup. "Now, that sounds like a pretty wild story, Detective."

Steve takes a large sip of his tea and says, "Thank you. It's good. Strong but good."

Dr. Ross says, "I'm glad you like it."

Steve puts the cup on the desk. "Which leads me to the main reason why I'm here. I hate to say it, but all roads lead to you helping this woman. She's been here as a ward of the state for a ridiculously long time. She hasn't been trouble since the fire. Then you accept her as a patient and all of a sudden she breaks out after all this time. And it looks like she leaves a trail of death no matter where she goes. But you helping her also seems ridiculous too. I mean, you're just a young, and pretty, I might add, doctor after all." Steve starts to cough.

Dr. Ross asks, "Are you okay, Detective?"

Steve grabs a handkerchief out his sport coat front pocket and says, "I'm fine. I'm—"

Steve continues to cough as Dr. Ross interjects, "Oh. I'm afraid I'm much more than that, Detective. How was your tea?"

Steve starts to sweat heavily and feels like the room is spinning. Steve asks as he stammers, "What di-did ya-you do…to…the…tea?"

Dr. Ross smiles as she answers, "I've gave you a family blend of tea that we give all uninvited guests. It's a mixture of black tea and hemlock. Used in a lot of spells and potions. Especially in the coven. It's been a recipe that's been carried down through the generations. I'm afraid it's quite poisonous, however."

Steve tries to control his breathing as he attempts to stand. His legs and arms have already shut down. In his last breath, he asks, "Who are you?"

Dr. Ross smiles as she looks over her helpless prey. Like a spider looking at a fly in her vicious web. She says, "I'm afraid you're correct, Detective. Please die knowing that you're correct. Of course I helped Angelica. I'm her only living descendant. Which is thanks to men like you who imprisoned her all those years ago. Now, you'll have to excuse me. I have to leave now. I have a pressing appointment with one of my patients." Dr. Ross smiles and walks toward the door leading to the hallway. Before she leaves, she turns off the lights and closes the door behind her.

CHAPTER 30

....

IT ENDS NOW

The agonizing long day for the crew drags into the evening as the sun begins to set over the large Midwest city. As the sunset sparkles and fades into the evening sky, Pet flies over the cemetery with Maddie secured under both of his hairy arms. The extreme shock, stress, and pain eventually leads to Maddie passing out in mid-flight. He lands in the front of the crypt as Angelica and Alek step outside. As Pet safely lands on the ground, Angelica is stunned to see Pet in such bad shape. She says, "My dear! What did those awful children do to you?"

Pet places Maddie on the ground. The movement from Pet's arms down to the ground doesn't faze Maddie who remains unconscious. Angelica looks at Maddie and exclaims, "Who is this? Damn you, you big hairy fool! You were supposed to pick up the little girl with the special gift. I have no use for this little one."

Pet whimpers as Alek interjects, "Maybe this little one can be of use to us."

Angelica asks, "What do you mean, my love?"

Alek grimly smiles. "In my youth I was an excellent fisherman. I could fish all day on the lake near my home. My father always believed that live bait worked better then dead."

Angelica says, "So, we keep this little one alive for now. And let our enemies come to us?"

Alek chuckles. "Yes. Keep her alive. A dead little girl can't be used to get what we want. A live one can hopefully work as an even trade."

Angelica hugs Alek and says, "You're a genius, my love. If we can use the clairvoyant little girl in our ritual, we can…."

Alek rubs the back of his hand against Angelica's cheek and interjects, "Yes. We can live forever and never worry again about losing our youth. Her power will give us eternal youth."

Back at Hinsbrook Hospital, Will and Annie sit with Tina as the doctor walks into her room. Tina is sitting comfortably, ordering food from the hospital menu. The doctor says, "Evening, folks. Do you mind if I come in?"

Tina says, "Sure. Please do."

The doctor asks, "How you feeling, Tina?"

Tina answers, "Doing just fine now. Whatever medicine you've been giving me in that IV bag seems to be working just fine." Tina points to Will and Annie and makes the proper introductions.

The doctor says, "Nice to meet you both. Is it okay if I go over the test results with your family in the room?"

Tina answers, "Sure. Whether you say it now or I say it later doesn't really matter to me."

The doctor replies, "Very well."

Annie interjects, "So, Doc. What's happening with Mom?"

The doctor says, "Well, you were experiencing some pulmonary issues. Basically a bad case of walking pneumonia. Nothing too major. I'm happy you were smart enough to call for help the moment you didn't feel right. If left untreated, it would have been much worse. The good news, just a standard treatment through some prescribed medications and of course a follow-up with a specialist will do the trick. Don't worry. We have a few specialists on staff here at the hospital."

Will asks, "When can she come home? Will she be discharged tonight?"

The doctor shakes his head and says, "No, I'm afraid not. I want to keep her here for one more day, just for observation, and then she'll be free to go home."

Annie adds, "Sounds good. Thank you, Doctor."

As the doctor leaves the room, Annie receives a text from Tommy's mom, Lisa. The text reads: "Hey, Annie. I've been trying to text Tommy. No answer. Curious if he was with your kids or I should try Robert's mother? Thanks."

Annie says, "Hmm."

Will can see the worried look on Annie's face and asks, "What's up, honey?"

Annie answers, "It's Tommy's mom. She is looking for the kids. Let me try Liam. At least try to figure out what's going on and give him an update on our status."

Annie attempts to call Liam. No answer. Annie, starting to get worried, calls Robert's mom. Robert's mom says, "Yeah. I wanted to call and see if I needed to add Liam and Boo to our dinner plans. I'm looking for Robert too. It's getting around that time that I need to start cooking. That kid has to get better at answering his phone and my messages."

Annie pauses and doesn't say a word. A look of panic consumes her face.

Robert's mom asks, "Hello? Hello. Annie, you there?" Annie finally says, "Sorry. I'll have to call you back." She hangs up the phone. Annie looks at Will and says, "Will. We have a problem. We need to leave and get home. Right now!"

The early evening falls over Chicago as Liam and Boo find their way back to the train station. They walk around some yellow police tape and several officers. They casually make their way onto an inbound train heading back into the inner city. As Liam and Boo approach the Cicero Avenue train station, Bishop Michael begins to receive a glowing signal from his silver cross as the S.W.A.T. helicopter begins to approach the forest preserve. While this happens, Bishop Michael receives a phone call from his headquarters. He covers his other ear and presses the phone closely to his head. The order informs him that they just discovered that Alek was once considered a very powerful master in the evil art of necromancy. The ability to transform and resurrect the dead.

The helicopter begins to hover and recon the perimeter of the forest preserve as Angelica begins to breathe in deeply and picks up a scent. Angelica, Alek, and Pet all take cover behind heavy brush and thick trees as the chopper attempts to locate them with their search light. Pet and Alek look up and see the tactical helicopter fly in a circular pattern close to their location. Pet becomes enraged at the sight and the sound of the flying metal chariot. Angelica rubs Pet's back and says, "I know, my dear."

Alek asks, "Is it those modern knights you talked about?"

Angelica answers, "Yes, my love. And I also detect someone else. That baby priest is with them. The knights are here!"

Pet continues to growl, just as Dr. Ross enters the cemetery. She says, "Hello...family. Sorry I couldn't arrive sooner."

Angelica, annoyed, asks, "Where have you been?"

Dr. Ross answers, "I was having a tea party with one of our enemies. Not to worry though. He won't be bothering us anymore."

Angelica points up to the circling helicopter and says, "We have other enemies to attend to, my dear. The knights have arrived."

Dr. Ross looks up at the helicopter and asks, "Does that mean we aren't going to perform the ceremony? The one you promised when I take my vows and become a true member of your coven."

Angelica answers, "Other serious matters are more pressing at the moment, my young student."

Angelica tells Alek her sinister plan in their native language. Alek nods his head and adds, "Indeed. Business first." Alek looks at Pet and says, "You. Take that steel eagle down to the ground. Make sure no one survives."

As Pet takes flight, Bishop Michael and the S.W.A.T. team make preparations to land on the ground. Bishop Michael says, "They have to be down there. My cross is glowing like a beacon."

Commander McKinley observes his live camera feed and says, "Nothing is coming up on our thermal imaging camera. Wait...I see a couple hot spots down there."

Bishop Michael shakes his head and says, "That device won't work on these monsters. Not even on their beast, I'm afraid. The warmth of life from their bodies died a long time ago."

At that moment, Pet soars straight up underneath the chopper. The pilot sees the glowing red eyes and performs an evasive maneuver before Pet is able to deliver a fatal strike.

Commander McKinley taps Chris on his shoulder. He points to Pet who gets ready to attempt another aerial strike. He says, "Chris! Do me a favor? Take down that bastard."

Chris says, "Absolutely, Commander." Chris attaches his safety line as he starts to sit along the floor of the chopper next to the open side hatch. He looks down the scope on top of his long rifle as the pilot positions the chopper. The pilot zips around quickly to give Chris a line of sight with his target.

The pilot asks over the intercom, "You good there, Chris?"

Chris replies, "Yeah. I'm good and lining it up now."

Pet turns toward the chopper. Commander McKinley looks at Pet and says to Chris, "Send it. Take it down!"

Chris fires a round. *BANG!* It hits Pet on his wing. Pet screams in pain and begins to fly in a serpentine pattern. Chris says, "I got him. But it didn't take him down."

Bishop Michael says, "You'll have to aim for his center mass. A direct hit should take him down."

Chris lines up for a shot but has difficulty as Pet continues to fly in an unpredictable pattern. Pet turns again toward the chopper. Chris lines up for his shot. Pet gets dangerously close to the chopper as Chris sends his shot. *BANG!* The round pierces Pet in the center of his chest. Pet releases a screaming death rattle and strikes the chopper's tail rotor before falling to the ground. Pet falls dead into the cemetery before he hits the ground with a loud thud. The tail rotor flies off the helicopter and spirals downward to the awaiting dark forest below. The pilot attempts to gain control of the chopper but to no avail. He knows that it's useless. The chopper continues to spiral uncontrollably down toward the ground. One of the members of the team flies out of the chopper and falls to his death. Commander McKinley screams, "Hold on! We're going down!"

The pilot screams into his intercom, "This is S.W.A.T. Airport Helo 1. Mayday! Mayday! Mayday! We're going down! We're going down! Send—"

At that moment, the helicopter slams on the forestry ground. The chopper rolls several times before the crashing momentum finally brings it to a halt. Flames and sparks fly from the chopper. Commander McKinley unfastens his safety belts and tumbles out of his seat. Bishop Michael follows suit. The commander checks his pilot. The pilot has died on impact. Bishop Michael checks another member of the team. He didn't survive the crash either. Chris coughs as he comes to.

Commander McKinley says, "Chris! You okay?"

Chris coughs some more and says, "A little rattled but I'm alive."

Angelica runs to assess Pet. Quickly she realizes that Pet is gone. She says, "Damn it! Pet is dead."

Alek says, "At least he finished my commands before falling."

Angelica adds, "They may be still alive, and if that priest is with them, they'll probably have weapons that are effective."

Alek asks, "What do you suggest?"

An evil grin spreads across Angelica's face. She looks at Dr. Ross. Angelica winks at Alek and says, "Why don't you perform a ritual and make use of the useless teenagers inside the crypt. Send them as a probe."

Alek smiles. "I love the way you think."

Angelica calls over Dr. Ross and says, "Now, my dear. There's not much time, but we have time to work our magic. Alek will be handling the proceedings."

Alek opens the crypt that is housing the decaying remains of Chloe, Lilith, and Blair. Alek takes Dr. Ross's hand and directs her to sit on the ground. Angelica says to Dr. Ross, "Now just close your eyes, my dear. Alek will take care of the rest."

Dr. Ross says, "I've been waiting years for this moment."

Angelica says, "Exciting, isn't it? Now, close your eyes and it will all be over soon."

Alek grabs the spell book out of the crypt and begins the ceremony. He waves his walking stick in the air, and a circular mist forms around Dr. Ross. He calls on the power of his lord and continues to speak in Latin.

As the swirling mist consumes Dr. Ross, she screams, "Wait! This isn't right! I've done everything you…Ahhhh!" Dr. Ross screams only for a moment and then silence. Her life energy leaves her body and travels through the purple mist toward the rotting corpses of the three teenagers. The purple mist encircles the three rotting corpses, and the bodies start to kick and rattle. Slowly, Chloe, Lilith and Blair rise from the ground and move toward their dark lord. The three zombie teenagers scream, growl, and moan as they are commanded by Alek to attack any humans around the engulfing smoke ahead. The zombies move toward the dark pushing smoke as Alek looks at the decayed remains of Dr. Ross. He walks next to Angelica and says, "Even your flesh and blood?"

Angelica shrugs her shoulders. "She's just a pawn helping her queen."

✦ ✦ ✦

Liam and Boo arrive at the Cicero Avenue train station. As they exit toward the main street, they see onlookers observing a rising trail of dark smoke towering over the nearby forest preserve. The sound of approaching sirens echo in the distance. Liam asks a nearby onlooker what happened. The bystander says, "A helicopter crashed into the middle of the forest!"

Liam looks at Boo and says, "Bishop Michael has to be in there. He needs our help. Let's go!"

✦ ✦ ✦

Alek walks up to a large puddle of muddy water. Angelica asks, "Thinking fog of war, my love?"

Alek nods his head. After a quick use of his magic, thick low-hanging fog covers the marshy heavy bush landscape. Alek says, "Let's give our girls a better fighting chance."

✦ ✦ ✦

Chris checks the status of his rifle. His rifle is in disrepair. Chris checks his secondary side arm weapon. Seems okay. Bishop Michael asks, "Does your weapon have the rounds with holy oil?" Chris nods his head. Commander McKinley checks his weapon. The weapon is okay but Commander McKinley is limping badly.

Chris assesses Commander McKinley and asks, "You good, Boss?"

Commander McKinley says, "I'm busted up a bit, but I'm still in the fight."

The fog drifts and engulfs the surrounding area. Soon, the remaining team hears the approaching sounds of groans and moans from something ungodly. Bishop Michael's silver cross illuminates greatly as the zombies approach the team and attempt to surround them. Bishop Michael says, "Prepare to defend yourselves, gentlemen!"

Commander McKinley asks, "What is it?"

Bishop Michael says, "Zombies. I recognize their death-rattling sounds."

Chris tries to get sight on his next target. Commander McKinley asks, "Anything, Chris?"

Chris says, "I can't see shit!"

The zombies lock on to Chris's voice and swarm onto his location like a pack of wild dogs. Chris attempts to fire his weapon but it's too late. The zombies take him to the ground. Chris screams for a moment but then silence as the zombies claim their first victim.

Bishop Michael and Commander McKinley move in to surround the zombies as they continue to feed. The zombies attempt to pounce and attack, but to no avail. Bishop Michael quickly dispatches two of them with his sword, and Commander McKinley eliminates the final one with a holy round chambered in his rifle. Commander McKinley looks away from Chris. He's visibly upset to see the horrific violence inflicted on his friend and team member. The bishop allows McKinley to walk away further before conducting an act of mercy on Chris. Bishop Michael approaches Commander McKinley as he wipes away the rotting ooze from his sword and says, "I'm sorry about your men."

Commander McKinley attempts to regain his composer. "He's was one of my closest friends. He was the godfather to my youngest son."

Bishop Michael places a hand on his shoulder and says, "Your friend is at peace. I made sure of it." The sound of approaching sirens begins to fill the air. The bishop says, "Sounds like backup will be arriving soon."

Commander McKinley shakes his head. "We need to end this before anyone else becomes a victim of these monsters. I'm with you. I'm still in the fight."

Bishop Michael nods his head as he checks his silver cross. It illuminates in the direction of Alek and Angelica. He says, "The light shows us the way. This is the end."

Bishop Michael and Commander McKinley follow the light to the entrance of the cemetery where they see Alek and Angelica waiting for them next to the crypt. Commander McKinley recognizes the little girl lying next to the crypt as she continues to remain unconscious on the ground. Commander McKinley wants to jump in and rescue Maddie, but Bishop Michael holds him back. Commander McKinley says, "That little girl lives in my neighborhood!"

Angelica pets the top of Maddie's head and says, "Oh, she does. And don't worry. She's alive for now. Unlike you'll be in a few moments."

Bishop Michael says, "We'll see about that, you unholy demon. Give the girl to us!"

Alek smiles and speaks in their native tongue, "Come and take her, baby priest."

Commander McKinley opens fire on Angelica as Angelica takes cover behind an old decaying tombstone. *BANG! BANG!* Commander McKinley says, "You take the guy. I got the witch."

Angelica smiles as she grabs her stick wand and waves it in the air. She casts a quick spell, sending a wave of sharp sticks toward Commander McKinley. The sticks sweep through the air and unload onto Commander McKinley. Commander McKinley screams out for a moment and then silence as he drops to the ground.

Liam and Boo hear the trail of gunfire and find their way to the cemetery. They walk through the entrance and find Bishop Michael getting surrounded by Alek and Angelica. Bishop Michael tries to move in on Alek and Angelica, but their combined power is far too great. He gets hit with several waves of evil magic, which forces the bishop to the ground. He gets hit with enough force to lift him up into the air. He loses the grip on his sword. It falls away from him as he lands on the ground. The hail of evil energy hits in all directions, which starts burning several dry bushes and leaves. Angelica laughs. Alek asks, "So...answer me this, baby priest. Where is your God now? Where is he when you need him the most?"

Bishop Michael almost gives in to every ounce of instinct left in his body, telling him to give up and be at peace. He flashes back to his time as a soldier and his slow recovery from being injured. He thinks about training Liam and Boo and remembers what he said to Boo. He remembers saying, "As long as you have air in your lungs, you can stand, fight, and defend your ground." Bishop Michael comes to a kneeling position and sees Liam and Boo as they approach the crypt.

Liam tries to assess Maddie. Boo asks, "How is she?"

Liam says, "She's alive. But she's out cold."

Bishop Michael smiles as he looks at Alek. "It's funny you ask that because right now I have never felt closer to God in my life."

Angelica puts her nose in the air and says, "Children?" She turns to find Boo aiming her bow and arrow.

Boo says coldly, "Witch." Boo releases the arrow. The arrow rushes through the air and hits Angelica in the center of her chest. Angelica flips into the air and lands on her back. She cries out in a last effort to ask for Alek's aid, but it's too late.

Liam runs to Bishop Michael's aid. The bishop attempts to order Liam back. Alek turns and strikes Liam across the face. The force sends Liam flying. In flight, Liam loses his war pick. Boo yells, "Liam!"

The radiant heat from the growing fire causes several other bushes and trees to engulf in flames. Out of the corner of her eye, Boo sees Misty. Misty points to the spell book and says, "Boo! Throw the spell book into the fire. Do it now!"

Liam tries to stand, but he feels like he is about to pass out. He stumbles and tries to get his bearings. He feels like his lungs are closing. His vision begins to spin, and he feels like everything is slowing down. He sees Boo and Maddie as Alek moves to approach them. Boo steps in front of Maddie and attempts to draw another arrow. Liam looks to Bishop Michael. He remembers what Bishop Michael said to him, "Remember, Liam. The last line of defense is self-defense." He sees his war pick next to a nearby bush. He stumbles forward and grabs it. From a kneeling position, he winds up the war pick and shouts, "Alek!" Alek turns toward Liam. Liam throws his weapon through the air. It spirals quickly toward Alek, and the pick end pierces Alek's chest. Alek stumbles back and drops to the ground. Liam says in a quavering voice, "That one's for Tommy. Leave my family alone."

Boo grabs the spell book and throws it into the fire. The spell book engulfs into a bright-green mist as Alek and Angelica scream out in terror as a green mist flies toward them. The mist engulfs both of them, draining them of all their remaining life energy. They both shrivel and decay as the mist sinks deep into the earth before it disappears. Their decaying skeletal remains are all that remain. Alek and Angelica are no more!

CHAPTER 31

YOU HAVE MY FULL ATTENTION

The fire continues to engulf sections of dry leaves, brush, and low-hanging trees. Boo runs to her brother's aid and grabs his inhaler. She helps administer the medicine before Liam passes out. The medicine kicks in, and Liam starts to regain his composure. Liam and Boo quickly make their way to Maddie's side. Liam, gaining back his strength, throws her over his shoulder. Liam with Maddie and Boo run over to Bishop Michael who comes to his feet. Bishop Michael looks around and says, "We have to get out of here!"

Boo says, "Well, the way we came in is filled with fire and smoke."

Liam asks, "Bishop, which way should we go to get out of here?"

Bishop Michael turns and sees a blue light flash and pierce through the smoke. A police cruiser makes their way through a small nearby forest trail. Bishop Michael smiles and says, "The light will show us the way."

Bishop Michael limps his way toward the police cruiser with Liam, Boo, and Maddie. An officer exits the car and shouts, "Sound off! S.W.A.T.! Anyone in here? Anyone left alive?"

Boo turns to Liam and says, "Help is here, Liam."

Liam smiles and says, "Yes, indeed."

Boo shouts out, "Hello! We're coming to you!"

As they approach, the officer helps Liam and places Maddie in the back of the cruiser. Bishop Michael says, "The members of the S.W.A.T. team are all down. But so are the monsters."

The officer quickly gets everyone inside. He informs dispatch he is exiting the forest with a few survivors and to have an ambulance report from staging.

Fire department crews move into the area to extinguish the flames. As they make progress, the police and other rescue crews search the area for the downed S.W.A.T. members. Maddie is taken to an awaiting ambulance with Boo. Liam follows Bishop Michael until another team of medics assist him into another ambulance. Bishop Michael waves to Liam and tells the medics, "This young warrior needs help too. He rides with me. I need to make sure he is united with his parents."

As Liam approaches, the bishop asks, "Where's Boo?"

Liam says, "She's with Maddie. She couldn't leave her side. She's riding with her to the hospital."

A couple of weeks later, Liam is walking hand-in-hand with Boo over to the baseball field. A sign along the dugout reading ALL-STAR GAME waves through the gentle breeze. Players gather in a circle around the mound before the opening and have a memorial service for Coach Phil and Tommy. The manager of the baseball club says to everyone, "This game is dedicated to Coach Phil. Who selected Liam and Tommy to be his All-Stars. In honor of that, one position will be left open on the roster for Tommy."

Liam and Boo look over to Tommy's family. They are visibly upset but are so proud of their son and his memorial service. After the memorial service, Boo sees Misty out of the corner of her eye and walks toward her. Next to Misty is the glowing spirit of Tommy. Tommy smiles as Boo asks, "Are you smiling about the All-Star selection?"

Tommy shakes his head, points to his family, and says, "No. I'm happy that Maddie is safe. Thank you for bringing her home."

Boo smiles. "Liam and I promised to make that happen."

Misty says, "We'll find the right time for Tommy to visit and talk with Timmy and Maddie. But for now, we wanted Tommy to be here and witness this ceremony."

Boo says, "These are the ceremonies worth witnessing."

Misty and Tommy give Boo a cool hug. Misty laughs as she says, "You'll never get used to that, believe me."

The All-Star Game begins and the players take the field. The opposing team takes the field first as Liam's team heads toward the dugout and gets ready to bat. Liam sees Father Luke walking down the park trail and gives him a wave. Liam says, "Hey, Father Luke. You here to see the game?"

Father Luke says, "Of course. I wouldn't miss it for the world." Father Luke looks around and says, "Where are your folks?"

Liam says, "Dad is around somewhere. I think Boo is talking to a friend, and my mom is working at the concession stand."

Father Luke says, "Perfect. Some food and refreshments sound great. I'll make my way over."

Annie sees Father Luke approach the stand. "Hey, Father Luke. What can I get you?"

Father Luke smiles and says, "Thank you. I'll take two hot dogs and a soda. There's something about summer, the smell of hot dogs, and baseball. It's like a holy trinity for me."

Annie gets Father Luke's food prepared as a man in a black suit walks behind Father Luke to get in line.

Annie hands Father Luke his food, then asks, "How's Bishop Michael? Have you heard anything?"

Father Luke answers, "Doing well actually. He's back with the order. Recovering slowly but recovering nonetheless. Any plans after all of this craziness?"

Annie replies, "Not really. There's only one trip planned this upcoming fall over Labor Day Weekend. Liam and Boo have a camping trip planned with the Scouts. They're really looking forward to it."

Father Luke replies, "I'm sure. Just to get away for some peace and quiet in nature sounds rejuvenating." Father Luke shakes for a moment.

Annie asks, "You okay, Father?"

Father Luke answers, "Just fine. Had a cold chill go down my spine. Don't you hate that?"

Annie nods her head. "Yup. I know that feeling all too well."

Father Luke pays Annie, grabs his food and walks back toward the game. The man in the black suit approaches the counter. His skin is pale, and his face lacks usual human emotion. Annie looks at the man with a suspicious glare and asks, "What can I get you?"

The man responds coldly, "Nothing for me today. I have all that I require." The man walks away toward the game.

Annie shakes her head and says, "That's weird. We don't need any more weirdness around here, that's for sure."

The man sits down at an unoccupied nearby bench. He closely watches Liam play baseball and Boo as she talks and laughs with Robert in the bleachers. A briefcase appears next to the man. He bends down, grabs it, and places it on his lap. Inside he opens a file and looks through several pieces of parchment. He says, "Well, well, well. So, these two little ones are going on a camping trip this fall. They've caused enough trouble. But now…now they have my full attention." The man puts the file back in the briefcase, closes it, and places it back on the ground. The briefcase disappears, and the man quietly stands up and walks away from the park.

Who is this mystery figure and what does he have in store for Liam and Boo on their camping trip? Find out on the next installment of the Liam and Boo Series in Book 4, *Harvest of the Midnight Pack*.

THE END